I0534516

JACK RECALLED

A Jack of All Trades novel

DH Smith

Earlham Books

Published 2017 by Earlham Books
Book design & cover art by Lia at Free Your Words
(*www.FreeYourWords.com*)

Text copyright © 2017 DH Smith

This is a work of fiction. Names, characters, businesses, places, events and incidents are either the products of the author's imagination or used in a fictitious manner. Any resemblance to actual persons, living or dead, or actual events is purely coincidental.

All Rights Reserved

ISBN: 978-1-909804-27-2

PART ONE:
DEEP IN EPPING FOREST

Prologue

In the misty forest air, a fox scooped at the leaf mould. Its paws threw back the soft earth beneath, seeking what it could only smell, until only its tail showed above the hole, flicking at the sprayed soil. Digging ceased when the famished animal got at the larvae-infested meat. Hunger trumped distaste, until at last full, the animal wandered off into the forest, vomiting all it had eaten in the following hour.

The next visitor was a brown, hairy mongrel, that stood over the hole barking until his impatient owner came off the forest path seeking him out. She found a bony hand and arm in ripped material, crawling with bugs, poking out of the soil. She jerked back, holding her chest, and leaned against a tree, wondering what to do. Keeping well back from the hole, recovering from her shock, she phoned the police. Once she'd told them what she'd seen, they asked for the location.

'I'm in Epping Forest.'

She had a problem giving clear directions, one tree being much like another. There were no landmarks visible. She could say where her car was, perhaps half a mile away, but was unsure which direction she had taken once she'd set off into the forest. But she had a whistle, she told them, one her husband had given her but she'd never ever used. They asked her to demonstrate it. The woman searched her backpack, found the whistle and gave it a blast. The effect was piercing even over her phone. She was told to remain where she was, to give them ten minutes, and then every minute give three blasts of a second or so each.

The woman stayed as requested, keeping well away from the hole, having no wish to see the appendage again. Her dog though remained curious and she was forced to drag him clear, putting him on a lead and tying him to a tree, where he barked and tugged to be free. She tried explaining, even as she shivered, hoping the police would come swiftly and release her from her civic duty. As bidden, she gave her regular whistle blasts, hoping someone soon would hear.

A track-suited runner came, a middle aged man, gasping, attracted by the whistle. She pointed out her find. Although impatient to be on his way, the man felt he could not leave her. So the two stayed, discussing who might be in the hole and how long the corpse had rested there. And how many others lay scattered about the forest. The smell wafted on the breeze, a smell of death, not of yesterday but not so long ago. As the runner said, the smell goes when the flesh goes.

The police came in about half an hour, a man and a woman in uniform. They took the details of the finder and the runner, and photographed them both, bearing in mind that murderers sometimes return to check the setting of their crime.

And let them go.

The area became a crime scene, marked out with police tape, with no one allowed inside its perimeter without permission, having to sign the book with name and time, and togged up in protective gear. A marquee was erected over the hole, and the ground within a few hundred metres' radius searched for anything that might be connected to the grave.

Two corpses were dug up over the course of the day. Both males, their bones showing through bug eaten flesh, remnants of clothes crawling with grubs. One body had lain on top of the other, the bottom corpse was in a clear plastic sack, the bones and flesh barely visible in a golden, cloudy soup.

Chapter 1

Not the best of days to be out, but necessity demanded. Who knew when the rain might stop? It had been pouring on and off for most of the month. At least his knee was holding out. Jack pulled down the zip on his jacket in spite of the rain, walking swiftly, head bowed, he was half hot, half cold, the exposed bits of skin feeling the chill. In his backpack was a stack of flyers, twenty or so in his wet hand, the remnant of 5000 he'd had printed 18 months back. He opened a gate, folded a couple as he went up the path, and posted them through the letterbox. Then quickly over the low separating wall, and on to the next house.

Jack of All Trades, the leaflet said at the head. His thirteen year old daughter, Mia, had taken a photo of his van with Jack beside it, hand on a ladder, toolbox at its foot. Not the best of pictures, his eyes half closed, making him look rather sinister. But as Mia had put it, builders are not expected to be models.

He was on Ham Park Road, across the road from the park, the thinning trees leaning at the railings as if trying to escape, heads thrashing in the wind and rain. Jack's woolly hat was saturated, water seeping into his hair, drips running down his face. His jacket had a hood but he'd refused to put it up as it made him feel like a horse in blinkers. There were no other pedestrians, just traffic throwing spray at him, wipers revealing dry, superior faces.

Hands emptied, Jack blew into the palms. How much of this posting was going to the wrong people? Some of the houses were owned by East Thames housing association. Useless leafleting them as the association had their own repair team. But he didn't know which they were. Then there were the private tenanted properties and they were useless too. The landlord would never see the leaflet. It was the owner-occupiers he was after.

He must get back to work, having had two months off with his knee, falling off that ladder. That'd teach him to rush, paint splashed everywhere. Which left a job half done, and no payment. He'd considered going to small claims court to get payment for the work he'd done, but the client insisted she'd had to pay a new builder extra to get them to come at once. She'd convinced him it would be fruitless. And so Jack had gone to the Job Centre to sign on. At first on crutches, even so, he felt they were suspicious of him. As if he'd borrowed them from a disabled person. As soon as he could, he'd changed them for a walking stick. Still limping, they'd pressed him to find work. He'd protested that he wasn't fit, and he'd had to go to his doctor to get proof for another two weeks off. As soon as that was over, they were at him again.

As if he didn't want to work. That was enough, more than enough. He'd signed off, deciding he'd get by one way or another. And managed a day here, a day there, but too little to make ends meet. He must get solid work. Put some money in the bank, so he'd have a cushion for the lean times. And to hell with the psychopaths at the Job Centre.

Jack strode up the steps of a house with four bells on the doorpost. In the shelter of the porch, he shook the water off head and face, folded four leaflets and put them through the communal letterbox, probably another waste of time, and clattered back down the steps just as his phone rang.

Maybe someone who'd picked up a leaflet. Cross fingers.

His ex, he read on the screen, no doubt from the warmth of her head teacher's office. He'd best reply or she'd only gripe.

'Hello, Alison.'

'Hello, Jack. Lovely weather out there. Wet play. Everyone's moaning.'

'I'm out leafleting,' he said, wiping the drips off his neck. He could imagine her in a swivel chair with a steaming coffee looking out of a window at the pouring rain. 'Can you make it quick,' he added. 'I'm drenched.' Knowing he would be whether he was talking to her or not, but at least he'd be drenched for some purpose.

'Can you have Mia this evening?'

The obvious; she always wanted something when she phoned. Well, he could lie, say he was going out somewhere or other, but he'd already hesitated too long.

'I've no food in the house,' he said.

'Get some.'

'I've no money. No work.' There, he'd said it. Let her have a go at him from her nice warm office, and he'd tell her how life was lived on the street.

Alison sighed heavily. 'I know things are tough,' she said. 'Mia told me. I'll lend you twenty quid. Lend, mind you.'

'Thanks.' He hated taking her money, another minus on his score card. 'You got a date tonight?' he added, eager to get her off his woes.

'Yes, I have. At the Theatre Royal.'

'Enjoy yourself. Is that everything?'

'Yes. I hope you get some work soon, Jack.'

'Do you think I'm not trying?' He instantly regretted his sharpness. 'Sorry. I'll expect Mia later.'

He closed the call. Unemployment made him grouch. Well, she'd lent him twenty quid and hadn't made too much of it, so she deserved some gratitude. And it'd be good to see Mia. He looked up at the sky, hoping there might be some improvement. The clouds were smudged charcoal, no break in the dirty grey. He'd carry on leafleting to the end of the road and leave it there. Go home, have his toast. There might be some scrapings of Marmite left. Black tea. He and Mia would shop when he got Alison's twenty.

And there was the hope, that evening perhaps, one of these houses might phone with an offer of work. Something small would keep the wolf from the door, up the garden path at least, although still howling. But a decent job, that's what he really wanted, say a week or so.

He stopped; he'd been walking automatically without looking, path, house, letterbox, pushing through the flyers, back down the path, next house. But this one he recalled. He hadn't thought about it coming up the path, engrossed in his own problems. But a foot on the steps, yes, that portico and the side door into the garden. He recalled too well. Anne's house. No place to leave a leaflet. He gave an involuntary shudder at the happenings two years ago.

'Hey, builder!' came a call.

Chapter 2

Jack turned and saw a woman, in the portico of the house next door to Anne's, waving a leaflet. She took a short step out, grimaced at the rain, and retreated to her porch.

'Hang on, madam,' he called. He stepped over the adjoining wall, to the foot of her steps. 'What can I do for you?'

She was tall and slim, her hair tied back, wearing jeans and T-shirt, her feet bare.

'You the builder on this flyer?'

'I am,' he said.

She was looking at the leaflet. 'Jack. That your name?'

'Of All Trades, for my sins.' He smiled, knowing there might be work here. Forget Anne and that hullabaloo. Concentrate. There might be a job in the offing. Could come to nothing, but you never know. 'I do a range of building work: carpentry, roofing, bricklaying,' he began. 'At reasonable rates. What can I do for you, madam?' Mia had told him never to say he was cheap. It sounded shoddy, she said.

'Can you do me an estimate?'

'What, now?'

'Well, you're here,' she said with a shrug. 'So what about now.'

Unexpected, but why not? It was the state of mind he was in, hardly a step or two out of Anne's, all those bad memories thrown up, trying to raise the energy to leaflet the rest of the road, and she'd beckoned. Broken his thoughts. He must get in business mode. This could be a job. Look confident.

'Now is fine,' he said. 'Show me what you'd like done.'

'You'd best come in.'

He climbed the few steps, out of the rain, through the porch and the open door. She waited in the wide hallway, by a double tiered shoe-rack, while he wiped his boots on the mat, and then set off down the hallway, turning into an open door. He followed her, and entered a long room that went from the front of the house to the rear.

The front section had a large sofa, two armchairs and a large flat screen TV. The garden end had an oval, dark wood table, reflecting the light from French windows, with four high back chairs around it.

She was looking at him, biting her lip. 'An awful day for leafleting.'

He shrugged. 'You don't get wet time when you're self-employed.' He tried to lighten up. 'It's only water, not sewage.'

'Let me have your jacket.' When he hesitated, she said, 'I'm not going to steal it. Just hang it up.'

He took it off, and held it out for her.

'And your bag,' she added, taking his jacket and then the bag. 'I'll put them in the hall.' And left him.

Jack looked at his boots on the carpet, a paisley pattern, thick pile. Well, she'd invited him in, and he'd wiped his boots. He brushed his hair back, it was pleasantly warm here. Might get a cuppa. And biscuits wouldn't go amiss. But go for it, Jack of all Trades, builder. Exude confidence.

He looked for a clue to what she wanted done. The long room had probably been two rooms once. Yes, there were doors to the hall in both halves. It was well decorated, with long, deep-green floral curtains at the front bay window. There were a number of brightly coloured abstract paintings on the wall, high book shelves to the ceiling both sides of a corner, the middle shelves taken up with a music centre. All very tidy. If he got the job, he'd better cover up the furniture. Whatever the job was. If he got it.

She returned. She had a towel with her.

'Here,' she said, handing over the towel. 'Wipe yourself.'

'Thanks,' he said, rubbing his hair, neck and face.

'I've put the kettle on,' she said. 'Your things are hanging in the hall,' then stopped and scratched her chin thoughtfully. 'I should really get a reference before I go any further. Sorry if I've been a little scatty...' She smiled. 'That's me all along.'

'Fine by me,' he said, putting the towel on the back of a chair. 'I'd do the same in your position. Do you know Anne next door?'

'What, Anne Tucker, the childminder?'

'Yes, her.'

'She's a good friend of mine. What work did you do for her?'

'About two years ago, I knocked down the brick wall, the one between yours and her place. And put in the wooden fence.'

'That was before I came back here. But it's a good fence, I'll grant you that. I'll have a word with Anne if you don't mind.'

'Not at all.' Though he wondered if he should have brought Anne up. It would tell her he was here, though if he got the work, she'd learn soon enough.

'Let's assume she gives you a good reference...'

The woman had put him on the spot for a reference. He hadn't spoken to Anne for two years. Had no wish to. But Anne certainly owed him a reference. A lot more than that.

The woman went to the middle of the room, facing the front window.

'I want a wall, here,' she said, spreading her arms across the room.

'There used to be one,' said Jack looking up at the ceiling. 'Two doors, one for each former room.' He pointed them out, adding, 'Why do you want the wall replaced?'

9

She sighed and turned awkwardly. 'Does it matter?'

'There are walls and walls. Different purposes, some thicker than others,' he said, already sizing up the job, beginning to think of plasterboard and wood lengths. 'Do you want a door in it?'

'No,' she said. 'Definitely no door. Two rooms completely cut off. That's what I want.'

'Not a sliding door?' he said. 'So you could make it a big room again, say for a party?'

'We don't have parties,' she said firmly.

He wondered who 'We' referred to. A husband, kids maybe. Who lived here?

'A permanent division,' she said. 'Two rooms. Soundproofed. Can you do me an estimate?'

Jack sucked in his cheeks, looking at the size of the space, thinking of time and materials. 'A soundproofed wall across from here to here,' he muttered as he stepped across the room touching the side walls on either side. 'Finish and decorate.'

'Yes. How much would it cost? How effective would the soundproofing be?'

'Not perfect,' he said. 'Sound would still be transmitted via the floorboards, and from the two side walls and ceiling.'

'Would I hear the TV from this room,' she said, 'if I were on this side?' going into the back space as she spoke.

Jack wanted the work, but was already uncomfortable. He'd done a job before that required soundproofing, and, although he'd read up on it and taken advice, and bought what he thought were the right materials, when finished the customer wasn't altogether happy.

'It's a big TV,' he said sucking his lips. 'Is it working off its own speakers or is it connected to the sound system?'

He walked across to the flat screen TV. It was facing the long sofa, the armchairs also focused at its screen. There were no external speaker wires coming from it. So just its own speakers.

'I would move the TV right to the end,' he said. 'Get it as far away as possible from the wall,' pointing to where an armchair was situated, near the front window. 'Sound falls off rapidly with distance. And move those speakers too.' He indicated the sound system of the music centre. 'I'd have them on the front wall.' He pointed out where they should go. 'As far away from the new wall as possible. Then probably it'd be OK soundwise.'

'Just probably.'

He was aware he should be more forthright, but sound could be hell to deal with.

'Depends how loud the TV is, depends whether someone likes heavy metal on full volume,' he said with a half laugh. He turned to her, appealing, 'There has to be compromise.'

She shook her head. 'My brother is not very good at that. He likes his football. Loud. And if he's got his mates round...' She clapped her hands to her head to emphasise the racket they made.

Jack knew he needed to up his game if he wanted the work. Never the best of salesmen, he must pull this together. Closure, didn't they call it? Don't hesitate. Too much truth never sold a secondhand car.

'It would be fine,' he said. 'A little sound spilling, but only at the noisiest of times. But the rest of the time, quiet as a spring meadow.' He hoped.

'You mean for nature programmes and for the Antiques Roadshow,' she said wearily, 'it'd be passable.'

'A lot better than passable,' he insisted. 'With some furniture shifting on this side, soundproof panelling in the wall, you could be in the new room, scream your head off – and no one would hear you. Like outer space.'

She looked at him oddly and sat on the arm of the sofa, obviously considering. 'Better than passable then,' she mused. 'Though it depends how you define passable.' She sighed. 'I do have noise-cancelling headphones for the non-passable times.' She stood up resolutely. 'I want it. I need my space. Do me the estimate.'

Her change of heart startled him. Here was a moody one. Which meant she could as easily change her mind. But go with it. Encourage. Except he hadn't come prepared.

'I need a pen and paper,' he said, apologetically. 'I was just putting out flyers, not expecting to do an estimate.'

'Yes, I've dropped you in it rather,' she said. 'But I'm sure you can cope.' She went to a drawer and took out a notebook and pen. She did a quick scrawl with the pen to check it worked. And handed them to him. 'I'll go and make the coffee. All right?'

'Leave me to it.'

Chapter 3

She spooned the coffee into the cafetiere as the water boiled in the kettle. Paul was off on one of his runs. Getting soaked to the skin. Well, she wouldn't find him a towel. Perhaps a bucket of ice cubes. She'd like to get the job fixed before he returned. Paul had sort of agreed, in his grunting non-committal way. Perhaps he'd catch pneumonia or drown in a puddle. Then she wouldn't need the extra room. The builder looked like he needed the work, so could be free right away. Or why would he be leafleting in this weather?

Maybe he wasn't much good. But there was something about him that seemed sincere. A cowboy would be more professional, would have all the spiel, but he almost seemed to be selling himself short. Well, he would. Anyone who calls themselves Jack of All Trades lacks some self belief. Unless it's a joke. Or irony. But irony doesn't work too well on a builder's leaflet.

She'd have to ask Anne about him.

Would Paul stop the job? He'd try. Might succeed. The house was half hers. But which half, he often said, and changed his mind all the time. I'll take the top floor, you take the ground, she'd once said in frustration. He'd said he wanted the top, and when she'd agreed, said he wanted the ground, and when she'd agreed (anything you want, damn you!), he said, let's keep it as it is.

The house bombarded her. Sound systems in every room, the running up the stairs, the mess in the bathroom. Paul, and his son and daughter, to hell with them, she wanted some peace. Her space.

She wanted to sell the house but Paul refused. He would not buy her out either. Stalemate, well for her, checkmate for him. The house was as good as his, as he wouldn't agree to anything she wanted. Except dividing the sitting room in two. Why had he conceded that? Maybe just to change his mind when she'd made all the plans. She'd kill him first. She would, she really would.

She poured the water into the cafetiere. And then stirred the grounds while sitting on a high stool, letting herself breathe. Slowly, in, out. Hear the sounds of the house, the drips of rain on the window, the crack of thunder. Perhaps the lightning would strike Paul. That evaporated her attempt at mindfulness. Paul destroyed everything in her life. Always had. Maybe she should just say goodbye to the house. Let the bastard have it. And go. Build a new life somewhere else. In Manchester, Birmingham, Edinburgh. The South Seas. Anywhere.

Except what would she do? An editor who couldn't use a computer. Violent headaches had forced her to give up her City job. Any computer blasted her brain cells, even laptops. She could just about bear a smartphone. TV was out, any electronic media with a screen, the rays had singled her out as their victim. Poked screws into her cerebellum and twisted.

Useless doctors, useless therapists. Was it physical, was it psychological – a reaction to a stressful job, they said. All of them at sea, or rather she was, on a raft surrounded by sharks. And her plan was to make a little hut on the timbers. A space where she could weep her heart out and work out what to do with her life. Paint, make pots, knit, sew samplers. Something that didn't involve computers. It would have to be something arty. Or marriage. But to whom? Better if she were working and had something to offer. Now she was nobody.

She'd been editor of the in-house magazine. Writing some of it, pushing for other articles, interviewing, taking photos, proofreading, using the desktop publishing program to put it all together. Everyone said it was marvellous when she took the mag round every Friday, turning the pages for their photos and articles. She'd be at the board meetings, the conferences. The hub of everything, working all the hours, knowing more about what was going on at the firm than some of the directors. Until the headaches, then it was time off, doctors, shrinks, back to work, and in a few hours agonized. She realised it was the computer, her head always in the screen, their proximity, the rays, the electronic particles or whatever they were, that drilled into her head...

That was then. Now, short of a head transplant, she must make her space. Do things in the space. Find out what she could do without electronic input. There must be something. She was still grieving her old life a year or more on. Part of the team, good pay, respect. Ah, respect. That back slapping; *you are important, we need you, Lynn. What a grand job you're doing.*

With no income, she'd had to give up her flat in Docklands and come back here, the house she and Paul owned, bequeathed by their parents. What a zoo! Almost as bad as being ill. Paul despised her, she despised him. And she didn't have much time for his son, her nephew Nick, his dirty bathroom habits and late night guitar riffs. His daughter, Dawn, was tidier, if pretty screwed up. Though how Dawn put up with the racket from her brother and father... But then she had other spaces to work in, like her college library, when she wasn't self harming, poor girl. But Lynn was here too much. Going over to Anne some evenings, but Anne had her own life...

Lynn closed her eyes. She would be an anchorite, walled up in her room. Away from human interaction, communing with the universe. Except they wouldn't feed her or take her refuse away. She wasn't saintly enough. So she'd starve, be a bundle of bones in rags with beetles crawling through.

Paul had had it all his way too long, pissing out his territory, encouraging his son to annoy her with his music and mess. Well, she must fight back. Stake her claim. Not lie there and be kicked. They would not show mercy, but take everything and throw her out into the street. Or lock her in the attic like a mad woman.

Fight. Instead of just yelling, put up a fence. That would surprise them. It had taken a year to get here. Well, she would stay her ground. Enough therapy, goodbye to quack medicine. *Tell me about the relationship with your parents. When did you start hating your brother?*

The day I was born.

She had poured out the coffees and put a few biscuits on a plate when she heard the front door open. That would be Paul. Not struck by lightning. Wet through though. Pity there wasn't enough coffee.

Chapter 4

Jack didn't have a tape measure with him. Of course, he could ask for one, but then he'd already asked for paper and pen. He didn't want to appear totally incompetent. Well, you don't have to be absolutely accurate for an estimate. His feet were more or less a foot long, so he pigeon-toed from one side of the room to the other, to get a rough length for the proposed wall. For the height, he stood against the side wall. He was five feet ten, call it six feet, so he held a flat hand over his head, turned and estimated the space above and added it on. Making it around ten and a half to the ceiling. He jotted down: wood – 2 by 1 uprights to the ceiling, 4 by 2 across the floor and ceiling to attach them to. Two layers of 13mm sound proofing plasterboard on either side of the wall.

And then he was stuck for the name of the metal strip. Used to keep the plasterboard off the wood and weaken sound transmission. What the hell was it called? He should've used it in that last job, over a year back. Bob had told him about it afterwards. He could phone him. Except if she walked in on him, he'd be admitting his ignorance somewhat publicly.

Make up a name for it. Sound blocking metal strip, noise muffling strip or whatever. Well, that's what it was, but clumsy names. He laughed at himself. How not to do an estimate: no pen, no paper, no tape, no internet to check materials and prices. He should get a smart phone, the last one had broken when he'd fallen off the ladder. Now he had a dumb phone. Not good enough, not when he was out and about. But the money wasn't there. It was that or food.

Resilient channel! That was the stuff. He congratulated himself on pulling that out of his stuffed attic memory. He had no idea how much it cost. Couldn't be much, call it fifty quid. Did it come in standard lengths or did you get it cut to size? He'd soon learn. And what was that other stuff? Rock wool, was it? A sound proofing filler to stuff in the middle, between the boards. Then cross fingers, arms and legs that it all worked. Must work to some extent. All that bulk and no door for sound to seep through. Don't forget sealant. He jotted a note. Sound was like water, seeking out any little cracks and joins to get through.

Must phone Bob this evening just to make sure he'd got it all right. Couldn't do it now, that would never do, voicing his lack of savvy in front of a client. He must be the assured builder, the one who knew exactly what he was doing. What a game. But this must be on the right lines, surely? After the botched last soundproofing job, he'd talked it over with Bob and read up sound insulation on the internet. And some of it had stuck in his thick skull. It got pretty technical, and wasn't easy to sort out how much was honest science and how much sales spiel for a particular product.

The front door slammed. Presumably someone who had a key. He was curious about who else lived here. Was she married? Though such thoughts about a potential employer weren't a good idea, but since when has sex been sensible? Get the job first, forget fantasies, settle for a coffee and biscuits. Back to the estimate. He could phone Bob tonight, go over the materials with him...

'Who are you?' came an weary voice from the doorway.

Jack turned. A man vaguely familiar, bent over, holding himself up by the door jamb. He was in shorts and trainers, an overlong T-shirt clinging to his chest, breathing deeply, obviously just back from a run. An obsessive, to be so rain soaked, droplets glistening in his dark brown hair, smeared on his legs and arms. Who else would brave the weather, but a fool of a runner or someone desperate for work?

'Jack!' cried the man.

He held out a wet hand, the other pressed against the support as if unsure he could stand unaided.

Jack took the man's hand. Heavens, he should know him. And snapped his fingers as it came to him.

'Alcohol Halt,' exclaimed Jack. 'Paul. I didn't recognise you in that gear.'

'Five times round the park,' said the man leaving the security of the jamb and sitting on the arm of the sofa. 'Out all weathers. Sun, hail, storm – I do my laps. Been sober four hundred and forty two days. And you?'

Jack grimaced. 'Not so hot for me, mate. I relapsed a couple of months ago. A woman I knew died, and I took the old remedy.'

'And did it work?'

'Of course not.'

'So why did you do it?' said Paul.

'Because I'm an idiot.' He laughed, having just considered the runner an idiot. Two alkie nutters. 'It set me off on a three week bender.'

'So how'd you get off it?'

'Max dragged me off to the Peak District. He near walked me to death, up and down the fells.'

'Didn't get you on his yoga kick, did he?'

'Tried to, but the lingo turned me off. He said forget what it's called, just do it. But I rebelled, so we walked up every fell we came to, got soaked and exhausted while he steered me away from every boozer. Four days of striding muddy heath land.'

'Well, you're sober now. Stay that way,' said Paul, spotting the towel on the back of the dining chair. He picked it up and began wiping himself down, beginning with neck and arms, his breathing less frenetic.

'Booze is not a remedy for anything,' said Jack.

'The gospel according to Max.'

Jack laughed at the saying they'd both recognised. 'He does have his headlines. But they do stick. Which I suppose is the point of them. You're looking well. If rather wet.'

'Thanks, Jack. I've swapped one obsession for another.' He was vigorously wiping his hair. 'Doing the London Marathon in April. I've set myself the goal of breaking 3 ½ hours. So I'm out training every day, seven days a week.'

'How d'you fit that in with work?'

'I run to work, run back again plus a few laps of the park. I'm working on the Isle of Dogs... Working from home next couple of days, so I can fit in the running during the day. Don't tell my boss.'

'Thought you had your own firm. Accountancy or something...'

Paul flapped a dismissive hand. 'Boozing did for that. You can't keep track of customer accounts and be in and out of the rehab. Just about staved off bankruptcy. Had to sell my house and come back and live here. Packed in my self employment, and now I kowtow to a tiresome boss. All damned targets and progress reports. I'm down for an assessment next week. He'll cut me down to size, that's the way he works. I refuse to be one of his toadies, out with him on his drinking sprees and buying an Arsenal season ticket.' He flapped his arms, still holding the towel. 'This is a miserable house, Jack. I presume you've met my sister Lynn?'

'I met a woman, but we never got as far as names. I was leafleting the street. Your sister, I assume it's your sister, called me in. Brown hair, sort of ponytail, slim, always moving, bare feet...'

'That's her, always walks around barefooted. I'm tempted to leave drawing pins around...'

'She wants an estimate for a soundproof wall here,' said Jack. He pointed out where it would go.

Paul took a step back as if he'd been struck. 'Oh, she's not still going on about that. For Heaven's sake. I half agreed to it the other day, when she was talking about it non-stop. I thought she'd forget it. Another of her madcap projects.' He threw the towel on to the sofa as if it was annoying him. 'Can you believe it! Where's all the money coming from?' He stepped out into the hallway and yelled, 'Lynn! What the hell is going on?'

The sudden anger told Jack this job might get no further than the estimate. What had he walked into? There were raised voices from another room, hers followed by his. Seconds out. A few phrases he could make out, but the gist though was clear enough. She wanted the wall, he didn't. It was down to who packed the biggest punch. Though she had waited for her brother to be out before she'd pulled Jack in with her 'Hey builder!' He'd been looking forward to his coffee and chat. Might get neither.

He'd almost had the job in his grasp. That's the way of it. Was it worth going on with the estimate?

No love lost between those two. Well, he wasn't going to walk into a family row. Let them fight it out. Shades of him and Alison a few years back. He smiled wryly, at least he was in the dry, might get a coffee, might not. Place your bets. He looked out of the window. Did he have a job or was he back out leafleting? The rain was darting into puddles in the roadway. At least he was dry, he didn't fancy getting soaked again.

Lynn rushed in with a tray which held a mug of coffee, a plate of biscuits and a small milk jug. She put the tray down on the low table in front of the sofa, flustered, breathing rapidly.

'Sorry about all that.' She indicated off with a flap of her hand. 'Please don't go. I want that wall. Just a tiff with my brother. It happens all the time.'

For a second their eyes held. What sort of appeal was this, he calculated, for sympathy or something more? And she was off before he or she could decide.

Keep calm, don't take sides. Enjoy the coffee, wonder about that glance. 'Please don't go,' she'd said. Meaning she wanted him to stay. To do her wall. Think no further. Eyes held for an instant and he was away, painting futures. Pushing a pram out of a cottage with roses round the door...

Jack had set himself on the sofa, stretching out his legs, and was pouring milk into his coffee, when the row restarted. It felt odd, sedately drinking, dipping biscuits, with a shouting match along the corridor. He shuddered; how people could hate each other. Brother and sister? You assume once they were adult they'd get over childhood antagonism. These two hadn't. Defending their territories like dogs either side of a fence.

Nice coffee though. Deep aroma. He knew that much, better than the instant he had at home. And not a lot of that at the moment. So enjoy someone else's warmth, coffee and biscuits. Take what comes. You never know what's in store. Twenty quid was due from Alison, better than the nothing in his pocket first thing. And this job? Anyone's guess. He might have to tap Bob for a loan.

Though he did know Paul. And she liked him. How much did that count for? Something, but measured up against their antagonism... How long could they go on for? Her yell, his deeper growl... They had a lot of insults in their armoury, years and years of it. Rows burnt out quickly in his experience. One party goes off in a huff. And then it's brooding silence. Worse than the quarrel. Can smoulder on for days, waiting for one or other to break. To apologise or throw crockery and get it going again.

Just supposing he got this job – what an environment to work in! He'd do it, shut up and smile. Let them knock rocks off each other. He wouldn't take sides. Think of the money. If this job was going to happen.

Jack dipped a garibaldi in his coffee, thinking of his empty larder. After Alison's twenty was spent, then what? A food bank, larceny... He could pawn his telescope. Sell some tools on Ebay. That was desperate stuff. And so short term.

Tonight, he should phone Bob about soundproofing and try for a loan. Never good. It so wounded a friendship. He must get all the leaflets out. And hope something came up. Phone around his contacts. You never know, someone might need a hand. A day here, a day there. Anything to tide him over.

Their voices had quietened. And then, as if they'd heard, came a shriek from her, a shout from him. With his hands round the coffee cup, Jack went to the window. The rain had stopped, there were patches of blue in the sky, the sun almost coming through. From the park opposite, the leaves of the trees were glistening and dripping on to the pavement. The clouds were gliding swiftly which could mean more rain on the way or the sky might clear completely. If so, maybe he and Mia could go out with the telescope tonight. He hadn't the fuel to drive to his favoured spot in Chingford, but they could go over Wanstead Flats.

Lynn and Paul came in, faces drained. A clear space between them, but a mutual exhaustion had decided something. Wet clothes were sticking to Paul, his hair standing up after its battle with the towel. Did Jack have work or just biscuits and coffee?

'What's been decided?' he said carefully.

She looked to her brother. 'You tell him.'

'No, you.'

'You thought of the idea.'

Paul's eyes lifted as if to indicate this was always her way. And might have set him off again, but Jack's presence mitigated his reaction.

'OK,' he said, raising his hands in truce. 'We'd like you to arbitrate, Jack.'

'On what?' said Jack, thrown by this. He thought they'd come to tell him what they'd decided, not make him referee in a grudge match.

'Does it make sense to put a wall there?' said Paul.

Jack eyed them both. It was a crazy position to be in. He wasn't neutral; he wanted the work.

He said, warily, 'In my experience people often make through-rooms, like this one. And sometimes regret it. You gain more public space but you lose a room.' He pointed out the TV and speakers. 'With all the sound equipment these days, people want walls back. Depends how many are in the house...'

'Four,' said Paul.

'And how loud they are,' added Jack.

'That bloody TV,' exclaimed Lynn. 'I'd like to put a brick through it.'

'I am entitled to watch television,' yelled Paul. He turned to Jack. 'You can see how unreasonable she is.'

'Take a walk in the traffic!' she exclaimed, and crossed her arms.

'OK,' said Jack. 'Let's keep it cool. If there's a noise problem, then one solution would be two sitting rooms.' It seemed a too obvious thing to say, childish even, like a mother handing out sweets, but he said it anyway. 'One for each of you.'

'Which the other can't go in, unless invited,' she said, getting in at once with the playground rules.

'This would be my room,' stated Paul, shaking a finger round the space to emphasise his territory.

'And this mine,' she said, going into the garden side and circling round.

They were looking to Jack, as if he had the wisdom of Solomon. He needed a baby and a broad sword. Or he could suggest slicing everything in the house in two. Every room, book, carpet, every plate and cup. It wasn't possible to live like this. Whatever he suggested might not work. But he wanted the job. Once done and he was paid, they could quarrel till kingdom come.

'It might up the value of the property,' he suggested, knowing money was often a decider. 'A big family, wanting the extra room.'

Paul shrugged. 'Everyone's going for through-rooms these days.'

'Some are reverting,' said Jack. 'With multiple sound systems, small rooms are on the way back.'

Paul scratched the side of his neck and bit his lower lip. A thought struggling to get free of aggressive guards.

'Do it,' he exclaimed at last. 'For peace and quiet. A Berlin Wall between us. Build it, Jack. I can't take any more.'

He was leaning against the doorpost, eyes closed, maybe already regretting the decision. He looked schoolboyish, on the defeated team, in his clinging shorts and T-shirt.

'Thank you, Paul,' she said quietly.

Paul harrumphed, then shook his head. 'I'm going to have a shower. Get some clothes on. This whole business is doing my head in. You two work it out.'

He gave a half-hearted wave and left the room. For a few seconds, neither spoke. Not wanting to be heard by Paul going up the stairs. A female cry sounded from the landing.

'Dawn coming down for lunch,' said Lynn. 'My niece, his daughter. She works hard and is so quiet. Too quiet. Do the noisy genes only go through the male line?' She stopped, then added, 'You heard what Paul said. Do it. You heard him?'

'Yes, I'm your witness.'

'So...when can you start?'

'Don't you want the estimate first?'

'Will it be less than a thousand?'

'Yes.'

'Then can you start now?' she said desperately, hands and eyes pleading. 'Get moving, so he can't back out.'

'I've got to buy materials,' he said. 'I need money upfront for that.' And then, considering his personal finances, he added, 'And half payment.'

He was unsure about pushing for too much, but he wasn't going to buy materials without their cash. Or rather, he couldn't. And the working money, though utterly necessary, also meant a commitment on her side. And didn't this job need it? If Paul changed his mind, he needed to make sure he, himself, wasn't out of pocket.

'OK,' she said. 'Give me a few minutes to get a few things. Then we'll go to the bank.'

Chapter 5

Dawn had crossed her father coming down the stairs. Running mad, she thought but didn't voice her criticism. All that effort and out in the rain too. Crazy. All for some meaningless goal in a crowd of thousands. At least it got him out of the house, out of her way. Tired him out.

She wasn't sure whether his expression had been disapproval at her or a leftover from the row she'd heard going on below. He threw his hands up as he passed her and headed for his room along the landing. One less to deal with, she thought. At ground level, she hugged the staircase newel, straining to hear the words coming from the sitting room. Her aunt's voice was clear but there was a man's she didn't know. They seemed chatty and she was curious who he was but at least he kept Lynn occupied. She must get to the kitchen without being seen. Lynn would only ask her whether she'd been cutting herself again. Those wearisome non conversations. Lynn tried, she could hardly blame her, but she didn't understand at all.

The necessity, the relief of it. Of course there was hurt and guilt. But was it any more senseless than running round and round the park until you could hardly stand? Yes, her dad would say, running is temporary. It's not self harm. Isn't it? she would say in one of those imaginary conversations she had with him. Aren't you simply pounding yourself to exhaustion, so you haven't the energy to think about what's really bothering you? Like your drinking and your putrid relationship with your sister, like working in a job you can't stand.

With her it was just a little blood from a razor. Relief in the pain. Something she could do. Couldn't stop herself

27

doing. You blame yourself for your parents splitting up, said one of her therapists. God save her from therapists. 'It was the best thing going,' she'd yelled at her, 'them splitting up. How can you live in a war zone?' Now her mother was safely in Australia. She'd talked with her on Skype last night. All about her college work and which universities she was applying to. She'd wanted to switch her off after five minutes, but on and on she went, her inquisition. And so hard to keep calm and smiling, to nod at her advice. Her mother who had left her for heaven's sake, gone to Australia with a professor who was more than fifty years old, who'd been married three times. Dawn wanted to say, he'll dump you in the Outback. If you want my advice – dump him first. But advice was one way, like heat, from hot to cold, like red blood from the heart to the arms.

Why was she living at all? Every day she wondered. The point of going on day after day, drifting to nowhere. For what? Like a caterpillar on a leaf, chomping and shitting. But who would, at least, one day become a butterfly. She wouldn't. She had metamorphosed into what she would always be. Useless and ineffectual. Nothing finished, lots of half done things scattered about. She coped, just about, with college work, might scrape into a university, one in the lower league.

To what end? To pass exams. She could take a gap year. A gap ten years? A lifelong gap. What is the point of this misery, she'd said tearfully to her latest therapist. Who'd had lots of practice with young adult angst, and suggested a career, fulfilling motherhood, or even both. There was that weasel word, fulfilling. Sneaked in, like a snake under a tent flap. Suppose it wasn't fulfilling? Like her father's job or his marriage or his relationship with his children. Then what?

How do you know if you don't try, said her therapist.

Dawn had ended up crying for half the session. 'I don't know how to try,' she'd exclaimed over and over. 'I haven't the will.'

'Then I'll help you develop the will,' said the therapist.

Dawn crept past the sitting room, the door half open, her aunt and the man continuing to chat, up the hallway and into the kitchen. She sighed with relief at getting there unassailed. Her territory now. She was hungry, having got up early, she always got up early, not like her brother Nick. He could sleep the whole day away, though not surprising, considering the time he went to bed.

She'd got her books out at 8 am, her laptop ready, wrote the title of the essay. Thought for a couple of minutes, lost track and cut her arm over the sink. She'd watched the blood drip and set over half an hour. Then did an hour of essay writing. And then she was stuck and her mind wandered, thinking about her mother. And she cut her other arm. Amazing how the blood replenished. You would think it would give up, know this was a losing race, but on it went, making more of itself in the bone marrow. Fulfilling its destiny in running down her arm and setting.

The point is the point. Living is *living*. She should write one of those pop books, full of how I went from trailer trash, addiction, and self harm to CEO of a multi national. With all those important things to remember, in CAPITAL LETTERS. All you have to do is believe in yourself and you can be President of the United States. Ra-ra-ra!

But there's only one every four years, and too many suits in the race. Besides, she wasn't even American, so she could believe in herself all she liked and she'd never be President of the United States. Alright then, first person on Mars. Or why not the biggest collection of blue elastic bands – so she could be in the Guinness Book of Records.

So difficult to choose what to be remembered for.

From the fridge, she took out the plastic box of bacon and placed two fleshy slices on to a plate. Then two eggs, and then to the cupboard for a can of beans. Finally bread from the bin. Two slices. She needed the sustenance. To write essays, to make blood so it could fulfil its destiny, and to give her the strength to tell her mother what universities she was applying to. And to think about whether to try for something or other, to make her therapist happy, or not.

Keeping half an ear to the hallway, not wanting to deal with her aunt who was hard to avoid, being at home all day. She'd encounter her soon enough; the kitchen was the place where everyone had to go. Most arguments happened here. Lynn always had something to pick her brother up on: the bathroom was a mess, a pan was burnt, the noise from his bedroom. Anguished guitar sounds, his doggerel rap to the window and walls. Dawn took pleasure in his noise. It was so horrible, she loved it. Her father bore it because Lynn hated it. Dawn would lay there, listening to the racket, enjoying the way the vibrations shook the house and heads of the occupants. And when it got too much for her, she would go into her hideaway, in the built-in cupboard, on its floor, under the rack of coats and dresses. She would lay out, close the door, put on her headphones and listen to white noise.

She liked her nest. It smelt of her. A womb she could stay in forever, dark as emptiness, with her and her only. With no necessity to do, succeed, fulfil the dreams she didn't have. Until hunger or the need to pee drove her into the light. The world of people, ambition and demand.

Her aunt came into the kitchen, with her head-teacher's face, bearing a tray of coffee items. Dawn used to think her beautiful when she would come over with birthday or Christmas presents, when she would read to her and Nick. But living with her did for that. The rows with her father reminded her of all those rows her mother had with him.

There's no such thing as beauty, she knew. Just need and illusion.

Lynn put the tray on the dishwasher and turned to her niece.

'That's a good lunch,' she said, looking over the laid out food.

'I never have breakfast,' said Dawn knowing her aunt already knew this, 'so I make up for it at lunch. Who were you chatting to?'

'A builder. His name is Jack. He's going to build a wall in the sitting room. Make two rooms of it, so I can keep away from your father.'

'Good idea. I heard the two of you this morning.'

'Sorry, dear.' Lynn sighed. 'I know it's hard on everyone. But we don't get on, never have, never will. It's just unfortunate we've been forced together.' She put her hand on her niece's shoulder. 'I'm so sorry you have to endure it. You have enough troubles.'

Dawn didn't reply. Not wanting to agree, and get into a conversation about her troubles. And get more advice.

'Has it been all right today?' said Lynn gently.

Dawn bit her lip and trembled. She needed to be a better actor. It didn't matter what she said now, the truth was revealed.

'Did you...? This morning,' asked Lynn.

Dawn nodded. And Lynn cradled her. Lots better than words.

'Poor you,' her aunt murmured. 'Oh my poor dear. I wish I could help.'

Tears were filling Dawn's eyes. Don't say any more, please, she thought. No advice. No telling me how to live my life. No looking at my arms.

'It's no good what I say,' soothed Lynn. 'I don't know anything myself and I'm twice your age. Look at me, jobless and useless.'

'You're not useless, auntie.'

Lynn kissed her on the cheek. 'Keep saying that, Dawn. Tell me I can do anything. Tell me I am superwoman. The world is waiting for me!'

Dawn laughed and separated from her aunt.

'You should write a book,' she said. 'One of those self help things. They sell well.'

She could give advice too. It was easy. She must do it more.

'I'll write one called How to get on with one's brother,' said Lynn.

'No, not that book.' She reflected. 'Or maybe half of that one. You know the first half – how bad your life was with him. From the moment you first opened your eyes and he stuck you with a pin. You can write that half.'

'But not what to do about it.' Lynn raised an urgent finger. 'Yet. Da da!' She sounded the drum. 'I shall build my wall. Or rather, the builder will. And in my space, I will make my new self.' She was fired. 'And I must go, dearest. I've got to get to the bank and get it all happening before your ogre of a father changes his mind.' She gave her niece a cuddle, then parted, getting as far as the door, before she had a thought. 'Is this study week or something?'

'It is,' said Dawn. 'It means our teachers have a week off, while we do lots of work.' And added quickly before her aunt asked, 'but I am doing it. Honest. Though I'm not sure about Nick.'

'Don't get me on to the subject of your brother. Must go. See you in a little while.' She blew her a kiss and left the room.

Chapter 6

DS Fayyad Kamani stopped the car, and peered out of the window. The rain had ceased though the pavement was wet, there were puddles in the gutter, and the trees over the park railings were dripping. He could leave his raincoat in the car for the short walk to the house. Fayyad was fussy about his suit, more important now, as he'd been made up to detective sergeant. Look smart, his father always said, and they think you *are* smart. Look scruffy and they think you're stupid. His father had nothing but suits, wore them in his sub post office in Seven Kings, mowed the lawn in his third best.

'This is the house,' said Fayyad to Detective Constable Amis, as he turned off the engine.

Fayyad was the senior. He had worked with Hayley Amis on and off for several years, and so they knew each other well, too well for her to call him sir following his promotion.

'We have to go carefully,' he said.

'Not to warn them off,' she agreed. DC Amis wore a navy blue dress suit with flat shoes. She didn't need the height of heels, being tall, and knew flats were better for pursuit.

'The fact that we are here at all tells them more than we'd like, but that can't be helped,' said Fayyad. 'Besides, we're not sure it's him yet.'

'Softly, softly,' she said, 'in case it's someone else.'

'That's the approach.'

They got out of the vehicle and Fayyad locked up. He looked up at the sky, swift cloud clearing in the chilly breeze. He straightened his suit and adjusted his tie. This could be a tricky conversation. A couple of times, he'd gone to places where he'd had to tell parents, in one case of a son's death, in another of a daughter's. So hard, what do you say, except you are sorry to have to bear the bad news. You offer condolences but they are hardly noticed in their grief. This wasn't quite the same, might end up the same, but not yet.

They went up the path to the house, climbed the steps and pressed the bell to Anne's flat. She answered, and, when they said who they were, she buzzed them in.

'I'll take the lead,' said Fayyad. 'We only say what we have to.'

'Got it.'

They went down the hallway, a young woman opened the flat door. Her hair was short, her pink lipstick slightly awry.

'We are here to see Bessie Brand,' said Fayyad.

'That's me,' she said, plainly nervous.

'I am Detective Sergeant Fayyad Kamani and this is my colleague Detective Constable Amis.'

They showed their identification. She looked at the cards briefly.

'I spoke to you on the phone, Miss,' said Hayley. 'About your father.'

'You said you might have news.'

'That's right,' said Fayyad. 'May we come in.'

'Sorry, sorry. How rude of me. Please come in.'

She was trembling, stepping from foot to foot, playing with her hair. Was it because of who they were, thought Fayyad, or was it because of what she knew? Hard to tell, the very presence of the police frightened people. We never bring good news.

They followed Bessie as she led them down the hall to the kitchen where there were four stools around a table. The room was tidy, a notice board with bills pinned to it. Recently decorated.

'Please sit down,' she said indicating the stools. 'Would you like a cup of tea?' Already picking the kettle up, just to be doing something.

'No thank you,' said Fayyad for them both. 'Please sit down yourself, Bessie. We have some things to tell you and then we want your help.'

Bessie looked around wildly as if someone might yet come to her rescue. And when no one did, she sat down on a stool, rubbing one side of her face.

Fayyad had taken out his notebook.

'You reported your father missing on 18th October 2014. You and Anne Tucker came to Forest Gate Police Station.'

'She's my boss. I'm a childminder,' she said rapidly. 'I live up there. Second floor. Yes, we reported him missing. We hadn't seen him for three days. Didn't know where he was. He was...' she corrected herself, 'is a taxi driver. The firm kept phoning me up. So me and Anne went to the police.'

'And you've heard nothing since?'

'Nothing at all.' She looked at them in alarm. 'Have you news? Do you know where he is?'

Fayyad took a deep breath. This was the difficult bit, but there was no other way. She was so patently uncomfortable, Fayyad wanted to put an arm round her as he told her. Professionally not wise.

'A body has been found,' he said, 'in Epping Forest. Male, badly decayed...' He stopped, aware of what he was saying, perhaps too much detail. But that's what happened to bodies. They decayed. Though he needed to be more delicate. 'Various tests indicate the body is about the age of your father and died about the time he was reported missing.'

'What's he doing in Epping Forest?' she exclaimed, scratching her hair.

Fayyad thought that a dense observation, but no, he reflected, unfair. Shock took people in different ways.

'We have yet to confirm whether it is your father or not.'

'It could be someone else, love,' added Hayley.

'Too badly decayed for visual identification,' said Fayyad. 'So we need a sample of your DNA.'

'You want me to pee in a bottle?' said Bessie, breathing rapidly.

Fayyad smiled for an instant, then culled it as inappropriate. 'Not necessary, Bessie. We just want a scraping from the inside of your mouth.'

DC Amis had put on a pair of plastic gloves and took from her pocket a plastic bag with a small canister inside and a wooden scraper.

She said, 'All I do is take a scraping from the inside of your cheek. It doesn't hurt.'

'Then what do you do with it?' said Bessie, staring at the canister that Hayley was taking out of the bag.

Fayyad knew some of the science behind DNA testing. 'You and your father share half the same genes,' he said. 'So your scraping goes to the lab. There will be cells in the sample with your DNA. We can compare that with the DNA of the corpse. If you fit fifty percent with him – then he's your father. If your sample is nothing like his, then you are not related. Until the tests are done, we can't be sure one way or the other.'

'Could be someone else then,' said Bessie. She was trembling again, her hands at her cheeks.

'Until we get the results, we can't say the body is definitely your father.'

Hayley unscrewed the canister with her gloved hands. She stood up. 'Open your mouth wide, dear.'

Bessie looked at them both like a frightened beast, then closed her eyes and opened her mouth wide.

'Just be a second,' said Amis, putting the spatula into Bessie's mouth and gently scraping the inside cheek. 'There,' she said, taking out the scraper. 'That wasn't painful, was it?'

'No,' said Bessie, her expression belying the word, as she watched Hayley transfer the saliva and cheek cells into the canister.

Hayley put the cap on, then took an adhesive label and stuck it on the canister, writing on it *Bessie Brand* and the date and time. She put the canister into the plastic bag. Only then did she take off the plastic gloves.

'We'll know in a few days whether the body is your father or not,' said Fayyad.

'Is it murder?' She hesitated. 'The man. Whether it's dad or not.'

Fayyad considered for a second, but it was too obvious not to give an answer; anyone could work it out for themselves. 'Bodies don't bury themselves in Epping Forest,' he said. And at once realised he'd told her that the body was buried. Hayley nudged him with her knee. Too late now. It was said. Well, it would be in the news soon enough.

'I want it to be him,' said Bessie.

Hayley looked to Fayyad, indicating she wanted to speak. He nodded.

'Why's that, dear?'

'He was a terrible man. He did terrible things to me. I want him dead.'

No one spoke for a short while. Bessie had covered her face with her hands, rocking back and forth. Fayyad wondered what her father had done to this girl. Beatings, incest? Both maybe. It had shocked him at first what people did to each other. But he was getting used to it. Not necessarily a good thing.

'I know this is difficult for you, Bessie. Thank you for your help,' said Fayyad. 'We'll be in touch when we know the results of the tests.'

He and Hayley rose. Bessie uncovered her face, looking at them helplessly as if they might suddenly turn on her. What on earth could he say to her? What had occurred between this girl and her father. He had told her he might or might not be dead. And she wanted dead, dead only.

'We're sorry we had to disturb you,' said Hayley. 'And hope we haven't brought back too many bad memories.' She had a light hand on Bessie's shoulder. 'But you do understand we have to make sure.'

'Yes,' said Bessie. 'It's your job.' She closed her eyes for an instance, then added, 'I do hope it's him, and not some other poor man.'

Chapter 7

Paul had showered. And felt better for it, warmed up after his run, less vulnerable now dressed. He'd washed off the row with Lynn. But was unsure what he'd done, the long term effects. Conceding that wall. Especially with a witness present. Lesson – never make decisions just after a long run.

He could have said no. Stuck to it. After all, he virtually had the sitting room whenever he wanted. All he had to do was turn the TV on and she'd scamper off like a hen that had seen a fox. Now he'd given up half of the room. It was Jack's presence that did it. He didn't want to be seen as oppressive. She'd played it smart by saying let Jack decide. And what else could Jack decide, he'd realised under the shower, than that there should be a wall. After all, that was his job. She'd caught him, weak after the run, not thinking straight. To hell with her. She could have the room, and let's see how good the soundproofing is. He'd give it a thorough test alright. Connect the TV to the sound system and turn it up full. And then where would she hide? In her useless room with its new wall, which she'd have to pay for. She wasn't getting a penny off him for it.

So let Jack build it. With her money. And see where that gets her.

He'd put on a blue long sleeve shirt and jeans. The advantage of working from home. No suit. No boss either. But he'd better do some work. He'd done a couple of hours before he went out on the run, but needed to complete the account and email it to the office. Lunch first.

It was difficult to find non hostile space. Anywhere. His office was competitive, here was a zoo, unless in this room where he worked as well as slept. But it wasn't sacrosanct.

Lynn could burst in anytime and then Nick in his bedroom, on his guitar, worse when his mate Tim came. At least he'd insisted they practise when he was at the office or watching TV downstairs, when, if they were really loud, he could don headphones. They bothered Lynn a lot more than him which was why he gave them a long tether.

Paul had the master bedroom. It had an en suite shower, something he was grateful for as there was frequently a queue for the bathroom. And Nick left it in a state. And from time to time, Dawn did her cutting there. Horrible, horrible, to find her sitting on the side of the bath, her arm dripping. He didn't know what to say to her. Fortunately Lynn was there last time. She took her to the hospital. He'd wanted to say, yell more like, straighten up, be sensible, stop this madness. Exactly the same things said to him when he was boozing. Useless verbage. So he'd tried being nice, soft, but then it would burst out of him, his anger at her. For doing that to herself, in his house, around him. What was the point of it? 'The only person you are hurting is yourself,' he'd yelled, then contradicted himself by telling her she was hurting him too, her mother, Lynn, her brother. Which was probably the point of it. If only she'd gone to Australia with Joan. Except they wouldn't have Dawn, her and that professor with his effete goatee beard. Off they'd gone and left him with two teenage losers.

If Dawn would kill herself, do it properly, then he could grieve over her, bury her and so forth. But no, it was this bit by bit. A dribble of suicide. This, look at my bloody arm, that's what you've done to me. Maybe he had. His drinking, being hardly ever here. And Joan was a cold fish. They should never have had kids. But there you are, done in a moment. Who knew the consequences?

He wanted the house, the whole house, to himself. Get rid of the kids: you're eighteen now! out of my hair, go to university in some distant northern town. Stay there. He'd send a bit of cash now and again.

He feared neither would go. Too soft here.

He couldn't deal with them and Lynn together. Deal with his sister first. Get rid of her. She was close to cracking up, he could feel it coming off her, crackling like electricity. Hear it in her hysteria. This new room, a last ditch effort. And when it didn't work, at that point – what else could she do but leave?

And the house would be his. She might own half of it, but what could she do if he wouldn't agree to sell? He'd have to sort the brats out, get them off his hands somehow. But leave that till it came to the top of the agenda. Lynn first.

People, damned people. How they got in his way! He wanted an empty house. Well, maybe a tenant or two, who he could evict when they annoyed him. Enough, enough, this buzzing headful. It was why he ran. To clear his thoughts. All he had to concentrate on was the effort of running itself.

He jotted down today's time on his progress sheet. Definitely speeding up, even with the rain. And yesterday out with the Sunday crowd, he was up with the fast guys, kept with them for the full fifteen miles. He'd never done that before. Quite a killer. Over Wanstead Flats, all the way across Leytonstone Flats and along the leftovers of Epping Forest that hung on the Woodford New Road like tired washing, past the North Circular, turning back at Woodford Wells and returning via Snaresbrook. He preferred the off road stretches, easier on the legs and not too muddy. Well, it wasn't yesterday, but would be from now on with all this rain. Mud didn't dry out this time of year, just thickened and churned with boots, bicycles and horses as you got deeper into winter. But he'd take the seasons as they came. Be hard, face the weather, no backing out for a storm or frost. That was his promise to himself. All surfaces, all elements, he'd do the mileage. If he could just keep off injury, then he'd break three and a half without any trouble. Maybe get closer to the magic three, so next year he could push into it.

He was ten, maybe fifteen years, older than most of the Sunday crowd, and he could still show them. Most of them were fair weather runners. Well, he'd take a bet, penny to a pound, that he'd be the first of them over the line come the marathon.

It was good to have a target. People to beat, a time to go for. Something difficult but achievable. He was obsessive, he knew that. The counsellor told him so, as if he didn't realise it himself. It was why he'd become an alcoholic. Blame the obsessive gene. Use it, said the counsellor, instead of letting it use you. Be obsessed with something you want to be obsessed with.

Like running. Like getting Lynn out of the house.

Dressed and comfortable, he went downstairs to the kitchen. He'd seen from his bedroom window Lynn leaving with Jack, so he'd be spared another encounter, though he wouldn't have avoided it. No, you must face her head on. And win. Every time win. Which was why the wall battle hurt. He hadn't won. But he would. He would make sure, in the longer term, it didn't work for her.

In the kitchen he encountered Dawn. He hadn't realised she was in there or he might have left her to it. But he'd walked in oblivious. She was clearing up her lunch things, wiping the table. One thing you could say for her. She did leave the kitchen clean, unlike somebody else.

Her blouse needed ironing, those jeans were ripped, but was that the fashion or were they just ripped? She was pale, he could see Joan in her, slim, could be pretty if she learnt how to smile. And wash her hair. Did it have to be so tangled?

'How was your morning?' he said, as cheerfully as he could manage, hoping for a positive answer so he wouldn't be dragged into her problems.

'Fine,' she said. 'I've got well into my English essay. I hope to finish it this afternoon.'

'That's good,' he said. 'Keeping up with your school work. Much better than your brother. I don't suppose he's even up yet.' He knew he wasn't but had to say something. Keep the conversation going, like any concerned parent.

'He was up very late last night.'

Paul knew that too.

'No problems with your teachers? Or the other students?'

'Everything's fine.'

He was glad she could lie to him. What on earth would he do if she told him the truth? Whatever the truth was. A version of not coping, in all the ways it could manifest. He'd known more than a few of them. Or that college was going badly. It was useless yelling at youngsters to work when they weren't. It never had any effect. They either did or they didn't. By the time they'd got to eighteen, they'd either got into the habit or they were wasters.

'I'm glad you're eating,' he said. 'That's the main thing. Look after the body.' He hesitated, then couldn't stop himself asking what he didn't want to know. 'You haven't been...you know?'

Why the hell had he said that? He didn't want her to tell him. What could he do about it? But it was expected of him, of parents, to ask, so he could say he'd asked, if asked himself by some therapist or doctor.

'I haven't,' she said.

He inwardly sighed. 'That's good. Me and your mother worry a lot about you. Lynn too. Don't think we don't care. Glad you've hit it on the head. Much better for everybody.'

'Yes.'

She was standing awkwardly by the table. He was aware he was barring the way to the door. He moved, he hoped without being too obvious.

'I'd better make some breakfast,' he said.

'And I've that essay to finish.'

She started for the door, when he called her back. He was fishing in his pocket.

'Here's a tenner. Treat yourself.'

'Thanks, Dad.'

She took the note and was gone.

Paul didn't move for a few seconds, listening for her footsteps up the stairs, wanting to be assured that this space was now his. That was her on the landing. And her door closing. Good. He had the space. And would hold it against all comers. He was quite pleased with himself; he'd asked Dawn all the right questions. OK, didn't get the truth, but who really wants that? Besides, she could have said it, he'd given her the chance. That was the main thing.

Lunch. And then get some work done.

Chapter 8

Jack had never felt comfortable in this cafe. The people who ran it were nice enough, mostly young people serving. Too many, it seemed to him. How could they make a profit? But they never hassled you. Although he always felt the other customers were looking at him, wondering why he'd invaded their space. They had degrees and read books he'd never heard of. Went to art galleries and to theatres. Guardian readers, like his ex. He was staring at a painting that was supposed to be of Wanstead Flats. Well, it had grass and trees but for some reason a huge, pinkish water lily in the centre. At least, he thought it was a water lily. That sort of thing. Lots of petals and floating in the water.

She saw him looking.

'Buddhist influence,' she said. 'It's about the oneness of everything.'

'I don't get it,' said Jack. 'There are no giant water lilies over the Flats. A few in the ponds but no bigger and better than anybody else's.'

'It's symbolic,' she said.

'Then why not a footballer or a pile of dog shit?'

She laughed. 'Why not? They are all part of the oneness. Whatever that is.' She shrugged. 'The artist sees the Universe as connected and we are at its heart.'

'We live on a tiny planet in hostile space,' he said. 'More than overdue for an asteroid strike.'

She stared at him fixedly. 'That's a strange comment for a builder.'

'What's a builder supposed to say? I'd better learn.'

'Cor, darlin', nice pair of legs!' She imitated the stereotype in over the top cockney, her hands shaping an ample bosom.

Jack blew a raspberry. 'Nah. That's Sun readers. I read the Mirror. We might think it, but we know when to shut up.'

She laughed. 'Considerate sexists.'

'Is it sexist to find someone attractive?'

'No,' she reflected. 'You're right. It's what you do that matters.'

They were carefully sizing each other up, no doubt about that, across the small table in the E7 Café. The room was fairly crowded, lunchtime, a buzz of conversation, ringing china and cutlery, somewhat stuffy with door and window closed. He thought of touching her hand and seeing what happened. Whether she pulled it away as if scorched or left it there. But he had four hundred and fifty pounds of her money in his pocket – and didn't want to jeopardise that. She was his employer. He need the job, the cash. Sex, love, would be nice. But it didn't pay the rent.

He said, choosing his words, 'You and Paul don't get on too well.'

Lynn gave a snort. 'Well spotted, Jack.' She sucked her bottom lip as if considering how much to say, then shrugged and continued. 'We hate each other, in short. Always have done, always will. My first memory was of him hitting me with a spade when I was two.'

'What did you do?'

'Throw sand in his eyes.'

He was aware of her hand on the table, so close, but their eyes had caught. There was a buzz all about them but they were in their own circle.

'All through childhood, we battled, me and Paul. If I had a birthday party, he'd spoil it with a tantrum. So I did the same to him. It ended up we couldn't go to each other's parties, one parent would take us off to a relative or something. We had separate holidays because they couldn't stand the two of us fighting. He used to rip up my dolls, I'd bury vital bits of his Lego. Amazing neither of us killed the other, but there was lots of blood. When we got to be teenagers, we stopped hitting each other. Just insults and belittling, stealing CDs, not passing on vital messages. What was considered vital anyway. Horrible and continuous pettiness. It was paradise when he went to university. I dreaded the holidays when he'd come back home. Relatives took great care to invite us one at a time. I never went to his wedding, arranged to be on holiday in Spain. But he came to mine, oh boy did he come to mine.' She stopped, her hand went to her cheek. 'I don't know why I'm telling you all this. Yes, I do. To stop Paul getting in first.'

'What happened at your wedding?'

Was her knee nudging his? Accidental perhaps, it was a small table.

'He got drunk. Dawn and Nick were there. They might even remember it. Aged three at the time. Anyway, the wedding. He insisted on giving a speech after the meal. And started off with jokes. Fine, fine. I thought I'll get away with it. He was the proud brother, proud of my first class degree at University, proud of my job in the City... And then began listing why he wasn't so proud. Whoring, drinking, drugs, cheating, stealing... My husband's mates had to drag him away, still ranting. I could have killed Paul then and there. I have never been so embarrassed, so hurt.'

'So why are you in the same house?'

She flapped her hands dismissively. 'Two divorces and a funeral. Our parents died in a plane crash in France two years ago. Enough already.' She held up a hand to indicate a halt. 'I can't tell you everything on a first date.' She clutched his hand fiercely in two of hers. 'You didn't think you were getting into this when you came in from the rain, did you?'

He pressed his knee against her.

'You took me in,' he murmured. 'And gave me coffee and biscuits.'

'There's a price for everything,' she said.

Chapter 9

Paul was eating his fry up, feeling guilty at his plateful. Two burgers, chips, beans, eggs, all piled up. Shouldn't he eat more healthily? But he was starved after his eight mile run, his row with Lynn, being nice to Dawn. It all took energy. Even crap food had energy. He should eat decent grub but you couldn't in this house. Everything was everybody's. The problem of the commons, he vaguely remembered from college. Like the sea or the unfenced prairie. No fences, no rules, just take what's there before someone else does. Like his first college flat. You couldn't leave a tin of beans in your kitchen cupboard, until everyone resorted to putting locks on. So sad, they couldn't work out something more sociable. Good job no one had a gun. They might shoot the locks off, then everyone in their beds.

Joan had got him out of it. And into something else, a long something else. The kids, setting up his business, lots of booze, losing his business, the divorce, more booze. Amazing how much of it he could no longer remember. Or perhaps how much he could. Not that it was worth remembering, losing the business, the house, just about getting out alive. The early stuff, well, love shmuv. And then... Tedium. That's what got him drinking, having to deal with his boredom. His increasing distance from Joan, the fighting kids. The tedium of home. Too much, way too much. And drink gave him succour. At first. An uncaring glug of years, at home, at work, flat out in the gutter. He'd been a champion drinker.

His legs were stiff, the calves aching. No wonder. Fifteen yesterday, eight today. Seventy miles a week. He'd cut it back to 30 after the marathon. Over the summer. Maybe computer dating. Before he got into autumn training.

How long might Lynn stay? She was pretty ratty this morning. Rowing with him over her space in the house, the noise, Nick's guitar playing, Dawn's problems. A lot buried in that word, problems. Who hasn't got problems? There was no doubt Lynn had too. And one morning she'd get up, pack a suitcase, and be gone. All he had to do was hang on. Pour in the aggro now and then. Turn up the volume on the TV. Get Nick to turn up his racket with that pal of his. And hang on.

Chapter 10

The children were on the carpet, eating slices of apple and orange, and drinking milk. A period of accord, concentrating on eating, though Bessie had to stop a little boy trying to take a piece of apple out of another's hand when he'd dropped his own. She gave him another piece, and took him to a calmer spot. Then joined Anne, who was tall, her face very freckled, hair light with a neat fringe at the front.

'So they told you they'd found a body,' said Anne, irritated by the children, who were quite well settled, but she had urgent matters to seek out. 'Did they definitely say it was your father?'

They were seated on adult size chairs, watching the children, near enough, should anything erupt.

'They said it might be him,' said Bessie. 'That's why they wanted a sample from me. She took a scraping from inside my cheek. To test, to see if it's a match with the body. Something like that.'

'They definitely said in Epping Forest?' enquired Anne, her stomach churning. She had dreaded this.

'Several times. The man, the Asian cop, he said he'd been buried in the forest... Definitely said buried.' She turned to Anne. 'It's him, isn't it? It's bound to be him.'

'I'd be surprised if it wasn't,' she said.

What would the cops do next? Had she and the others been careful enough? Could everyone be relied on?

She thought back to the night. The night she'd smashed Frank on the head. He was on top of her, in the midst of attempted rape, having pushed his way into her flat, and forced her down on the sofa. She'd grabbed what was handy and whacked out at him. When he'd weakened his hold, she hit him again and again, until the vase smashed to pieces in her hands. She'd slid out from under his immobile body, blood all over her, and sat there numb.

Maybe five minutes later, who knows how long? she'd felt for a pulse in his wrist. Nothing. Blood was pouring out of his head down the side of his face, puddling at his collar. Dribbling on the sofa, and running on to the floor. She couldn't call the police. Out of the question. She'd been banged up for two years in a bungled investigation when her husband was murdered. And now this. A second killing. They would never believe it was an accident. They'd make sure they had her dead to rights this time. She'd been unable to move, or do anything. Overwhelmed by the corpse and what it could mean for her. And then Jack turned up, for what he'd supposed would be a romantic evening... And was anything but.

'What will they do?' asked Bessie. 'When the tests show it's him.'

'They'll be back here, all over us,' said Anne, clenching her fingers in frustration. 'Question each one of us. Over and over. No let up.'

She was exhausted at the thought. They'd be here alright. Her worst nightmares confirmed. And find out who she was. Her time in jail, conviction overturned but now associated with a second corpse. Though if it was just her, she'd manage somehow, but it was all the others she'd dragged in. Too many.

'What shall I say?' said Bessie.

'Tell the truth about everything,' she said. 'Except when it comes to that night. You slept through it. Your dad didn't come home. That's all. You went on with your life. Did what you normally did.'

'Nothing about cleaning up?' said Bessie.

'Of course not,' she snapped. The girl exasperated her. 'Cleaning up what?'

'Nothing.' Bessie corrected herself. 'Of course, nothing. But it's OK to say I helped you in the nursery?'

'That's fine. Everything was normal. Except your father didn't come back. You helped me in the nursery. Did Nancy's shopping for her.'

'I took out her cat litter, I washed the dishes... I do miss her.'

'She was old, Bessie. Everyone dies. She'd had a good life.'

Anne didn't really know whether Nancy had or hadn't. But it's what you say. She'd been an old lady who lived upstairs; Bessie was her main visitor. Went to her every day. Not to speak ill of the dead, but it was no bad thing Nancy wasn't here. One less to blabber. This could so easily go wrong. For her, for Bessie, who still needed guardianship even though she was in her mid 20s. Her father had infantilised her. And done worse, so much worse. Then there was Jack who she'd drawn in, along with Maggie and David. None of whom knew what was about to befall them.

'What happened to Bert?' Bessie interrupted her thoughts.

Anne sighed. This was so complicated. If they'd found Frank, then they'd found Bert. Buried, aptly, in the same grave. So many fingers in the pie. All it needed was one of them to say a word out of place. And it could all tumble out. Good cop, bad cop, they knew how to do it. She'd experienced it, how they lied, put words in your mouth.

If it came out, and for hell's sake, let it not, but if so she would say that with Frank it was self defence. True, true enough. But how to make that stack up? Every murderer says it was self defence. So the cops assume everyone is a liar. Frank was a rat, she would say. He was raping her, she grabbed what was at hand. True, absolutely true. But then there was Bert. Bert had found out by following Maggie and David to where Frank was buried. And so she'd pretended love, slept with Bert out of necessity, and planned his murder. That was never self defence. A stabbing pure and simple.

She'd virtually put Bert and Frank out of her mind. Safely buried, deep in the forest. No longer. Unless it was someone else. They were still testing. But how many bodies are there in the woods? There was a chance it could be someone else. She and Bessie had reported Frank missing. Could just be they'd found a body in the forest, buried about the same time, but someone else completely.

'Did they mention Bert?' she asked.

'No, just Dad. They didn't say anything about Bert.' She pondered, scratching her chin. 'How come he died too?'

'It happens,' said Anne. Especially if you make it.

The cops would only say as much as they had to, she thought. That was the way they worked. Best assume the worst. Be prepared and assume it was Frank they'd found. Be a pleasant surprise if it isn't. But go on as if it is. Then she'd be ready for them. And if they found Frank, they'd found Bert too, both in the same grave. It seemed tidy at the time. Apt. Stupid in retrospect.

She was thinking a hundred thoughts at once. Beginning a thought, going that way, waylaid, then another direction, incoherent zigzags. Take control. Work out what to do, what to say. How to behave. Be consistent. Whatever that means.

She'd had practice with the police. But the others hadn't. She had to control this situation. She must speak to Maggie and David. Get them on the book. Jack too. Bessie hadn't been involved in the murder of Bert. Nor had Jack. So, keep them ignorant of it. For self preservation. All they knew was that Bert had disappeared. Nothing of the how. Keep it like that. Bessie was the weak link. The cops had terrified her.

Anne liked her a lot, but she wasn't the brightest cherry in the bunch.

'If they come back, and I'm pretty sure they will,' she said, 'just say Bert came to see you a couple times asking where your father was. You made him tea...'

'Do I tell them what he did to me?' Her eyes were welling.

Anne clasped her, feeling Bessie's desperation in the rapid beating in her chest. Bert had raped her, had been taking over the flat, her life. How much need Bessie say of that?

'Oh, the men in your life, dearest. I am so sorry...'

'Don't be!' Bessie exclaimed. 'I'm so glad they're gone.' Warily, she added, 'I have the feeling that Bert is dead too? Is he?'

'Don't ask me,' said Anne. 'Then you won't have to lie about Bert. You can say what he did to you. But you don't know anything about his disappearance, so you have nothing to say about that. He came. He did nasty things. He went away, never came back, and that's all you know.'

She released Bessie, aware of her own palpitations. Could she take all this again? But what was the choice? It had a course to run. Don't panic. Such trite advice, when she simply wanted to flee.

The children were finishing up, oblivious of grown up talk of death in the forest. Of adults seeing the forces of law and order homing in, preparing their alibis. Cups empty, fruit gone, demanding attention, new play.

'My boyfriend knows none of this,' exclaimed Bessie. 'I don't know what to say to him. He'll be asking me questions. What do I say to him, Anne?'

'Let's clear up,' said Anne, rising. She looked out of the French windows. 'It's stopped raining. We could go over the park. Talk more in the playground.'

Chapter 11

'We have two options,' said Jack.

They were seated in her car, having just embraced.

'Which are?'

'Go to my place. It's just round the corner. Or go off and buy materials.'

'You choose,' she said.

Said in such a way, with such a direct look, that Jack knew exactly what she wanted. When such moments come, grab them was his instinct, but there was a tiny voice of commonsense. He needed to get the job past the point of no return. Buy the materials, then get the work underway, so Paul found it difficult to say stop. He had to work or he'd be back out in the rain going door to door. But then again, there she was, there he was. Both willing. Such things didn't happen that often.

'Let's toss for it,' he said, taking out a coin. 'Heads, my place. Tails, buy materials.'

He flipped the coin, caught it and turned it on the back of his hand.

'Tails,' he said as he uncovered the coin.

She put her hand over his. 'Do you mind, Jack?'

'Of course, I do. But we can't do both. And I need to get your job started for my own selfish money grubbing motives. Like food and rent.'

'I need it started too,' she said. 'Quickly underway, so Paul can't pull it back.'

'So let's buy materials,' he said, culling his disappointment.

'I'll come with.'

'I never thought you weren't. I live round the corner. Let's pick up my van. And head for Jewson's in Stratford.'

Chapter 12

Detective Superintendent Nikki Martin surveyed the incident room. It was a few minutes before they were due to start the meeting. She always had a measure of excitement at the beginning of a major incident, though there had been many. There was team building, the various directions of investigation which she must orchestrate. There was the drawing together, picking out the important from the dross of facts. Making sense of it. And with luck, the homing in.

Or the alternative, losing it. Not making sense of the muddle. You never knew at the outset; this could be one of those cases. Or not. There were people, evidence, often surprises. You never knew.

She was stocky, middle aged, with short blonde hair, natural in colour, the grey hardly showing. She wore a skim of make up. There was no disguising her aging, it would take more than blusher. Besides, she was a career cop, not married, relationships from time to time but work had taken precedence which was why she was not in a relationship now. Policing hours never helped. She'd had ambition when she'd first signed her forms, had never regarded herself as ordinary, and as such had to be forceful to rise through the ranks. She couldn't be less, as there were egos here, testosterone in bulk, ready to push her off the ladder and clamber over her, should she falter. She hoped to make it to Chief Superintendent in the next year or so, and with luck, Commander. She doubted she'd get any higher before retirement beckoned, but then again, ranks shifted, some fell out of favour and some caught the Commissioner's eye.

A result, that was the key, the building of a reputation, brick by brick. Today, tomorrow; take the praise with an eye to the next rung on the ladder. There was the reverse, of course. Spending months on a case that frittered away inconclusively. Nothing to hang on anyone. Or to have your eyes glued to one suspect, letting the others fade away, ending up with no one in the frame and a complaining Commander. Budgets, resources, easy to justify when you got a result. But nothing? There was always the temptation to make sure you got something. To force a suspect into the evidence, and maybe with a little persuading of witnesses, add to the fit. She decried this. It was not a result to jail the wrong person, she continuously told herself. Though there were cops who would never admit an error, grumbled at the miscarriages of justice, complained about lawyers' tricks and dumb juries. Cops who shouldn't be cops. Then again, you could get away with it. Get a result and win praise and promotion. And then 15 years down the line, when it turned out to be a miscarriage of justice, you were several rungs out of reach, or long gone.

She was beyond the point of not sleeping for fear of past mistakes catching up. Experience, you might call it. She must have jailed a few innocents in her time. Statistics said so. But never purposely. And in the end, it was the jury and the legal system that jailed the innocent along with the guilty. That cloudy concept – beyond reasonable doubt. What did beyond mean? Reasonable? Doubt? Every word questionable. It was here, in incident rooms like this, amid the hue and cry, they would persuade each other they were onto the killer. The group mind. Beware, beware.

Always the excitement at the beginning. A new group to make, starting with the gory details, building a case, sometimes a leap in the dark, you might call it intuition but really it was experience, a nose for the key details. Of course she'd made mistakes. Justice can never be perfect. You try to make things fit with the evidence you have in hand. And there's almost always holes in it. Just don't try too hard. You submit what you have, and then it's down to the lawyers. Some of the guilty will get off, some of the innocent will be banged up. Inevitably.

She sat on the table at the front, having taken off the navy jacket of her dress suit and put it on the back of the chair. She wore a white shirt, with a small blue scarf at the neck, the female equivalent of a tie, less strangling, less old school. She glanced at the time. Give it a minute. And looked over her notes. There were about 14 or 15 present at the hastily convened meeting. She would get more in the team if they made progress. Notice boards had been set up, photos of the bodies and the forest site were on them, names scrawled. There were six desks, all filled by officers, computers on each. Other officers stood around, drinking coffee or water, or just waited, chatting. All non uniform. This was the local murder squad of the Criminal Investigation Department at Forest Gate Police Station.

'All right, everyone,' DS Martin began, her voice raised. 'Let's get underway.'

The room straightened. Chatter stopped. She waited until everyone was looking in her direction. She stared out a last chatterer, saying nothing but making clear her displeasure in a look. Satisfied, she continued.

'This is the first meeting of Operation High Beech,' said DS Martin. 'This is our Major Incident Room. For the time being at least. I know it's not as big as we'd like it. But there are other investigations ongoing, and this is the best we can do for now. Consider this home. So let's see where we are. The bodies were only found two days ago, but there's been some movement already. Forensic tests tell us the bodies have been there about two years, plus or minus a couple of months. We know one of the bodies is Bert Long who was reported missing by his family, October two years ago. His

DNA is on record and matches that of one of the bodies. He'd been jailed for grievous bodily harm. Charged with rape twice but found not guilty on both occasions. He was a member of England First, a racist party, as you well know. Its leadership are attempting respectability, they wear suits anyway, but some of the rank and file are, let's say, not above dirty work, so there's an obvious point for our investigations. The other body, we think might be Frank Brand who disappeared about the same time, but as matters lie, that's to be confirmed...'

'We've been round to his daughter's place, ma'am,' called Fayyad from the back of the room, 'and taken a DNA sample from her inner cheek.'

Hayley Amis, standing next to him, held up the bag containing the canister. 'Here it is.'

'Get that to forensics as soon as the meeting is over,' called Nikki. 'Make it top priority. We do need to know whether it's Frank Brand or someone else entirely. Keep an open mind for the time being and wait for proof. To move on.' She searched for faces in the room, and having found who she was looking for said, 'Potter and Kennedy, I'd like you to question Bert Long's family. They have a butcher's shop, I think. And then follow through with the England First angle.'

'Straight away, ma'am?'

'Yes. The less they are prepared the better. But go gently. They can be a difficult crowd.' She looked to the back of the room. 'I believe you have something for us, Davis?'

'Yes ma'am. The site around the grave in the forest is still being explored by crime scene. But I was involved with the bodies. And I can tell you, they are a stinking, mouldering heap. Utterly foul. The stench gets in your hair and clothes. Especially the bottom corpse, whoever it might be. Possibly Frank Brand...'

'Keep an open mind, Davis,' she admonished.

'Yes, ma'am. Whoever-it-is is a semi-rotten mass floating in a soup of piss-coloured liquid inside a heavy duty builder's bag. But on the outside, in a fold of the plastic, we've found a fingerprint.'

'After all this time?'

'I was amazed myself, ma'am. No others. Just the single print. But as I've said, it was in a fold, so had some protection.'

'Good work, Davis. Is the print on record?'

'No, ma'am.'

'Then we need to fingerprint everyone we question. Keep it low key. Assure them that all fingerprints will be destroyed after the investigation is complete. And with luck, we might get a result, in spite of the time lag. The priority though is identifying the second corpse.'

Chapter 13

Lynn was chirpy, bouncing along, as she helped unload the lengths of 4 by 2 timber, balancing one at a time over her shoulder, carting it up the path and stairs and laying it out in the hallway. The door of the house was wide open as they came and went, her car parked in the drive.

The rain was history, the pavement drying out. There was broken sunshine, a lively breeze lifting her hair. It was good to be working, instead of wondering what to do with the days, months, years ahead of her. What shall I do, plagued her each morning. She'd never considered manual work, not seriously, not having done any, but she was reflecting on it now. Carpenter, electrician, plumber. There must be quite a few who would prefer employing a woman builder. A woman on her own, say. There must be women's firms. So why not? There were courses. She could begin with doing free work, like now, show willing. Maybe a longer period with Jack, maybe not. Depends if their affair got off the ground. There were complications either way. Assume one job with Jack, then see. Maybe more with Jack, if she hadn't gone off the idea. But it was a good way to find out. See if it could work for her.

Oh, but she felt good! A beam over her shoulder made her feel like a real worker. She could at last see a way out. Hope on the horizon. And perhaps she was falling in love. She'd best take care there. In her situation, she was vulnerable, too needy. Oh, she could fall badly. But Jack seemed OK. Bright for a builder. Though what did she know about builders? She had no friends who were builders, certainly never been out with one. And this one was keen on astronomy. That was almost weird. How did that happen?

But then again, she might have to examine her prejudices. Something to look forward to.

He wasn't married. One pitfall avoided. Had a daughter, thirteen years old. You could never tell with teenagers. The daughter might feel Lynn was competition, so resent her. Take that as it comes. Be nice to her, if she was allowed to be.

The timber was all in the hall. Together they brought in the sheets of soundproof board. They were weighty. Jack had loaned her a pair of rough leather gloves. This work could certainly chip your nails. She'd cut them short tonight. A lot of lifting involved, she could see why you might want to work in a team. Though Jack seemed to manage. But give him fifteen years and he might have to team up with some younger guys. By then she'd be running her own building firm. Could employ Jack. Or, a sudden thought, Dawn. Might be what the girl needs, some manual labour. They push everyone to pass academic exams as if that's the only way to a career. Someone's got to build the houses, repair them.

She laughed at herself. All this after an hour or two. What might she be like in a week! An evangelist for the construction industry.

Lastly they brought in the bits and pieces, the nails, the screws, the bags of rock wool, the lengths of resilient channel. She looked at the mass, against one wall of the hall, tumbling into the centre. It took up a fair bit of the passage. She didn't mind, but knew someone who'd create a fuss.

She said, 'Can we get some of this in the cellar, Jack? I don't want to annoy Paul.'

'Point taken. Where is it?'

She led the way to a door one side of the hall. She opened it. 'There.'

Jack looked inside. There were steep stairs with a low headroom down to the cellar. He noted the light switch and turned it on, and went down the steps. The cellar space was under the whole house, filled mainly with junk, discarded furniture, tea chests, broken shelves, smelling of dust and cobwebs. He noted the stopcock by the narrow front window and the fuse box close to the bottom door. You never knew when you might need those. It never ceased to amaze him how many householders didn't know where their stopcock was.

He shifted some chairs, stacked them up, then pushed back a sideboard. That would do; he wasn't here to tidy up, just make space for his gear. Jack came back up to the hall.

'Let's get everything down except the boards,' he said. 'Too much hassle getting them down the stairs. With luck we'll fix them in tomorrow. Leave them tidy against the wall for now.'

He was aware of saying 'We', and her not disagreeing. Could be good, very good. Could have its complications, but he discarded such negativities. It would go swimmingly, and likely meant plenty of coffee, lunch too. Though he must keep Paul sweet, as his acceptance had been grudging. Be matey, talk football. Ask him about his running.

They began taking the materials down to the cellar, starting with the timber. She at the top, handing them down one at a time to Jack at the bottom who stacked them tidily. There she was, above him, part of a team. It was so good to be working again. Proving to herself there were other jobs than looking into a screen and getting bombarded with rays. She enjoyed passing the beams down the stairs to him, his face smiling up at her, hands stretched and ready. Then the long strips of resilient channel. And was sorry that part of the job ended. She could have passed down timber all day long.

Fairly soon, everything was down, except the soundproof boards that were staying up. They were both in the cellar. It was all stacked tidily. She smiled at him, he at her, and they came together in an embrace. Connecting. Wanting. She was overpowered, seeking his essence, the pleasure and depth of him. Oh, she hungered. Skin, lips, her liquid self boiling in passion. She gasped, grasped, her tongue in his mouth.

The doorbell rang.

They unglued, gazing at each other as if caught in the forbidden. Jack laughed.

She was annoyed. 'This house, always the way in this house.'

Jack sat on a tea chest. 'Give me a mo to cool down.'

She was climbing the stairs, calling out, 'Hang on, whoever you are, I'm coming.'

Always the way, she thought, as she clambered up to ground level. But then again, sex here, above or below ground, wasn't a good idea. Not with Paul around. She could bear Nick and Dawn, but not her sneering brother. She'd have to talk to Jack about his place. It was obviously going to happen. She wouldn't allow it not to.

At the top, she dropped her gloves by the cellar door. And looked along the hallway. At the open door was Tim. Annoying, no one important. She'd hardly spoken to him before, always with her nephew, Nick. The pair, she referred to as the noise makers. But he was here on his own.

Behind her, she could hear Jack climbing the stairs. Once at her level, he tapped her on the shoulder.

'Got to go, Lynn. Need to tidy my place before Mia arrives. I'll be back at eight tomorrow morning.'

Neither moved for a little while, held by each other's eyes, hands with effort held back. She could see he wanted her as much as she him, but there was the presence at the door, there was his daughter coming. The world homing in.

'Your mate will be ready at eight,' she said. And laughed at the rhyme of it, at her light-headedness.

He half whispered, 'Never looked forward to work more.'

And left her, striding up the hallway, as if once deciding they must part then he must do it quickly. For a few seconds, she felt abandoned. As if what had been building had been suddenly kicked down. She shook herself. Of course it hadn't. It was her impatience. Need. Slow up, slow up. Always better not to rush these things. There were other people coming out of the mist. Let this affair be paced. Better for both of them, she thought, not quite believing it, but she had a job, sort of, a partner. And was, once again, filled with hope.

She went to the front door, where Tim waited patiently. He seemed smaller on his own. He was wearing baggy jeans, obviously too long for him, and a bomber jacket with the arms folded back at the cuff, the zip undone revealing a T shirt on which she could make out a print of a band with their instruments. He had a torn backpack over one shoulder. Was it designer scruffiness? Or poverty.

'Hello, Tim,' she said. 'Can I help you?'

'Is Nick in?'

'I'm afraid not,' she said, having seen her nephew rush out while they were bringing the timber in. 'Anything I can do?'

He scuffed one trainer behind his ankle as if reluctant to admit something to the older generation. Mixed race, she thought. And wondered where his parents came from. The sort of thing that is rude to ask, but he was a beautiful light brown, his eyes doleful, quite penetrating. She had never been this close to him before, he was always part of Nick.

'This is difficult. I don't know whether to say,' he said, sucking his bottom lip. Were there tears in the corners of his eyes? He shrugged wearily. 'I've been evicted.'

'I'm sorry,' she said. 'Can't you go back home for a while?'

He gave a short laugh. His teeth were yellowish, could do with a dental visit.

'I haven't got a home,' said Tim. 'I grew up in care. Thirty-seven foster parents. Most of them wouldn't recognise me.'

'Thirty-seven!' She was aghast. The poor boy had been passed on all his life. No one wanted him.

'Do you know who your parents are?' And regretted saying it. Nosy, prying. But she sensed a story. An Oliver Twist horror.

'I don't,' he said. 'I could find out, I suppose. They can't keep it secret anymore. But do they want to know me? They dumped me when I was one year old. Do I want to know them?'

He had more depth than she'd allowed. Why on earth was he knocking around with her thick nephew?

'Come in and have a coffee,' she said. 'I don't know how long Nick will be.'

And she led the way along the hallway, to the kitchen. She'd been interrupted, dropped back into the mortal world. But she still had the promise of the gods, in her lightness and smile.

The kitchen told her she was back on earth. Along with Nick's detritus. She wasn't as pained by it as she usually was. She was high and felt protective of this young man. And Nick was his friend, maybe his only friend. The leftovers she threw in the bin, the crockery in the dishwasher. She'd do the pans later, and placed them by the sink.

While they talked she made coffee with toast and marmalade. He ate it rapidly and most of the biscuits. She guessed he didn't eat too well. No parents, evicted.

'Are you at NewVic with Nick?' she said. Newham Sixth Form College to anyone not from the area. 'What do you do for money?'

'I work in the casino at Stratford, waiting tables, clearing, late at night.' He saw her looking at his clothes. 'Oh, not in this rubbish. They have a uniform. I've a locker there. A clean shirt every shift.' He laughed. 'Get most of my food there.'

'But you've been evicted.'

He was quite the saddest person she'd ever met. Wistfulness poured out of him. It melted her. Or maybe that was just the mood she was in. Receptive. Wanting to share her good fortune.

'I was in a Council flat,' he said. 'Three of us, out of care. But that got impossible. Thieving, fights. They sold my clothes and beat me up. So I left. And I found a squat on Water Lane. You know, back of Stratford. Been there a couple of months. The water is on, but I have to use candles for light. I come and go by the back fence so no one knows I'm there.' He halted, remembering her question. 'Well anyway, I was doing some course work in Stratford library for a few hours this morning. And then got really tired, I didn't get home till four this morning after work. So I thought I'd go back to the squat and get my head down for a few hours. When I got there, there were these three black guys.' He shrugged to indicate the inevitability of what happened next. 'And that was that. Take over. I'm out on my ear.' He pulled at his ear, a sort of plea. 'I was hoping to see Nick. Maybe stay here a couple of days...' His eyes appealed. 'Until I can find somewhere else.'

She thought for a second, but he had captivated her. Caught her at a good time.

'I can't see one more would make much difference,' she said, instantly liking the idea..

'Oh that would be so good, Mrs Atwood.' The joy shone in him as if he had a light switch, with just two settings. Sad and ecstatic.

'We've a box room,' she said thoughtfully. 'Full of junk mostly.'

'I'll clear it out,' he said eagerly.

'Where's your things?' she said.

'At the squat. It's all rubbish. They've got it all. Won't let me back in. But I'd like my books back. They're no good to them.' And then close to tears. 'And my guitar. It's the only damn thing I've got worth anything. I can do without the rest. Even my books. But my guitar...'

'They can't do that,' she exclaimed. 'Simply steal everything.'

He shrugged. 'They can. What can I do? Call the cops? To a squat?' He shook his head vehemently. 'Say goodbye to that place. Count myself lucky, I got two months out of it. It's just the flaming guitar.' He closed his eyes; she could see the little boy in him, passed on from foster parent to foster parent. 'Two weeks' money it cost me. Electro-acoustic. Bollocks...' Then caught himself. 'Sorry, Mrs Atwood. I didn't mean to swear.'

'I'm Lynn, not Mrs Atwood. And you have every right to swear, considering the way you've been treated.' She stood up. 'Come on, Tim.'

'Where we going?'

His eyes were the most beautiful, olive green. Thirty seven foster parents. It was unbelievable.

'To get your guitar,' she said.

Chapter 14

'The bell doesn't work,' said Tim.

They were at the house. The ground floor windows had metal shutters over the front, the top were free with closed, dirty curtains. The privet hedge at the front was scraggy and untended. Cans and chicken boxes littered the small front yard.

Lynn rapped the knocker hard, twice, the sound echoing through the house. Alarmed, Tim stepped well back, as if her actions were nothing to do with him. She waited at the door, unsure who would answer, if anyone would, and what she would do if they did. She had grabbed her black three-quarter length coat and woolly hat when she left her house, but was now too warm. Or perhaps it was the uncertainty.

The door opened slowly.

A black man, bulky, untidily dressed, with dreadlocks, stood there. A smell of weed wafted out.

'I guess you're not the pizza guy,' he said with a grin. 'Do you want me to join your church?'

'I've come for this young man's papers,' she said politely, with the brightest smile she could fix. She'd thought start with the papers, the guitar depending on the lie of the land. 'If you don't mind.'

He frowned. 'I don't know anything about papers.'

She was leaning on the door, or he would have closed it on her. The hallway was very brown in hue and smell, almost disappearing in the dark, though she could see light flickering from the open door of a side room.

'He was living here,' she said indicating Tim at his safe distance, 'before you moved in. He's at NewVic. You know the sixth form college on Prince Regent Lane in Plaistow.'

'I know NewVic.'

The man was perhaps in his 30s. He had a couple of teeth missing, his nails were dirty, bitten to the quick. She had the feeling he did weights or at least used to, and could remove her with one hand if he chose to.

'He was in care,' she said, seeking something that might engage the man. 'Had 37 foster parents. Just a kid trying to make something of himself.'

The man didn't say anything for a second or two, then said, 'I was in care. Passed on and on like an old sack.' He sucked his teeth noisily. 'Papers you say. There might be papers.' He scratched the side of his face. 'You'd best come in.' He pointed out Tim. 'You stay there, kid. I'll deal with your minder.'

He held the door wide for her to come in. She hesitated. She didn't know this man or who else was in the house. She turned to Tim.

'I won't be long,' she said. And then a whisper, 'Call for help if I'm more than five minutes.'

And went in, past the man as he held the door open for her. She stopped halfway along the passage and waited while he closed the front door. She was now shut in. If anything happened, she didn't know what help Tim might be. Whether he would call the police. Did he have a phone? She hadn't really considered anything, being so energised, feeling nothing was beyond her.

A silly illusion. She was flesh and blood; she had no magic. But at least the man knew someone was outside. A slight protection. A pea shooter against a polar bear. Stay polite, smile. No threats. Lynn worked to quiet her breathing, her legs hollow. Could he sense her fear?

With the front door shut, the hallway was almost in darkness but for the small window above the door and the flickering light from the side room. There was a stale, sweaty smell, mingled with marijuana and urine.

71

'You've got some balls,' said the man, squeezing past her, pausing against her breasts long enough for a trickle of pee to run down her leg, then moving on. 'But you're stupid.'

He went into the lit room. She followed, not knowing what else to do. It was a front room of the house, one of two either side of the front door. There were shutters on the windows, the only light a couple of candles. There was no furniture but sofa cushions on a reddish, threadbare carpet. Two men were seated, smoking weed, legs splayed out. One bald, with Somali type features, the other wearing a battered cowboy hat.

'Who's the chick?' exclaimed Cowboy Hat.

'Hello,' said Lynn brightly, more animated than she felt. 'Don't let me interrupt you. I've just come for papers my friend left behind...'

'What's with the papers?' said Cowboy Hat to the man who'd let her in.

He shrugged. 'Just college stuff. From the kid who was here. Nothing in it for you, man.' He laughed, showing his gapped teeth, and pushed his friend on the shoulder. 'Unless you fancy A Level English, or want to fathom the cognitive psychology of your drug-stewed brain box.'

'There's some fat books there, man,' exclaimed Cowboy Hat. 'We could sell them to college kids.'

'No one wants books,' dismissed the Somali with a flick of his fingers. 'Tablets or phones maybe. Who bothers with books?'

In a darkened corner Lynn saw a guitar leaning against the wall with a broken string. She suspected it was Tim's. Dare she ask? She could offer to buy it. Maybe not right now. Get the papers, they'd be no use to them. Then see. The guys were high, step by easy step, she might yet get what she'd come for.

'They're in the other room, the papers,' said the man, indicating out of the door with his head. 'Come on, baby.' He took her arm. 'Leave these scumbags.'

She let him lead her, turning at the door.

'Thanks, guys,' she said as she left them, remembering to smile. And joined her guide in the hallway.

Cowboy Hat yelled, 'Give her one for me, Benji!'

Her heart leapt in panic. Was he joking or serious? She could hear them hooting. Man-joshing, she hoped. Harmless. The way a group of men joked, elbowing, pretending. She looked to the front door, just three or four strides, but locked. And the man, practically beside her, his face barely visible in the shadow. He was by the door of another room, dark inside, a few chinks of light leaking from the shuttered window.

'In here,' said the man, indicating the room. 'The papers. His clothes too. You can have them. A bonus.' He chuckled.

She thought, no way am I going in that room. And knew she must leave, or live to regret it. Her legs were shaking uncontrollably. She must control her fear. Pretend control, and innocence, as if she didn't suspect the worst. Hoping it wasn't too late.

She put a head in the doorway, 'I can't see a thing. I need a light.'

The man was scouring her, tongue lolling in his cheek, a hand resting on his flies.

'I need a light,' she repeated. 'I won't be able to find anything.'

'Always better to see what you're getting into, lady,' he said. And went into the other room.

'Let me have one of those candles,' she heard him say. 'The chick's afraid of the dark.'

Laughter.

She raced for the front door. The latch was fiddly, her hands as if encased in mittens. She couldn't get it to turn.

73

The man came out into the hall with a lighted candle, looking for her, not seeing her at first.

'I got a light, baby.'

Then spotting her at the door, he dashed for her.

The door opened. And she was instantly outside, and in a few rapid strides on to the safety of the pavement, breathing as if she'd raced 400 metres, blinking in the sunlight. There was Tim, close by. He sidled up to her. There were pedestrians walking by. Witnesses. An old lady with a basket on wheels.

The man came to the door, still holding the candle, the flame flickering in the outside air.

'Not totally stupid,' he said, waving a gold ringed finger. 'I'll get the papers.'

He shuffled back inside as if going to bed by candlelight, leaving the door half ajar. Lynn was several yards back, on the pavement, bent over, hands on the knees of her jeans. They were damp with her pee. She was breathing rapidly, knowing if she had stepped into the room, the door would have closed on her, he'd have blown out the candle....

How dumb can you be! How unaware of your own safety... She'd felt so alive after working with Jack, as if she could walk on water. Raise the dead.

Tim patted her on the arm, saying in a hushed voice, 'You never should have gone in there. They're drug dealers.'

She nodded, tears welling. Her legs were shaky, she was shivering. Who on earth did she think she was? As if being middle class, white, and educated, was a talisman she could hold before her, shrivelling them. But she'd been the one shrivelled. It was their space. They'd booted out Tim. And so she, the fairy godmother, came with her wand and rose petals. Usher, usher, all fall down.

'I saw your guitar,' she managed to say, wiping her eyes with the back of her hand. 'But I think we'll leave that for today.' And tomorrow, and next week. She could buy him one. Two, a dozen. From a large emporium with fifty fluorescent lights blazing overhead.

The door opened. And the man came out, his arms filled with a bundle of papers, pads and a few text books. He dropped them on the step where they scattered in a jumble of handwritten script and typing. Smiling as he swayed between the door jambs, he looked her up and down.

'Pity we didn't get to know each other better,' he said, blowing a kiss. 'I got a lot to give, honey.'

Terror locked her. A hare frozen in headlights. He could so easily drag her in. Her scream would be short. Would any passers-by respond?

The man laughed, she knew that he knew. He pointed out Tim, wagging a threatening finger at the young man.

'You tell that mate of yours we want to see him. Get me?'

Tim held up shaky hands indicating passivity. 'I'll tell him.'

The man took a step back, gave a baby wave, and stepped inwards slamming the door.

Chapter 15

Jack was washing the dishes in his kitchen sink. He'd left them from the morning and the evening before. Mia was coming, some semblance of tidiness was required. Though he was barely aware of the soap and water as his hands worked independently. Quite a day. From rain to sunshine. He had a job and Lynn would be working with him tomorrow. She'd been so chirpy carrying timber, he couldn't help laughing at the image, as if it were a game for her. Let it be. The newness of it. She didn't need the money as badly as he did. That's when the playing stopped.

It was an odd relationship. He was her gaffer and she was his boss. He'd better do a good job. No short cuts. The situation had other risks. He didn't know her, she didn't know him. Once they did they might find they didn't like each other. Then again, this job was only a few days. They only needed to like each other that long.

Such pessimism. Then again, if you are prepared for the worst then you might get some pleasant surprises. If your gloom doesn't throttle it.

He poured away the water and dried his hands. The dishes he left to drip on the draining board. He no longer had a tea towel. Had a couple last year, Mia had bought them at a Christmas bazaar, but they'd got covered in oil when he was working on the van. And hadn't been replaced. He really should get some more if Lynn were to come over. Tomorrow night, so why not? Maybe it was time to find the vacuum cleaner.

Being next door to Anne. That was an uncomfortable coincidence. A couple of times he'd considered going round. Saying hello. Sooner or later, she'd spot his van or see him going in and out. And he'd like to see how Bessie was getting on. But that whole scene two years ago, he wanted to forget. The body was buried. Let it stay that way. What really did he and Anne have to say to each other? Other than remind each other of an event that neither wanted to discuss.

The flat door slammed. Mia. Forget Anne, responsible father mode. The last she'd seen of him, he was down in the dumps. Now working again, not one of the despised. Though he wouldn't mention Lynn. Too recent news. And who could say how it might go?

He went into the sitting room where Mia was slumped on the sofa, an exhausted teenager after school, a stuffed backpack next to her. Her figure was beginning to develop, hormones coursing, confined and berated all day. She was in school uniform, navy blue trousers and jumper, pale blue shirt, her jacket over the arm of the seat.

'My teacher,' she exclaimed, 'picks on me all the time. She knows I know the answer, so she always asks me. You can bet on it.' She imitated, 'No hands up, 9R? But I'm sure Mia can tell us.' She rolled her eyes. 'So what can I do? If I give the answer the other girls have a go at me for being a smartie.' She sat up on the sofa. 'Can I help it if I know it and they don't?'

'What did she ask?' he said.

'What is a black hole?' she said wearily. 'First she asked the class: who has heard of a black hole? And everyone put up their hand. Of course, everyone had. Then she asked us what one was. And no one put their hand up. So she asked me – and I told her about neutron stars and gravitational collapse and event horizons... I should have shut up.'

'So why didn't you?'

'If you know, you don't want everyone to think you don't.' She puffed out her cheeks. 'I've a reputation to look after. Status. But is it worth it, I ask you?' Instead of waiting for a reply, she began pulling something out of her pocket. 'I've got something for you...' And handed over a screwed up banknote. 'Twenty quid. Mum knows Mrs Patel, the school secretary. I was called out of class, I wondered what I'd done this time, but it was nothing. Mum had phoned her, and she gave me the money. It's like the Mafia, my school. She's the snitch who tells Mum what I'm up to.' She looked at him quizzically. 'Why you always broke?'

'I'm not broke,' he said defensively. 'Cashflow. You know my work. Always waiting payment. Or rather, I was when I spoke to your mum this morning. Then I got a payment. See here.' He took out his wallet, opened it, showing her it was full of banknotes. 'That's self employment for you. Either no work or too much. Broke or rolling in it. You know I'm getting back after my knee trouble. Besides, it's not the best of times for building work.'

'You had all that hassle at the dole office.'

'Don't bring them up. They give me nightmares.' He put his money away. It was a comfortable wodge in his pocket.

'I'm starving,' said Mia stretching. 'What we got to eat?' She was up and about to go in the kitchen.

'Nothing.'

That stopped her at the door.

'Nothing? Nothing at all?'

'Old Mother Hubbard's got there before you.'

She rushed into the kitchen. He could hear her rifling about, cupboard doors opening and closing. He wondered what Lynn was up to. Whether she was weighing him up or was too busy arguing with her brother.

'Half a mouldy onion,' she called out, 'no bread, some scrapings of Marmite, a bit of marge, no milk, no eggs, no tea, no biscuits, no fruit, a sprouting potato, a tin of something without a label...' She came in holding the silvered can. 'What's in it?'

'Tomatoes, I think.' He'd find out in the morning, whether she'd been thinking of him all night, or had cooled down. He mustn't get carried away.

'Not much good by itself,' she said, thumping the can on the table. 'It's a bit much. I come home, totally exhausted, bitched at by teachers and the creeps in my class – and now we have to go shopping.'

'It's only up the road.'

'You go,' she said. Then reflected, 'No, you'll get the wrong stuff. You need looking after! Time you got a girlfriend.'

He laughed. How she looked like her mother. The questions similar. Not the time to tell her there might be someone in the offing. He grabbed his coat, eager to be out of the house.

'Come on. Let's stock up.'

Chapter 16

It was a windowless space, hardly more than a deep cupboard. There would just be room for a single mattress and a chair. But that was fine. Tim only had the clothing he wore and the college books and papers that Lynn had salvaged. Say goodbye to the guitar. Well, he'd never expected Lynn to get it anyway.

In the box room, there were a heap of suitcases, a rocking horse, a dolls' house, a black bag of clothing that got him excited until he found it was girl's stuff, box games – Monopoly, Scrabble, Cluedo, jigsaws. Various shoes, sandals, Wellington boots, a pair of trainers. He tried them on. Tight but if he stuffed them with newspaper overnight, they might stretch, a darkroom enlarger, boxes of books and old magazines. A hefty desktop computer with a monitor. He might be able to get that working. Everyone had moved on to laptops these days. He'd had one but it got nicked when he was in the Council flat, so maybe he'd borrow this one.

He drew the items out into the hall, gradually emptying the space. Lynn had said he could put some of it in her room, and there might be room in the loft. He'd need to get a move on as he'd gathered from Lynn that there could be a problem with her brother Paul. Tim had heard them quarrelling when he was with Nick yesterday, and other times when he'd been round. Nick always turned up the sound to drown them out. The next row could well be about him. So get on the move. The more gear shifted, the more it looked like a room, the more likely he could persuade Paul to let him stay. Tim wanted this place ship shape by the time Paul got back from wherever he was. To be settled, neat and tidy. That always helped.

He had his tale of being kicked out, might soften up Paul. Lynn would back it up. Though that might not be a lot of help, considering her relationship with her brother. Nick would speak up for him. But who listened to Nick? Would Dawn put in a word for him? No, she wouldn't. Never got on with her. Moody bitch. But it was Paul he had to convince. He and Lynn had the big say so in the house.

Just a few days, insist it was just that. He could help out Nick with his college work. Yeh, that was a good line.

Just a few days. And once in, keep quiet, be the good boy, so they'd get used to him. And maybe let him stay. He couldn't see them charging rent. So there it was, all to play for, a room, food, warmth, light. And no one to turn up one morning and throw him out on the street.

Nick came up the stairs as Tim was piling up a tower of cardboard boxes full of papers. He stood at the top of the steps, bent one knee, put his fingers in an imagined rectangle of a film screen.

'Take 69. Cut!'

'Where have you been?'

Nick was in the corridor, dancing round him. 'Take 42. Cut!'

'I came looking for you.'

'Reaction shot. Cut!'

Nick's jeans were a mass of square, tidy patches, as was his denim shirt. They weren't covering holes but were part of the design. He and Tim were the Apatches. Tim had had a similar shirt and jeans, now lost at the squat.

'I got kicked out of the squat,' said Tim, lifting out a large TV set and placing it by the wall in the hall. 'They gave me the push.' He recalled the last words said to him. 'You know the guys. Your dealers. You didn't put them onto my squat, did you?'

'No.'

Tim eyed him, unsure whether to believe him. Nick was an idiot when stoned. Could have told them his full life story. Either way, he needed Nick's help.

'Lynn said I could stay a while,' he said.

Nick had settled on the carpet and was idly picking at a spot. His face was a mass of them; he'd tried creams, pills, liquids and picking them, but they wouldn't leave him. He would stare in the mirror, count them when he was stoned.

'I had this idea,' exclaimed Nick. 'I could wear a mask. We could be the Avenging Apatches.' Then realising what his friend had said. 'You're gonna be here. We'll get the album done quicker.' He indicated his room with his head. 'What about a go through now?'

'I've got to do this, Nick,' protested Tim. 'I can't leave this gear out in the hall.'

'I spose so,' said Nick deflated. 'How long will that take?'

Tim shrugged. 'I haven't looked in the loft yet to see what space there is. I've got to see Lynn about what I can put in her room...' He stopped. 'Besides, my guitar's been nicked.'

'You're joking!' Nick was aghast.

'Wish I was. The guitar, the amp and leads. All in the squat.'

'Then you can forget about them. They're monsters.' He stood up and indicated his room. 'Let's not talk about them. Come in my room. Let's have a smoke. Play some music. You can do the bongos.'

'I've got to get this stuff shifted, Nick. Want to give me a hand?'

Nick looked in the box room. 'All that?'

'I've got to shift it before your dad gets back.'

Nick shook his head. 'I got phoning to do. Sort out some deals.' He headed for his room, then stopped. 'You haven't got any money, have you?'

'Got about a tenner.'

'Forget it,' said Nick. 'A tenner won't help. I wonder if Dad'll sub me.'

'How much d'you need?'

'Eight hundred. I told you.'

'You didn't.'

'Yes I did.' He shrugged. 'You haven't got it anyway.' He pushed open the door of his room and blew out his cheeks. 'I have to do some phoning around.'

PART TWO:
THE GOOSE BEING COOKED

Chapter 17

The pictures had gone from the room, knickknacks taken off the sideboard and mantelpiece, half-filled tea chests were scattered about. It was depressing, a room being undone, the living taken out of it, even as the family attempted to go on with their daily commitments.

Anne was in an armchair, coffee mug on the arm. David and Maggie who lived on the top floor of the house, at least for the next few days, were on the sofa. Lenny in his babygro was crawling in the playpen, which Maggie had drawn closer to her.

'So Frank's body has been found,' said Maggie, rubbing one of Lenny's hands. 'And if Frank has, then so has Bert.'

David sighed heavily. 'I'd hoped this was all done with. Safely buried.'

He was a tall, black man, Nigerian parentage, acquiring a belly due to too many pastries in his sedentary job as area manager of a coffee chain. Work in law was a memory; he couldn't get articled, and so had to give up any hopes in that direction. The fill-in job had proved permanent.

David had taken off his tie; he was still wearing one of his expensive work shirts, the sleeves rolled up, as he'd been packing while Maggie had cooked their dinner. There was much to do, to be ready for the removal van at the weekend, when they were moving to a three bedroom house in Manor Park.

'I can't believe how stupid we were,' said Maggie, handing Lenny some train carriages. 'Three adults, with everything to lose, going off to bury a body. Bonkers.'

'Like happy go lucky students during rag week,' exclaimed David.

'I'm sorry,' said Anne curtly. 'But Frank was raping me, so I hit him. Do you blame me for that?'

'No,' said Maggie. 'Well done. All the better for poor Bessie. But it's the next bit I'm complaining about. Our involvement.'

'All the racket in the hallway that night,' exclaimed David. 'If only we'd slept through it. But we came down to see what was going on. The whole house there. Like a Halloween party. There was the screeching cat with a tack in its throat from a meatball, Bessie and Nancy near hysterical, and you and Jack dragging out the body in that big plastic bag...' He gave a short laugh and shook his head. 'You couldn't make it up.'

'We should've called the cops, then and there,' said Maggie. 'Now get the engine, Lenny. Good boy. We should have called the cops.'

'Well, you didn't,' snapped Anne. 'However you replay it, you didn't. And two bodies have been found in Epping Forest. Not just Frank's. You can blame me for him, but I won't take the blame for Bert.'

'You and that damned key,' said Maggie turning on David. 'Take the Duplo out of your mouth please, Lenny. That's it. Good boy. Give it to me.' She wiped the sticky brick on her skirt. 'Get the bus and dinosaur... A Nigerian keyfob! Dropped in the forest, I ask you. You might as well have left our name and address.'

'You left your phone.'

'In the car, darling. He had to smash the window to get it.'

David scowled, but swallowed any reply.

'Bert followed the two of you when you went back to look for the fob,' said Anne. 'He was a sharp bugger. He thought, what's that teacher and her husband up to, in walking boots on a weekday morning.'

'I'd spotted him in the car park by the forest,' said Maggie. 'Drinking tea. I thought he was a commercial traveller or someone stopping for a break...'

'He followed you all the way to the grave. Watched you going round and round it, searching for the keyfob. Which Bert had already pocketed. Oh he was a smart, slimy lizard...'

'Who you slept with,' said David.

'And you killed.'

'We're all in this up to our necks,' sighed Maggie. 'Once you'd told us what Bert was planning, did we have any choice?'

'He was smart. Just not as smart as you, Anne,' said David. He gave her a mock smile, just short of a grimace.

'Imagine what would have happened, with your keyfob, David, your phone, Maggie, found at the grave by the cops. How would you have talked your way out of that one?'

Maggie closed her eyes. 'I remember when he phoned me, on my own phone. I was sitting exactly here on the sofa, when he told me he had the keyfob as well as the phone and knew exactly what we'd done to Frank. I nearly died on the spot.' She shook her head. 'However could you sleep with the slimeball?'

'Better than jail, I assure you,' said Anne. 'It was necessary.'

'It was,' agreed David. 'Had to be done. He had so much on us. I don't regret stabbing him. A very unpleasant man. Except when I see Lenny putting the train together – and I think, suppose me and Maggie get fifteen years apiece, he'll grow up without us.'

'Don't!' exclaimed Maggie, throwing up her hands.

'We can't evade it,' said David. 'I killed Bert. Stabbed him while you were kissing him, Anne. All set up at the grave.

Then we buried him with his mate.' He gave a snort. 'What a clever plan!'

'I suppose I could get a smart lawyer and argue that the two of you forced me into it,' said Maggie. She imitated a defendant in the dock. 'There I was, milord, six months pregnant, emotional, with a bully of a husband in league with the lady downstairs...'

No one laughed, all eyes on the toddler assembling the wooden train track, his mother handing him the sections, the engine and carriages waiting patiently.

Anne pondered whether she could trust them. If it all came out, they'd have their own lawyer. Couples support each other. The nuclear family, cleaving together. She could see them darkening her name in order to get off. To be with their darling Lenny. Telling the jury that she had killed Bert as well as Frank. Two against one. But there was Jack, of course... Don't forget Jack.

'The builder's around,' she said.

'You don't mean Jack of All Trades?' exclaimed Maggie.

'The very same,' said Anne, thinking, as she spoke, of what she ought to do. She must have one ally. 'He's working for Lynn next door. I saw his van outside.'

'Good God,' said David. 'What a can of worms! Another one for them to question.'

'I haven't spoken to him.' She bit her lip. 'We had a short lived relationship that didn't end well.'

'Am I surprised?' said Maggie.

'He has to be told,' insisted David. 'So he can prepare himself.'

'I realise that,' snapped Anne. 'But I thought talk to you two first. He and Bessie don't know anything about Bert's killing.'

'Just us three witches on the heath,' said Maggie with a wry smile.

'It's difficult to talk of one without the other coming up,' she said. 'Why Bert just disappeared from the scene. He'd forced himself into Bessie's place. Took her over. King of the castle. Then disappeared.'

'And we know why,' said David.

'It's a spot Bessie keeps picking at,' said Anne.

'Let her pick,' said David. 'Just don't give her any facts. And the same for Jack. He's got to be told what's going on. But only with Frank. He was with us dumping him. Just don't mention the complication of Bert. He doesn't need to know.'

'I'll talk to him tomorrow,' said Anne.

'Just don't sleep with him,' said Maggie.

'Why not?'

'You might fight when you break up,' she said.

'One of you gets embittered and goes to the cops,' joined in David. 'That's what happens on TV.'

'Then let's hope you two stay together.'

Chapter 18

There was a light wind over Wanstead Flats. The sun had set a couple of hours before, leaving a line of bluish light on the western horizon. Jack and Mia had parked halfway down Centre Road, the road that split the Flats in two, in the small cinder-covered car park, the only car there. They were togged up for an autumn evening in Wellington boots, anoraks, and woolly hats. On their hands, father and daughter wore fingerless gloves, so they could manipulate the telescope dials.

The car park was close by the road, useless for decent observation with the streetlights and car headlights. They headed into the Flats, as far away from lights as they could get. Never far enough, this was the city after all, with its light polluted skies. Just the best they could do. Jack cradled the body of the telescope in his arms, Mia had the mount over her shoulder, as they trudged over the bumpy grass. This was rough land, mostly grass and wild flowers, long past flowering, with a few gorse bushes here and there. They aimed for the edge of a football pitch; there were more than 30, marked out in lime, the goal posts up permanently this time of year.

Jack was relieved to be out under the autumn skies. There was a resistance, once home, having eaten, easy to slouch in front of the TV. But the skies had cleared after the earlier rain, and he knew he'd be invigorated once set up in the open air. Too busy searching with the scope to worry about tomorrow. Space held him, the immensity and wonder of it, knowing we were travelling at a 100,000 kilometres an hour, an hour! round the sun. How was that possible! Why weren't we simply thrown out like sand grains from a bucket?

It was an odd hobby for a builder, had been remarked too many times. He was beyond being insulted. As if all builders were all the same. You had to earn a living somehow, not everyone went to college. That didn't make him stupid, though he'd met plenty of stupid people with degrees.

Stupidity depends on the beholder. Going out on cold nights to look up at the sky for hours on end, to some that would be their idea of hellish vacuity. As it had been for a couple of girlfriends, who'd come once and left him to it. As had his ex, Alison. But then anything he did had become poison to her. Though she'd got him into it.

After a row, the unbearable silence, the flat too small for both of them, he'd go out into the garden. And noted night after night, overhead was a lozenge of a constellation. He had no idea what it was called. It had one especially bright star, nameless to him. It was order in his chaos.

He bought an astronomy magazine. In the centre pages was a star map. The lozenge, he saw, was called Auriga, the charioteer. He imagined the shape to be the reins to the horses. And from the map, he picked out other constellations close by, Gemini, with the bright stars of the twins, Castor and Pollux. And of course, the glory of the winter sky, Orion the hunter. With his bow and his belt.

Once he and Alison had split up, Mia had picked up the astronomy mag he'd left lying about. And then both had gone over Wanstead Flats, she pointing out as much as he. He'd bought a second hand pair of binoculars. And both marvelled at the Pleiades, like a diamond crown against the deep purple of space. They'd found the nebula in Orion's dagger, after much effort, simply a red smudge in binoculars, and wanted to see more.

Which led to him buying a telescope. Utterly stupid, if one is comparing stupidities, considering his finances at the time. A recovering drunk, trying to put together his life, to pay the rent once he and Alison had separated, to keep up his van and to buy tools, shelling out over seven hundred pounds for a telescope. For a telescope! It left little for food that month, but he'd reasoned, it left nothing for drink either.

Mia and Jack headed for their spot. The place they considered theirs; they had no challengers, just beyond a copse of trees, on the level ground of a football pitch. A runner came by in a baggy tracksuit and woolly hat pulled low over the forehead. The occupant might have been a man or a woman, their shape smothered in cloth. There was a dog walker far off, a silhouette against the night sky and, further away, beams of cars and streetlamps, the enemy.

Mia set up the mount. She'd done it many times. It had to be steady and level. Jack put on the telescope, tightening the screws, checking again for level. If the night was clear, sometimes they drove out to Chingford, by Epping Forest with its darker skies. There, Jack would align the scope to a known star, but there was little point here. They weren't going for deep space. Too much light pollution. It was the moon, the planets, the obvious stuff. There was little subtlety in town observing.

'It's awfully cloudy,' said Mia looking up at the sky, turning about.

'A few stars,' said Jack, pointing them out. 'That must be the handle of the Plough.'

'I wish the moon would stay out.'

There was a half moon, always good for observations on clear nights, but tonight fighting the patches of near black cloud.

Mia turned the scope to the moon.

'Gone!' she exclaimed, as cloud floated over it, leaving a smudgy glow in its wake.

'Wait a bit,' said Jack. 'It might come out again. Let's look at the star chart.'

He removed his magazine from his backpack, and turned to the centre pages showing the stars and planets visible this month. His hand torch could switch to white or red light. The red, they used when one of them was observing.

'So what's happening late October?' she said, coming over to share the magazine.

'Venus, dominant in the early morning,' read Jack. 'Jupiter, bright enough to outshine any night time star, best at 5.30 GMT...'

'Both useless. We're not staying nine hours,' she retorted. 'Let me see.' She took the magazine and torch from him. Her mother would have told her off for grabbing. But he was glad of these shared moments. Her eagerness cheered him as he recognised it in himself, and let her take the lead, looking over her shoulder at the magazine.

'Mars is a morning object,' she went on, 'Uranus – forget that, we'd never find it.'

'Possible,' said Jack.

'It's tiddly,' she said. 'Took us over an hour last winter and wasn't worth it. Saturn... I love Saturn. Oh,' she read the comments on the planet, 'too low for serious observation.'

'The moon's out again,' exclaimed Jack, 'Quick, quick.'

She went to the telescope.

'I've got Clavius,' she cried. 'And I can see the small craters in it. Do you remember what I used to think?' She laughed at her younger self. 'I imagined each one had a moonman in, who would pop up as if out of a manhole! When even the tiniest is ten miles across.'

Jack smiled. 'I remember. It's difficult to tell the scale from a telescope. Everything is bigger than you think.'

'Clavius is over 200 kilometres across.' She looked up from the eyepiece. 'If you were in the middle of it you wouldn't know you were in a crater. The walls would be below the horizon.'

He enjoyed her sharpness, and could see how it might get her in trouble at school, where knowledge of boy bands was the tops, not knowing about moon craters.

'You could jump ten feet high,' she exclaimed, still at the telescope eyepiece. 'Even with the weight of the suit and the backpack. You'd be a sixth of your earth weight.' Then aware she was hogging the telescope, 'You look.'

Jack took his turn, seeing Clavius and nearby Maginus with its two monkey ears, as Mia called them, actually smaller craters.

'In that gravity, you could fall off a ladder and not come to much harm...' he said. 'Maybe I should volunteer to build a moon base.'

'You might rip your spacesuit with your hammer and nails. Then your blood would boil.' She reflected. 'Or freeze.' She was looking up as cloud came over the moon. 'We're losing it. Losing it. Gone.' She returned to her earlier thought. 'Definitely freeze. I read in the mag, the astronauts would moonwalk near sunrise, the sun hardly up.'

'Be hard to rip a suit,' said Jack. 'Three or more layers, for protection and to keep the cold out.'

'What would the temperature be?'

'100 below, Celsius. Colder even. The astronauts have heaters in their backpacks.'

'I remember now. There was a picture in one of the articles. Lots of thin tubes going through the suit with hot water circulating. Must be like a hot massage.' She was watching the smudge of moon, hoping it would break out. 'But then the moon surface would warm up. Quickly. As the sun rises. And the cold would flash off – and in no time it would be past boiling point...'

'Too hot, too cold, worse than Goldilocks,' he said.

'And they'd have to be back in the ship.' Mia turned to her father. 'I think we've lost the moon for tonight. Do you think we could find Andromeda?'

'There's a bit of the Square of Pegasus...' he pointed out.

'Not enough of it,' she said. 'Forget it. I don't think the Andromeda galaxy would be up to much on the Flats.'

'Need dark skies for any details,' he agreed. 'Find something else.' And gave up the scope to her.

Mia searched about through the small finderscope on top of the telescope. And came upon the double stars, Alcor and Mizar, in the handle of the Plough, but lost them as cloud came over. One of those nights. At least it was just the Flats. It would have been a whole lot worse trekking off to Chingford to walk up a muddy hill for no viewing.

They called it a night. They hadn't expected much and hadn't got it.

Chapter 19

The box room was like a tent, the more so because Tim had so little. Just his papers and a couple of text books. It was sparse. Only the single mattress, covered in sheet and duvet, a matching pillow. Both so clean. A chair which could just about fit by the bed. He'd taken off his shoes, his socks were smelly, but he had no others now that he'd lost the rest of his clothes. Though truth be told, he'd had no other socks. He would have a word with Nick who had a lot more than he could use. Wouldn't miss a pair or two. Of anything. Underwear, vests, shirts.

Or just take some. Nick wouldn't care, or know for that matter.

He laid out flat, head on the pillow. Such a high space. He stretched his arms out to the sides. He was too close to the right wall. He shuffled on the mattress to the midpoint of the room. Yes, he could just reach both walls with his fingertips. He sat up and looked about his territory. What he needed in here was a socket. Then he could get that computer going. With a double socket, he could have a bedside lamp too. Nick had one he never used. Then Tim could close the door, do some college work. Headphones and an MP3 player. You can get them dead cheap. The one at the squat wasn't cheap. Forget it. Gone.

He must keep his stuff to a minimum. Though he could use one of those suitcases he'd put in the loft, keep it in Nick's room for any clothes, once he was kitted out again. His only real regret was the guitar and speaker. It had a good sound. He could play it acoustic or electronically. It was a comfort. At the squat he would play for hours by the flickering candle light. Tunes he remembered, and then improvising, going through his repertoire of chords, extending them. The music tutor had gone too. He was about halfway through it. Still, he could buy another one of those anytime.

He'd need a front door key too. Best talk to Lynn. He was working at the casino tonight, eleven till four. He couldn't be ringing the bell at four thirty in the morning. Still, a space, his. It had been an awful afternoon, when he'd got back from the library to find those three guys in his squat. A takeover, they'd called it. And slammed the door in his face. That was misery, and, not knowing what else to do, he had gone to Nick's. And with Lynn's help had got this. He sniffed the duvet; it smelt so clean. He could always borrow Nick's key if it came to it. Get one cut soon as he got some cash. He sniffed the duvet again. It smelt of pine needles.

'What's going on here?'

Paul was in the hallway outside, in a grey suit and tie, looking as if he'd just come in from a business meeting. He put his briefcase down on the hall carpet and stared at the young man laid out in the box room.

'What's going on here?' he repeated, brushing back his thinning hair.

Tim sat up. Lynn had said she'd deal with her brother but she wasn't here. He sucked his lower lip. Charm offensive was called for.

'Lynn said I could stay for a day or two,' he managed to say. 'I won't be any trouble. Lynn said...'

'To hell with Lynn.' He threw up his arms. 'That's my cupboard. What have you done with my papers?'

'They're perfectly safe, Mr Atwood. I put them in the loft.'

'And who told you to put them in the loft?' He was gripping the door jambs, leaning into the room, looking at the little that was in there.

'Lynn said it would be alright...' He wanted to get out of the room (or was it a cupboard?) but he couldn't, not without pushing by Paul. He'd like to stand up, but even that seemed forbidden. 'She said so long as the papers are tidy and easy to get to.'

'I use my papers all the time. I can't go scrabbling about the loft!'

Paul came out of the doorway, and Tim lost sight of him.

'Lynn! Lynn!' he heard him shouting from up the corridor. 'Get up here. Let's sort this bloody thing out.'

Tim took the opportunity to get up and go out into the hallway. Paul was at the head of the stairs gazing down. Nick came out of his bedroom. He had a faint smirk and was wobbly on his feet, obviously high.

Paul marched up to his son. He pointed out the box room.

'What d'you know about this?'

Nick smiled at his father benignly. 'A cool space. Tim'd make a good tenant. Give him a rent book.'

His father stared at Nick, not knowing if he was serious.

'It's illegal,' he retorted. 'A fire risk. Against health and safety. There's no ventilation.'

'There's an airbrick, Mr Atwood,' ventured Tim. He hadn't ventured far from the room, leaning against the wall for protection.

Paul turned on Tim, pushing his face into the boy's. 'I don't give a monkey's whether there's an airbrick or not. I want you out. And I want you out now!'

And then Lynn was there. Tim hadn't seen her coming up, being too intent on Paul's attack.

'Leave him alone,' she declared, pulling Paul away.

He turned on her, his usual adversary. 'That's my cupboard!'

'Since when?'

'Since forever. I keep my papers there.' And then as if aware this wasn't his strongest argument, changed tack. 'It's a cupboard, not a room. You can't bring all and sundry in and put them in a cupboard.'

She recoiled as he sprayed at her.

'Don't spit at me.' She flapped her hands in distaste. 'Have some compassion, Paul. For goodness sake. He's a poor boy, down on his luck...'

'Tell social services. It's nothing to do with me. There are four of us already in the house. Only this morning you were complaining about it being overcrowded. Against my better judgement, I gave in to you splitting the sitting room in two... And do I get any peace? No, you want more. I knew it. Now it's my cupboard!'

'It's not yours,' declared Lynn. 'And Tim's been evicted.'

'How's that my concern!'

'He's had fifty foster parents!' Tim didn't correct the overstatement. 'He's not a wastrel. He's at Sixth Form College. He does night work for his keep.'

'I will not be pushed around, Lynn.' He was waving a finger at her. 'There's no room in this house. You cannot pick up every waif and stray. I will not give up my cupboard because you have been soft-soaped.' He turned on Tim and pointed to the stairs. 'Out! Out! And take your damned guitar with you...'

'It's been stolen, Mr Atwood.' He slipped into sadness mode. It was a trick of his that sometimes worked. He could even well up tears. Though he hardly needed acting now. 'I've lost everything,' he went on. 'My clothes, my guitar, my other pair of shoes...' He didn't have another pair of shoes but it suited his case to have lost them. He was fighting for his right to be in the world.

'I'm sorry about your guitar, I'm sorry about your clothes, I'm sorry about your shoes...' Paul was fiddling in his trouser pocket. His hand came out. 'Here's twenty quid. But you can't stay here.'

Tim went to take the note, but Lynn snatched it first.

'You vile beast! Have you no sympathy at all?'

It occurred to Tim that she wasn't his best ally. On his own, he might get a couple of days out of Paul. But not with Lynn's help.

'This is not Battersea Dogs Home!' Paul yelled.

She poked her brother in the chest. 'He's not a dog, but a human being. I know you well enough; you'd let a dog in. Buy it dog food. But a kid who's been brought up in care all his life... Not you. You need room for your useless papers!'

Dawn's door opened. She stood there resting on the doorpost, shaking her head at the melee. Behind her, Tim saw a laptop with writing on the screen on the desk by the window.

'Can't you find somewhere else to have your row?' she said wearily. 'It's worse than a Moroccan bazaar!'

'Tell your aunt.'

'Tell your father.'

'I know what's going on,' she said. 'The whole street knows. It's about him.' She pointed out Tim. 'About whether he has the box room or not.'

'And what do you say?' asked Lynn, seeking support.

Dawn was looking Tim over. His best forlorn expression.

'I'd say butter wouldn't melt in his mouth,' she said scornfully. 'I've seen him at college... I know him well enough. You'd better lock up anything valuable. Don't put your purse down.'

'Thank you, Lynn,' declared Paul. 'My daughter has at least seen sense. Do we invite a thief into our midst?'

'I'm not a thief, Mr Atwood. I might have been accused, but it wasn't me.'

'It never is you, is it?' snapped Dawn, a finger wagging at him. 'Those sad, weepy eyes. He could convince an angel to jump in a furnace.'

'But not you,' said Nick. 'You're too clever.'

'Shut up!' she snapped. 'The bugger took my phone.'

'I never. I swear it.' He looked around to everyone, appealing.

'You did. I know you did. Here's one person you can't fool, Tim.'

'Nick! Did I take her phone?'

'Not as far as I know.' He was leaning on the doorpost of his room, somewhat on the outside of the row. 'He hasn't got a phone.'

Dawn instantly got down and was patting both Tim's pockets. He stood still and let her. She put a hand into his pocket.

'Aha!' she declared. 'What's this?' She pulled out a phone and looked at it. Turning it over. 'It's not mine.'

'Apologise,' snapped Lynn.

Dawn shrugged. 'I don't know where he got that one. Some other poor sap. I bet he didn't buy it.'

'I bought it from The Phone Shop, last week,' he said. 'I could show you the receipt, it's with my gear...' It wasn't, but who would know?

'Do you think he should stay?' said Lynn to Nick.

Everyone turned to him, awaiting his response. Nick cringed at their expectation. Too many people. He gazed at Tim who was nodding at him.

'Yes,' he said at last. 'I want him to stay. He's my friend. We write songs together. We're forming a group. He won't be any trouble.' He stopped, exhausted after his speech.

'Two against two,' said Lynn, as if she now had a majority.

'I'm not going to be the big, bad baron in this.' Paul turned on Tim. 'Two nights you can stay. Two! Get that number?' He held up a pair of fingers. 'No longer. And if anything disappears, I'm calling the cops. Get me?'

'Yes, Mr Atwood. I'm not a thief. You won't know I'm here.'

Chapter 20

Lynn was busy in the kitchen. Without her usual irritation at the overnight mess, she put the dirty crockery in the dishwasher. She rapidly washed the dirty pans in the sink, wiped them and put them away, almost skipping, eager to begin work today. She knew her jeans were a little tight for working in, but her others were even tighter. She must get something looser, this figure hugging stuff was no good for manual work. Dungarees! That's what you wore. All those pockets for pencils and screws. She imagined herself with her thumbs under the shoulder straps, looking confident, ready to work. A mid green, with a few paint stains. Well, they'd come. You could hardly buy a pair ready stained.

She looked at her feet, oh this was no good, bare feet. She'd have to have some footwear. Around the house, she went around without shoes. Her feet got dirty but then she showered night and morning. And was so much more comfortable. But boots were needed. She had some walking boots somewhere. Not that she'd been walking for years. Meant to. But they were somewhere in her room. Feverishly expensive. Oh her City days, when she could buy without looking at the price...

She was so looking forward to working with Jack. Picking up from where they'd left off yesterday down in the cellar. Wrapped round each other, so much passion, it could so easily have happened then and there, sprawled, uncaring in the dust and cobwebs. He was so physical, so bright for a builder... She must stop thinking like that. What did she know about builders? Other than they wore overalls and climbed ladders.

A pity Dawn and Nick would be about. Study week. She could hardly take him to bed with them prowling. Then again, bedroom door shut... And to hell with it, they were eighteen year olds, hormones racing like crazy, what did they think their aunt got up to? It was her house, half her house. She shouldn't be dictated to by a nephew and niece.

Why should she pretend to be asexual just to please them?

The kitchen clean, she hit the cooking, doing three things at once. Kettle on for coffee, toast in the toaster, eggs and bacon in the frying pan. Normally she only had muesli for breakfast with some fresh fruit but today she was a builder, and a builder must begin the day with a good breakfast (and boots).

Tim came in, nervously, his hair ruffled, wearing the only clothes he had. She'd like to buy him some underwear and socks. And that T-shirt was so grubby. Perhaps she could put him in a dressing gown and shove all his clothes in the washing machine. Except she was working today. Oh he was so beautiful! That smooth, milk-coffee skin, those eyes, the sadness in them melted her. She felt for him, the poor boy. Years of being sent from home to home.

'Breakfast?' she said.

'Yes, please,' he said. 'I've been up a while, but didn't know what I could have, considering...' He didn't go on but she knew he was referring to Paul.

'Come in, eat what and when you want,' she said. 'We both buy the food. And I don't eat half what he eats, so you have some of my share.'

'I want to get out and go to college this morning, work in the library, before he comes. Least he sees of me the better.'

He gave a half smile which made her shiver in sympathy.

'Paul's out for a run,' she said. 'With luck we'll both miss him. Not that he'd spend much time in the kitchen with me in here.' She was breaking two more eggs into the pan, adding extra bacon. She felt so maternal. It was madness.

'Can I help?' he said.

Oh those eyes! She wanted to press him to her.

'Butter the toast while it's warm,' she said. 'How's college going?'

All that concern. She wanted to know everything about him, buy him clothes. Look after him.

'Quite well,' he said, buttering the toast. 'Most of my papers we got from the squat. Thanks for that, Lynn. It was very brave of you.'

'Quite stupid really,' she said. His story yesterday had made her so protective that she'd felt invulnerable, superwoman, until she'd actually gone into the squat, and knew within seconds it was an illusion. She was relieved to get out in one piece.

'There's my course work for psychology,' he said. 'I've been working on it for the last month. I thought that had gone. Luckily...' He held up a computer stick. 'This was with the papers. It's got all my work on it.' He stopped, bit his bottom lip as if considering, then said, 'That old computer. Does anyone want it?'

'That relic of a desktop?' she said with a shrug. 'Have it. We've all moved on to laptops. Don't even know whose it was. I don't suppose anyone will notice.'

He sighed. 'Except I've got to be out tomorrow.'

'You're staying,' she said with finality. She flipped the eggs and bacon onto two plates.

'Paul said two days.'

'And I said you were staying.' She put the plates on the table. 'He's got two kids here. I'm on my own. But I own half the house, so by rights I can bring someone in.'

'He's got a fearful temper.'

'So have I. One to match his. I win some, I lose some. This one I will win. Besides, you've got Nick on your side. Is he getting up? Sit down, let's eat.'

She took cutlery from the drawer, placed the cafetiere in the centre with two mugs and gathered up Tim's toast.

107

'I don't think Nick will be up for a while,' he said.

'It's study week or something. Isn't it?' she said, recalling what Dawn had told her.

'It is, but you can still go in and use the computers. You can stay all day. I've lots to do. And I want to keep out of Paul's way. I mean to get good results, so it's fine by me. Nick has more or less given up. I think he'll get kicked out at the end of term.'

'Does he know that?'

'He doesn't care. Says his future is in music.'

She gave a grim laugh and poured out two coffees.

'I've heard him. He likes it loud, he likes to shake the rooftops. Do you think he'll shake the rock world?'

'You never know.'

'But do you think he will?'

'No. Though we're writing some songs together.' He stopped and corrected himself. 'Well I'm writing them, Nick adds stuff when we try them out.'

'Good stuff?' She was crunching toast. It was so nice to have friendly, awake company at breakfast. This was going to be the best of days. First, Tim, beautiful boy. And then Jack.

'Sometimes.'

The front door slammed. But there was always her brother. It had to be him.

'That'll be Paul back from his run,' she said. 'Just eat your breakfast and don't worry.'

She could feel the fear in Tim as he watched the door. She wanted to stand over him with a cricket bat and swing out as her brother entered. Instead, she wiped egg with a piece of toast and pretended Paul wasn't there when he entered, breathing heavily, exhausted, in a crumpled T-shirt and shorts. He held onto the doorpost with one arm, bent over as if that was the finishing post.

Lynn and Tim ate their breakfast without looking at him. She wished she had turned the radio on. It would have been some sound, any sound, to drown out his awful breathing.

Paul straightened up, and massaged the back of his neck. She knew he wanted to be congratulated for his efforts, in going out so early, pushing himself so hard before work on his eight mile run, or however long it was. But although he wanted it, she knew it wouldn't be welcomed from her. In truth, she thought it rather stupid, pointless, although she had to admit she might have admired the tenacity in someone else.

Paul slouched across the room. She concentrated on cutting her bacon into neat pieces, almost sickened as he passed by at the intensity of his sweat. But she would not show it. He was in the room, but they'd got here first, sitting firmly down, claiming the territory. It was theirs, theirs alone. He knows it, she thought, and will leave. She was used to controlling the kitchen.

He was behind her at the sink. She didn't look, dipping a piece of bacon into egg yolk. Tim had his head down, taking his cue from her. Silence was required. Hers aggressive, his timid. Water was running behind. He was guzzling like a stray dog. That was how she saw him these days, all animal smells, dirty underwear, the soiled dishes he left behind, without a smile or joke, any encouragement to make her feel he was human.

Water droplets flicked her way, she ignored them. Easily she could have said something, begun a row, but Tim was here. She was his protector. The guzzling ceased. The long armed ape strolled out of their territory, across the kitchen to the door, glanced back, frowned at seeing them together at his table, eating his food, breathing his air, and left them. Leaving behind a smell of hostility.

Chapter 21

Jack arrived at the house at eight in the morning. The closest parking place was outside Anne's place. It was there or fifty yards up the road. If she hadn't noticed him yesterday, she definitely would today. But maybe, he reflected, she wanted to see him even less than he wanted to see her. It hadn't been a good time for either of them. Though her making out with Bert had puzzled him, such a lowlife. Then he'd disappeared. Curious.

Time past. Forget it. Just say hello, ask how she's getting on, the minimum.

He was out of the van quickly. The sooner he was in the house, the better, less chance of an encounter with Anne. Which would happen. But not yet.

He rang Lynn's bell and she answered almost immediately.

'Hello, Lynn,' he said with an eager smile. 'I can see you're ready for work. Smart boots.'

She was wearing her walking boots, brightly polished brown leather.

'I've hardly worn them,' she said looking down at the boots, slightly abashed. 'Two days in the Lake District a couple of years ago. Might as well press them into service.'

She pecked him on the cheek.

'Is that all I get?' he said.

'Too public here. Besides, we need to get the wall started before Paul changes his mind.'

She was being sensible. Just as well one of them was, the work needed to get on the move. He'd got half payment, he'd better justify it.

They began by bringing up the timbers from the cellar. Once it was all out, he and Lynn went out to his van to get his toolbox, stepladder and workbench. Realising he should've brought it in first thing, then he could've avoided Anne. But too late. She'd come out of her house and was on her top step. She was in jeans and T-shirt, short hair, freckled, hardly any change in her from the last time he'd seen her.

'Hello, Lynn,' she called and waved to her friend.

'Hi, Anne. I'm a builder today.'

'I can see you are,' said Anne. 'And I know your boss. Jack of All Trades!' She smiled broadly. 'It's been a long time.'

'Hello, Anne,' he said. 'Still childminding?'

It was a daft question as a mother was bringing a small child up her path.

'Still childminding,' she said. 'Bessie is with me.'

'How is she these days?'

'Much better,' she said. 'You'd be surprised at the change in her.'

And then became involved with the mother and toddler who had climbed the steps, greeting them both. Just before she went back into the house, she turned to Jack. 'I'd like to talk to you later, Jack. If that's alright.'

'Fine,' he said. 'I'm next door.'

Anne went in.

Lynn had the toolbox. She said, 'Did you have an affair with her?'

Jack blew a raspberry. 'Hardly.'

'What's hardly an affair?' enquired Lynn.

He shrugged. 'We began. Then she ditched me for another guy.'

Lynn gave a short laugh, then said, 'So what does she want to see you about?'

'Not to apologise, I'm sure.' He kissed Lynn on the cheek. 'I haven't seen her for two years. And don't mind if I never see her again.'

'That bad?' she said.

'We didn't part on good terms. Let's get this stuff in. Before she's out again.'

A car had drawn up with a mother and infant at the front. Anne had returned to her front step, in greeting mode.

But it took another trip outside as worksheets had to be brought in. Lynn volunteered, to save him any embarrassment, she said. He suspected she was a little jealous, their own affair hardly underway. But Anne was too busy greeting parents and children to say any more to them.

Once everything was in the house, Jack gave Lynn the sheets to cover the furniture, and any items in range of their work.

'These could do with a six months' soak,' she said, grimacing as she sniffed the sheets.

'Been too busy,' he said uncomfortably. But she said no more and laid them out tentatively. It was one of the discomforts of working with your employer, who might be less critical if she wasn't laying out the sheets herself.

Jack set to measuring height and width of the wall to be. Yesterday, he'd simply paced out the width of the room and estimated the ceiling height. Now he needed the exact measurements. And then noted that the carpet went through...

'I'm going to have to cut the carpet,' he said.

'Do what you have to do,' she declared. 'I want that wall.'

He set her marking up timbers, having shown her how to use the set square. Leaving her to it, he used a timber length as a straight edge and with a knife cut the carpet across the room. And then peeled both sides back, far enough to reveal the floorboards and to give work room.

Jack locked the electric saw on the portable bench and was soon immersed in the job, sawing to size, the whine of the saw minimising chat. Every so often he'd glance at Lynn, and was pleased that she was doing well. You don't really want to tell your client off.

A little later, he noted she had sawdust in her hair, and was scratching it in, on her knees in a pose of concentration, marking up rapidly. An attractive builder, difficult to keep his mind on the job. She looked up and caught him watching her.

'What you looking at?'

'I like the yellow highlights in your hair,' he said, lifting his goggles.

She shook her hair and sawdust flew out. 'Oh, it's making me sneeze.' She tried to hold back and then it came out in a blast. 'Look what you made me do.'

'There's a mask in the toolbox,' he said.

'Cissies wear masks,' she said disdainfully, continuing with her marking up. 'When do I get to use the saw?'

'End of your apprenticeship,' he said, zipping off a wood end.

She rose and came over to see what he was doing. He sawed off another end.

'What d'you think?' he said.

'I could do that,' she said.

'After tea break,' he said.

'It's coffee.'

'Tea,' he said with finality. 'Coffee is for white collar paper pushers.'

'You drank it yesterday,' she said.

'I needed the work.'

'You mean I shouldn't believe anything you said yesterday?'

'Sixty per cent of it was true.'

'Not bad for a man.' She returned to marking up. 'Tea break,' she said with deliberate emphasis, 'at ten?'

'Fine by me.'

They continued at their separate jobs, she feeding him the uprights to saw to size. He liked working with her and wondered whether it had a future. But knew it could only last as long as their relationship. And that had barely begun. Besides, he didn't know her. This was the easy bit. And should you really fantasise while you saw? Health and safety.

The pessimist in him, predicting the end before it began. Maybe this time, something more lasting? He was looking forward to tea break, to toast and a chat. With a worker, a client and a woman he fancied.

Jack left the sawing, so as to give her some to do after the break. And set to screwing a crosspiece of 4 by 2 on to the floor, going from wall to wall, through the floorboards and into the joists. And then up the ladder, Lynn with a broom supporting an end, he screwed a crosspiece to the ceiling.

With the two crosspieces in place, Jack began screwing in the 2 by 1 uprights. Lynn had finished marking up and he set her working from the other end.

'We do one side for one wall,' said Jack. 'Then a space and the other wall. Two walls made up of soundproof board attached to the uprights. We fill in the middle with rock wool.'

'It's quite simple really,' she said. 'A skeleton. Then you put the skin over it and fill it.'

'Regretting employing me?'

'Not yet, though I might do the next one myself.' She laughed. 'I could fill the house with walls. Like a maze. Much more interesting. Get Paul well and truly lost.'

She suddenly shut up as Paul was at the door in his grey suit, briefcase in hand. Had he heard? Lynn's face had tightened, obviously wishing he wasn't there to listen in. Jack wondered what was in the briefcase, knowing that not so long ago it would have held a bottle of whisky and little else.

As if giving up on an invitation to enter, Paul took a decisive step into the room. He put down the briefcase, sucked his cheeks, and appraised the work. Lynn scowled as she was screwing in an upright, making no attempt to hide her displeasure.

'Coming on quickly,' said Paul to Jack, man to man.

'Well, now I've got a mate,' he said, indicating Lynn, 'it's full steam ahead.'

Jack came down from the ladder, having fixed an upright at the top. He tested it for firmness, top then bottom.

'Good.'

Lynn had taken up the drill. She set it whirring and drilled a couple of holes, then seemed to turn it on her brother, almost like a space gun. But he wouldn't be evaporated.

She said to Jack, 'I'll make us coffee.' Then corrected herself with a brief smile. 'I mean tea.'

She left them.

Jack noted Paul lightening up as soon as she'd gone.

'So how's this wall going to work, Jack? I mean, I can see it's a wall, a barrier, but how will it block sound?'

'There's a four inch gap between the uprights on both sides,' he said. 'That'll be filled with rock wool. That'll be sandwiched with a double thickness of soundproofing plasterboard.'

Aware, as he was speaking, that he'd intended to phone Bob last night about fitting a soundproof wall, or failing that look it up on the internet. But Mia was there, they'd gone out on the Flats, and he'd simply forgotten.

'I'll be intrigued how well it works,' said Paul.

Me too, thought Jack, scrabbling to recall after the last time he'd fitted a wall, and had complaints, and read up on it.

'It's about weight,' he said. 'Sound is vibrations; the more weight in the wall the more the vibrations lose energy as they pass through.' He knew too it was about frequency and wavelengths but didn't understand that too well, but he'd have a go anyway, as he was sure Paul understood even less.

'It's the lower frequencies that have the most thump,' he went on. 'You know, drumming or bass guitar. Rock wool is good at cutting out those frequencies. And the resilient channel...' He held up a long strip of the perforated metal. 'This is attached to the uprights, and the soundproof board is attached to it, not to the wood. It breaks the sound transmission...' And other bullshit, he thought.

'I'm sure it beats egg boxes,' said Paul, obviously having had enough of the technical spiel, to Jack's relief. 'How you getting on with my sister?'

'Lynn's OK,' he said carefully. 'She works hard.'

'Do you fancy her?'

'I can't think that way,' lied Jack. 'She's a client. I don't go around sizing up every customer. That's how you lose work.'

'She could do with a boyfriend,' said Paul, strolling about the room, straightening the covering sheets here and there. 'Someone to take her off my hands. Get her out the house once and for all.' He turned to Jack. 'You up for it?'

'I'm employed to make a wall. From here to there.' He stretched his arms across the space. 'That's me, mate. And then I'm off to the next job.'

Paul came close and looked him in the eye.

'I could make it worth your while,' he said quietly.

They were a couple of feet apart, Jack saw his seriousness. And knew not to take sides in this brother-sister war.

'I'm not sure what you're saying,' he said, though he more or less did.

'Befriend her. Screw her. Encourage her to leave this house... Permanently. I'd pay you for your time and trouble.'

'Enough,' exclaimed Jack, raising his hands to indicate a halt. 'I'm a builder, not a gigolo.'

'She likes you, mate.' Paul patted him on the shoulder. 'I've seen you looking at her. Be pleasant work.'

'Yeh, well,' he said awkwardly, 'I've other fish to fry.'

'Lucky you.' Paul was about to sit on the sofa arm, but hesitated at the grubby sheet, then decided it was bearable and sat down. 'I tell you, Jack, she exhausts me. Yesterday, well, you know all about this wall. We'd briefly discussed it the night before, came to no solid conclusion, and then she's doing it. Going hell for leather. The woman's crazy, I tell you. Then in the afternoon, she brings some homeless kid into the house. Gives him the box room. I never know what she's going to do next.'

'It's difficult living with people,' said Jack, endeavouring to stay neutral, but too aware that Paul was doing a poor job at selling his sister. How much, he wondered, had he been prepared to pay? Did he really think Jack could get her away?

'We own half this house each. Our parents died in a plane crash.'

'Lynn did mention it.'

Paul threw up his arms. 'What a situation!' He rose and strolled about the room. 'OK, I admit, it was my fault that my business went bust. I drank myself stupid. Lost my house, lost my marriage. You know the story.'

'I lived it,' said Jack. Only too aware of his last year with Alison, and his part in their crumbling marriage.

'So I had to come back here,' he said. 'No choice. Circumstances forced me and Lynn together. Neither of us wanted it. I went bust, she got ill, and here we are. For all that's holy, here we are.' He sat down again on the arm of the sofa, but was instantly up again. 'I don't need telling it's a nice house. Plenty big enough, I'm sure all the homeless families would tell me.' He stepped towards Jack in appeal. 'Are you absolutely sure you won't consider my offer, Jack? Five thou. Cash.'

Jack was surprised at the figure, might have asked for details but Lynn entered with a tray. Jack noted that, although there were three of them, on the tray were only two mugs of tea and two bacon sandwiches. It was obvious who wasn't included. Five thousand! But for an impossible job. He couldn't imagine getting Lynn to do anything she didn't want to.

It was never a serious offer, he assured himself. Paul would back out. And Jack would end up looking an idiot who would get slammed by Paul and Lynn, if she ever learned of it.

She handed Jack a plate with a bacon sandwich and a mug of tea, just in case there was any confusion about who they were for. She took her own off the tray.

'Excuse me,' Jack said to Paul indicating the sandwich. 'I'm famished.'

'Don't mind me, Jack. I've eaten.'

Jack attacked the sandwich, placing the mug on a rung of the ladder. He'd had only a slice of toast before leaving the house that morning. He was never hungry first thing, about 10 am it usually hit him.

'It's going to take away space,' said Paul thoughtfully, holding an upright and examining the distance between those on either side.

Jack put his sandwich on the plate. 'Let me calculate,' knowing he should have done this beforehand.

'No, Jack, you eat your sandwich.'

'No, legitimate question. Let me figure.' He picked up his notebook. 'Let's go from one side to the other.' He jotted as he went along, pointing out items with his pencil. 'One inch of soundproofing board, half an inch of resilient channel...' He doubted Paul actually cared but went on to fill the vacuum, and to do what he should have already done. 'Then one inch of upright, four inches filled in with rock wool. Ditto, ditto, ditto on other side. That's...' He checked the figure to make sure. 'Nine inches.'

Paul indicated nine inches between his hands. 'That's a chunk of space to lose.'

'Any wall takes up space,' insisted Jack. 'And soundproofing takes up more.'

'Who's going to lose most?' he said, putting his hands in the space, trying to calculate.

'It's exactly equal,' snapped Lynn. 'Symmetrical. Four and half inches your side, four and a half my side. Share and share alike. Family.'

He ignored her. 'It's one thing talking about a wall, Jack, it's another seeing it taking shape. Suddenly the sitting room is chopped in half. Space is lost. I see the carpet's been sliced.'

Dawn came in. She was wearing a bright orange, long-sleeved top and blue jeans ripped at the knee. Her hair was shorter than last time Jack had seen her, cut ragged. A home, amateur job.

She said, 'Ah, this is where it's going to be. So quick. I'm amazed. This'll be two rooms in no time.'

Jack said, 'It's not load bearing. So no brickwork. That's why it's speedy. And Lynn's been helping. Saved me a lot of time.' Lynn smiled at him; he wasn't sure how Paul was taking the compliments to his sister, maybe approving. After all, he wanted Jack to take Lynn away. Far, far away.

Dawn walked about the space, going in and out the uprights like a country dancer, avoiding the ladder where Jack had his mug of tea and plate.

'His and hers,' she said. 'Will I have to knock on your door, Lynn?'

'You will. But I'll let you in.'

'Will you lock it?'

'With a big key.'

She turned to her father. 'Will you turn up the TV, just to annoy her?'

'Of course not,' said her father, as if anything so childish had not occurred to him. 'Besides, it's built to stop sound.'

'Only from the TV room,' said Dawn. She pointed upwards with a finger. 'What about Nick and Tim upstairs?'

Her father looked upwards, as if to peer through the ceiling. 'Is your brother up yet?'

'Silly question,' she said with a smirk.

'As for Tim,' he turned to face his sister, 'he is going tomorrow. Don't you try to baulk me. And I don't want him back.'

'There speaks the arch fascist,' exclaimed Lynn. She was seated in what would be her room, on one of the chairs by the large table which now had its leaves folded down. 'The boy has never had a thing, brought up in care, passed from foster home to foster home, he gets evicted by some bullies – and my brother can't wait to throw him onto the streets.'

'Have you suddenly discovered the homeless, Lynn?'

'One homeless boy. He has nothing.'

Paul threw up his arms. 'The Virgin Mary is in our midst.'

'Tim's a thief,' said Dawn.

'Please don't say that, Dawn. You can't know for certain,' said Lynn.

Dawn shrugged. 'Everyone at college knows he's a light-fingered tea leaf.'

'Is there proof?'

Dawn blew a raspberry. 'You don't need proof when he's always around when stuff goes missing.'

'Doesn't sound like proof to me, Dawn.'

'He's a thief I tell you. Don't let those soft brown eyes fool you.' And so, not to be argued with in her certainty, she left the room.

'I shall lock my bedroom door,' said Paul. 'I'm not having a thief stay in the house.'

'There's no proof,' declared Lynn. 'Simply prejudice.'

Jack was silent, drinking his tea and eating his sandwich, wishing they would have their row elsewhere. He had no idea who this Tim was. A thief, a poor boy brought up in care, about to be homeless. Some of those things.

'Definitive proof is not required,' retorted Paul. 'This is not a court of law.' He had gone to the door. 'This is my home, the home of my daughter and my son... We don't need someone living here accused of stealing. Suspicion will do.' He turned into the hallway. 'I've things to do. One more day and night. Then he's away. I don't care where.'

He left the room.

'You should've been a hangman!' yelled Lynn, rushing to the door, shouting at her brother's back as he went up the stairs. 'A concentration camp guard! Chief torturer for the Borgias.'

She came back into the room, suddenly deflated and began to weep. Hands in her face, she aimlessly wandered to the front window, body heaving. Jack crossed to her and took her in his arms. She held him to her and kissed him solidly on the mouth. He melted with the sensation, legs hollow.

She broke away. 'Not here. Not with him upstairs.'

He wanted more, but this was not the place. Not with Paul about, with his daughter, what's her name. Wasn't there a son too?

'Do you want to come over this evening?' he said.

'Yes, I do,' she exclaimed. 'But I must make sure Tim is alright. My brother is such a bully.'

'We could get a takeaway from Moon House,' he said.

'Then you could show me your telescope.' She laughed. 'How apt.' She was sitting on the arm of the sofa and had picked up her tea. 'I don't know what you must think of us.'

'I don't judge other people's rows,' he said, taking up his own tea and sitting by her. 'They never solve anything, not that I can be one to lecture.'

She took his hand. 'Do you think I could work with you, Jack? I don't just mean here. Is it a possibility?' She held up a hand. 'Don't say anything. It's too soon I know. But I need a way out. I'm too much in this house. I need to work outside.' She had a sudden thought, pointing to what would be her room. 'That could be the works office. Just the office, I'd need to be out and about, working on site. Making walls, putting in the plumbing. I must research women's building courses.' She kissed his hand. 'I am so enjoying working with you. I know it's not art. But it's practical. Making new spaces, putting roofs on them. The mystery revealed.' She laughed. 'You must think me an idiot.'

'No, but keep the mystery hidden,' he said with a laugh. 'Some of the things I've covered up, may they stay that way forever.'

She stood up. 'Now I'd like you to show me how to use the electric saw. So I can cut off my brother's head.'

Tim entered. He had on a backpack stuffed full of books.

'Hello,' he said. 'College was closed. They had a flood, so I went to the Stratford library for a couple of hours. Thought I'd come back for some lunch, if that's alright.'

'That's fine, sweetheart. But you'd better not go upstairs. My brother's there, not in the best of moods. Not that anyone is this morning. But he's going out for another run shortly. Stay here until he goes.'

He nodded. 'Thanks, Lynn.'

Jack rose from the sofa. He would have liked Lynn alone, but it didn't seem possible in this house. He wondered about the young man. Lynn was motherly towards him. He must be the one Paul had objected to. What was his name?

'Are you Jack of All Trades?' said Tim with a broad grin.

'I am. Working here.'

'I saw your van. I'm Tim. Staying here a little while.'

Jack held his hand out. 'How do you do, Tim.'

Tim took his hand. As they shook, Jack was held by his handsome, brown face, his deep brown eyes. Almost hypnotic.

'I can see it's a wall you're making here,' said Tim, when they broke. He was fingering the posts. 'Seems rather thick.'

'Why don't you explain to him, Jack,' said Lynn. Tim was looking at Jack's notes on the table. He wouldn't make much sense of them, thought Jack.

There was a rapid padding down the stairs, and a few seconds later the front door slammed. Lynn went to the front window, one hand on the glass.

'There's Paul, out to run himself soppy, as if he needs it,' she exclaimed. 'He calls it interval running. It doesn't make sense to me. He does one run, has a break, does another. Why can't he just do one long one?' She waved a hand dismissively. 'Who cares! It gives us an hour's peace.' She turned to Tim. 'You've got the kitchen to yourself, sweetheart, with no risk of interruption.'

'I'll go and eat. Can I make you anything?'

'We've eaten,' she said. 'You help yourself. I'll be in here with Jack if you need me.'

Chapter 22

DS Nikki Martin completed the booking for *As You Like It* at the National. She and Joyce went to the theatre once a month, though more than once she'd had to pull out due to an investigation. Another time, she'd got to the theatre ten minutes after the performance started, having to persuade the young lady at the door to let her in, and then had to make her way in the dark, and find her seat somewhere in the middle of the row, annoying too many of the audience.

But it was the treats that broke up her over-concentration on work. Out of the station, life could be lonely and dull. So plan ahead. Do things. An art exhibition, the theatre. Though the big exhibitions could be so crowded. She and Joyce had worked out a technique. Book for the last showing of the day, and then let the crowd drift ahead, be purposely slow. And then you had the exhibition more or less to yourself. Their tardiness might annoy the staff, but both were tough enough to ignore them. Joyce, Head of Social Services, had a hide like buffalo, and horns to match when she needed to use them, but mostly dealt with altercations on their days out with ultra politeness, as if she was utterly unaware they were causing any inconvenience.

An incoming email caught her attention. Just as well she'd booked the tickets before. This had to be dealt with at once. The investigation had taken a leap. She phoned Fayyad on his mobile number. She knew that he was somewhere in the building, but a quick phone call was much easier than chasing around for him.

'Where are you?' she said.

'In the canteen, having a quick cuppa. Anything up?'

'Yes,' she said. 'Get here as soon as you can. The daughter's DNA proves it's Frank Brand.'

'Be there in a couple of minutes.'

He was. And took a seat opposite her, the desk between them.

'So it's definite,' said Fayyad.

'Proved,' she said. 'One body is Bert Long, the other his mate Frank Brand.'

She liked Fayyad, especially in his cricket whites and had spoken in his favour of his promotion. She was a cricket umpire herself, having been a spin bowler when she was younger. Everyone knew she had favourites, but then so what? Who didn't? Just make sure they were good at their job.

'I've had a quick look at Frank's details while I've been waiting,' she said. 'A member of England First. A friend of Bert Long. And the two end up in the same grave.'

'His daughter hates him, ma'am,' said Fayyad. 'Got that much on our visit. Didn't pursue it, as the body might have been someone else.'

'Of course. Any thoughts about why she hated him?'

'She lived with her father until he disappeared. And it was clear she wanted the corpse to be him. No doubt about that. She was afraid of him. Which suggests violence. Hayley reckons sexual abuse too, but it wasn't in our remit to dig any further.'

'Understood. But we will now. Is the daughter still at the same address?'

'Same place. And there are others in the house. I'm not sure how many but it's quite a big house.'

'We'll need to question everyone who was in that house two years ago when Frank disappeared. Start with the daughter. What's her name?'

'Bessie Brand.'

'Let's have Bessie in for questioning right away. You and Hayley pick her up and bring her in to the station.' She reflected for a second. 'No heaviness. It's an invitation to give us information.' And added with a wry smile, 'Use your charm.' She bit her bottom lip in thinking mode. 'We have two bodies, murdered and buried in Epping Forest. And now identified. We need to move quickly before everyone puts their defences up. Bring her in.'

Chapter 23

Dawn was on the 104 bus, upstairs in the long seat at the back, legs stretched out and feet on the seat opposite. She'd been picking at the dried blood on her arm, but a middle aged black man had come and taken a place on the long seat at the opposite window. And she'd pulled down her sleeve, covering her scars.

Though why shouldn't she reveal them to the world? They were a true part of her. She'd made them, a map of her suffering. Others hid their feelings, she should roll up her sleeves, and say this is me. I bleed because it's the only way I can show what I am.

It would be cowardice to hide her scars, she persuaded herself. And so rolled up her sleeve, slowly, almost teasingly, to her shoulder. Out of the corner of her eye, she watched the man. He saw her arm, grimaced and turned away, looking out the window. She kept her arm in plain sight. He couldn't miss it. She knew he would be curious. She was enjoying this, knowing she'd captured him. He wasn't really looking out of the window, just trying to escape seeing her. Well, she wouldn't let him.

He turned back from the window, saw her arm, and threw his arms up.

'What are you doing to yourself! Stupid woman,' he exclaimed.

And was up, out of the seat, marching down the almost empty top deck to the front of the bus, where he sat down again.

She'd won. She had the back seat to herself. This was her territory. He'd reacted in horror. Good, that was the reaction she enjoyed. Not the busybodies. Like her therapists. All with their theories. Telling her why she must stop. She could never make them see that she didn't want to stop. That stopping would be giving in. They were stubborn in their demands. Fixed. Blind.

She had a body. And her body was hers. She could treat it how she wished. Therapists were fascists. Wanting to control her. As if mind control wasn't enough. Body control too. That was society's way. Mind and body conformity. She'd been lectured by teachers, nurses, doctors, therapists, her father. Her mother in New Zealand, thank goodness, was safely out of touch. She could stay that way. Pity the others weren't too.

Yes, they housed her and fed her, but the payments they demanded were over the top. Her father was a brick wall of No. His face, his arms, his eyes. He didn't even have to say anything. Though he was quite easy to avoid. All his running and work. He didn't really want to be bothered, and she didn't want his strictures. So she would pretend to be working too, when in reality she was online, talking to the ones who knew what it was like. How the world wanted to control you.

Nick mostly ignored her. Well, that was fine. She ignored him too. A lot of the time he was too stoned to see anything anyway or blasting his head off with sound, or both. He knew she hadn't been going to college for the last month, but didn't care. But that lowlife, Tim, he watched her too much. He'd tell Lynn. And she cared much more for her than her useless father. What more could he say to her? Take up running like me. Or get drunk like I used to. He'd even suggested she go join her mother in New Zealand. Why? For what point? When her mother couldn't get away fast enough.

But Lynn was the one person in the house who half understood. Didn't demand of her. Let her be. But she was being taking in by that boy. That sly fox. Couldn't she see what he was? What he wanted from her?

Clearly not.

It was amazing what people couldn't see. Didn't allow themselves to see. They parroted the same phrases, as if repetition made them more true. How ignorant people were. Locked in their unknowing.

She liked this route. The long route south. Very Asian to begin with, down High Street North with sari shops and Indian restaurants. Mostly men came up top of the bus, a few younger women in hijabs; burqas stayed downstairs. Then across the Barking Road into High Street South, more mixed race here. She had spread across the seat, legs stretched out, daring someone to say something, her scarred arm out. From up here, she could look down on the people in the streets, going where, doing what? Busy ants with no real purpose in themselves, but they had their orders, go where you are told to go. They knew so little.

And across the Newham Way into Docklands. Down along Beckton Park with its abandoned supermarket trolleys and on to the once docks. A couple of weeks ago, she'd seen her father running down here, along a dock basin. She'd already got off the bus, he hadn't seen her. How stupid he looked, did he never see himself? Didn't he know what an idiot he looked to other people, running to stop himself thinking, simply to come ten thousandth in the London Marathon? Some time of hours and minutes that meant nothing to anybody.

Once he'd come back to the house so exhausted, that he'd collapsed on the top step. She sort of understood that. The need to force your body beyond itself. But when she'd told him it was similar to cutting herself, he told her she was talking rubbish. Her usual nonsense. She should straighten up, lift herself, not continue playing the victim.

What an idiot he was, believing he was free, a puppet dragged along by his strings.

She got off the bus by the Woolwich Ferry. The sky was dark, with low smudgy cloud, reflecting in the water. There was the foot tunnel entrance, a huge red brick roundel, like a giant's toilet. Sometimes she'd come back that way, under the Thames, through the porcelain sleeve. It felt like passing through a sewage pipe, before the flush.

There were lorries and vans queuing to get on the ferry. She enjoyed walking along the pavement, past the impatient drivers, one of the few foot passengers. Two ferries were on today, fat bugs that plied the Thames, a river apart at the moment, they would meet in the middle.

She waited at the head. A ferry had just come in, the quay was being lowered to meet it, with its road and passenger walkway. After a few minutes the bar at the far side was raised and traffic began to come off the ferry. Foot passengers could go on at once, the on traffic had to wait until the ferry was empty of vehicles. She ran along the vibrating metalwork, and stepped on to the ferry. First again.

All hers.

She went down the stairs into the bowels, feeling the thump of the engines as it beat like her heart. There were open rooms with ancient benches round the sides for the hundreds of dockers who fifty years ago crammed on the ferries to go to work in the docks. There would be at most ten people down here when the ferry left, with space for three hundred or more. She loved the roominess. And would walk about, down here, in the five minutes before the ferry went, exploring the deck as if she were on a cruise ship going to Patagonia, rather than an insignificant ferry going back and forth from North Woolwich to South Woolwich, a journey of less than four hundred yards.

She took her place at the end cargo gates. There was never any cargo. They were like horse gates, maybe three times as wide, open at the top, where she could lean over as the ferry turned in to the river to begin its crossing. A little way out, the ferry had to turn about, to get its front facing the far side, and then it would head over. To the west was the Thames Barrier, pier heads out of the water like seals waiting for giant beach balls, beyond – the skyscrapers of Canary Wharf.

It was mid river that she dropped it, as if by accident, a little thing, a little splash.

Chapter 24

Fayyad and Hayley drew up at the house on Ham Park Road. He turned off the engine.

'Let's be extra careful,' said Fayyad. 'She's rather fragile as it is.'

'Yes, I saw that the other day,' said Hayley. 'She doesn't want to be reminded of her father. Bad memories there. But there's a good chance she knows something about his death.'

'Be helpful and kind,' said Fayyad. 'We'll get more out of her that way.'

'Like two ministering angels,' said Hayley.

They alighted and locked up. The car was on the park side of the road; there was little traffic. A breeze was blowing leaves along the pavement with many yet to fall from the trees overhanging the fence. Fayyad and Hayley crossed the road and walked quickly to the house.

The buzzer was answered by Anne.

'Who is it?'

'It's the police for Bessie Brand,' said Fayyad.

'One moment,' said Anne.

They waited at the door, under the high porch, turning, looking about them. There were a few pink roses left in the circular flower bed in the front garden. The grass was overlong and half covered in damp leaves. Fayyad looked up at the upper floors.

'I wonder who else lives here,' he mused.

'Four bells,' said Hayley, indicating the bells on the door post. 'Anne is on the ground floor with her childminding. Bessie has a room upstairs, yes, Brand.' She pointed out the name. 'And there's Khan and there's a fourth bell with no name on...'

'That's my mate's van,' Fayyad interrupted, pointing to a vehicle.

There, just up the road, was a van with Jack of All Trades painted in blue on the side. A ladder, a bucket, some tools, were also part of the design, as if the artist was nervous of drawing a person, objects allowing less complaint.

'He must be working in one of these houses,' mused Fayyad. 'My mate, Jack Bell. We were at school together. Last I saw of him, he was having a tough time of it workwise. Looks like he's got something round here. Good for him.'

The front door opened. And there was Anne with a child in her arms.

She said impatiently, 'You were here only yesterday. Is this harassment? Why do you want Bessie?'

'That's between us and Miss Brand, if you don't mind,' said Fayyad. 'We'd like her to come to the police station with us.'

'What!' exclaimed Anne. 'Just like that. Drop everything and come to the station.'

'It's important,' said Fayyad. 'Please tell her.'

'Is she under arrest?' said Anne.

'No,' said Fayyad. 'We simply have some questions for her.'

'Then she can't come,' exclaimed Anne. The child was pulling her hair. 'Stop it, Damon. You turn up out of the blue, no notice,' she went on, holding the child's hands off her face and hair, 'not caring that we have seven children to look after. There must be two adults present. How on earth can she go with you? Health and Safety. I couldn't cope with all these children on my own.'

Fayyad looked at Hayley, suppressing his feelings. She was certainly being protective, but she had a point, even if she was less than polite expressing it. Bessie wasn't under arrest and so he couldn't compel her to come to the station.

He said, 'When do your children leave?'

'The last ones leave... Stop pulling my nose, Damon. Stop it!' Damon started crying. 'And we have six more just like this,' she added above the racket. 'The last ones go about six thirty. But after five thirty I can cope on my own. Come back then.'

And she began to close the door. Fayyad put his foot in it.

'We'd like to speak to Bessie Brand, out here, if you don't mind,' he said.

'I do mind,' she said. 'And I've told you why. I've a nursery to run. I've been out here too long already. Come back at five thirty.' She pushed at the door. 'So if you'll kindly withdraw your foot...' Fayyad did so. And she slammed the door.

'Cow,' he hissed.

'She has got seven kids,' said Hayley.

'And no manners.' He was looking at the front door as if wondering how to break it down. He turned to Hayley. 'I'm suspicious. I have a feeling something's going on in this house...'

'Could be she's got seven kids and she's harassed.'

'Or she's hiding something. And if so, that's not the way to behave when the cops come. What's her name again?'

'Anne Tucker.'

They had drifted down the path on to the pavement. Fayyad was looking back at the house thoughtfully.

'We'll check her out when we get back to the station. See if we've got anything on her.' He looked at his watch and turned to Hayley. 'Now what do we do? I suppose, go back to the station, come back late afternoon. What d'you think?'

'We could stay a while, watch who goes in and out,' said Hayley.

'We could. Maybe have a chat with them... Ah!' he suddenly pointed out. 'Talk of the devil. There he is. My mate, he's just come out of next door, gone to his van. I'll have a word with him. He might know something about this house. You wait in the car, Hayley, while I have a chat. Better if it's just me.' He waved his arms and yelled, 'Jack!'

Jack turned on hearing his name. He'd come out to get his phone, which he thought he might have left in his van.

'Fayyad! You old dog.' He strode to his friend. They shook hands. 'Who you sleuthing today?'

'That place,' Fayyad indicated with his head. 'Do you know anything about the residents?'

'There's a childminder downstairs. Anne's her name.'

'What's she like?'

Jack was aware, this was a cop asking the question, not simply his old friend. He wondered too what he was doing here. Why he wanted to know about that house in particular.

'Anne, well...' he said, pretending his acquaintance was slight. 'She can be a bit difficult. Got a temper.'

'She has that all right. Doesn't like cops.'

Who does, thought Jack, but didn't say.

'She's got a young girl working with her,' went on Fayyad. 'Do you know anything about her?'

'Bessie, do you mean?'

'Yeh, that's her.'

'What's she been up to?' said Jack. 'Nothing serious I hope.' But he was already fearing what Fayyad might tell him. Jack knew too much about Bessie.

'Well her dad disappeared a couple of years ago,' went on Fayyad. 'And we've found him.'

'What? He's back?' exclaimed Jack, knowing that he couldn't be, but guessing Fayyad knew that too.

'A dog walker found him in Epping Forest. Or rather her dog sniffed his hand poking out of a fox hole. It's a crime scene now,' he said. 'Two bodies turned up.' He tapped his nose. 'Keep that to yourself.'

Jack was electric, calculating, thinking ahead. It had happened. Frank had been found. And identified. The cops were nosing around already. Of all the places to be working! His legs were shaking, he did his best to still them. He was aware of Fayyad looking at him. Was he waiting for the answer to a question he hadn't heard?

'All this'll be a shock for Bessie,' he managed to say, hoping that would suffice.

'She half knows,' said Fayyad. 'We came the other day. And told her we thought the body could well be her father. And now we can confirm it. The wonders of science. Do you know who else lives in the house?'

'There's Maggie and David on the top floor,' he said, knowing he mustn't hide that he'd worked there. It would only look suspicious when they found out. 'And an old lady, what was her name?' He shrugged. 'Forgotten.'

'How come you know this?' said Fayyad.

'I worked there,' he said. 'Couple of years ago. I put in the back fence, in the garden.' All too easily checkable with the agents. Though there were two bodies, Fayyad had said. Had to be Bert. His sudden disappearance. How on earth did he end up buried with Frank?

'Did you ever meet Frank Brand?' said Fayyad.

'Once,' he said. Though he might have added alive, as he'd seen too much of him dead. 'I saw him putting tacks into meatballs in the backyard.'

'That's a strange thing to do.'

'He was out to kill the old lady's cat, in a painful and horrible way.'

'Sounds no great loss to the world,' said Fayyad, his tongue lolling in his cheek as he looked up at the higher floors of the house. 'You working nearby?'

'Yeh, next door,' said Jack, 'for the next few days.'

'That's convenient.'

For whom, thought Jack. Not him. The last place he wanted to be, seeing the cops traipse backwards and forwards, as they most surely would be, questioning, homing in on any little discrepancy, coming back to question further. It was like a rolling avalanche, heading his way, set to overwhelm and bury him. He would have to talk to Anne; he couldn't avoid her any longer.

'You still with the crime squad?' he said. A silly question, considering Fayyad's knowledge and interrogation. But he was desperate to take the focus off himself.

'Meet your friendly neighbourhood bobby, Detective Sergeant Kamani,' said Fayyad, puffing out his chest. 'Forest Gate CID. Promoted two weeks ago.'

'Congratulations,' said Jack, not ready to pat his schoolmate on the back. 'Good to chat. But I must get on. Great to see you, Fayyad... Work to do, you know. Keeping the wolf from the door.'

'Perhaps I could come to your place this evening,' said Fayyad. 'Get a statement. As you were around when Frank disappeared. So you could fill out the picture. Say eight o'clock?'

'Fine, fine,' said Jack. 'See you then, mate.'

He gave Fayyad a playful tap on the shoulder and headed back to his van. This was awful, awful. There were so many people involved. What do you say, what do you keep back? He had the feeling he hadn't done so well.

Chapter 25

Lynn was sawing, Jack was putting in the uprights. Thank heavens he had work to do. Or he'd be a punch ball to his thoughts. Whatever happened, he must stay sober, or the cops would utterly confound him with their questioning. Who knew what he might admit, slurred tongue, slurred mind.

He'd told Fayyad he was there at the time. That was the right thing to do. He must look as if he had nothing to hide. Fayyad was coming around this evening. And then he remembered - he'd invited Lynn over.

That wouldn't work. He couldn't cope with the two of them. He should have asked for Fayyad's number. Put him off. But he couldn't deal with Lynn in this state.

He was drilling holes and screwing in the upright supports. The work was simple, repetitive, allowing him to think but keeping him from being overwhelmed. Sitting at home on his sofa would be unbearable. He was bad at dealing with stress, one reason he preferred to work on his own. No boss over his shoulder.

Lynn wore goggles, her hair tied back in a band, concentrating on the wood passing through the saw band. He was grateful for the racket. She couldn't come tonight. What excuse did he have? Double booked for something. Well, that was the truth, but he couldn't tell her actually who with.

What a mess.

There were five involved. Himself, Anne, Bessie, Maggie and David. All hoping earthworms had eroded the evidence. But the worms hadn't had time. And Fayyad was coming over this evening, and not simply to catch up on old school mates.

Fayyad said he wanted to see Bessie. The body was of her father, after all. And she would tell them who was around two years ago. Confirm what he'd already told Fayyad. He must tell as much truth as he could. Just have them thinking he'd been a builder there for a job, nothing else. Soon enough Fayyad would be talking to Anne, Maggie and David. Could they stick to their stories?

Bessie was a worry. She'd be asked about her relationship with her father. And the ground could crack under her. Once in tears, she might say anything.

He should phone Anne, but couldn't find his phone. Annoying. It hadn't been in his van. He was almost sure he'd left his flat with it this morning. Work calls might be coming in. Alison may have called. Well, losing that call was fine, but work mattered. No, it didn't. All that mattered was that Frank had been found. That was the priority. Work would be useless if he was in jail.

Where was his phone? If he was going to make up an excuse to Lynn, he might need it. Quite how, he hadn't worked out. Pretend a text had come.

Jack put down the screwdriver.

'Lynn,' he called out.

She stopped the saw, and flipped up the goggles.

'Yes, boss.'

There was nothing for it, he'd have to tell her.

'I'm going to have to call off our date this evening,' he said.

'Oh,' she exclaimed. 'I was so looking forward to it. Why?'

What could he say? Another girlfriend? Too late, too complicated. Oh what the hell, tell her.

'The police are coming to see me.'

'What have you done?' she said in alarm.

'Nothing.' The first of many lies. 'I was talking to a cop outside...'

'I thought you were a long time.'

'Bessie's dad has turned up. Dead, I mean. Found in Epping Forest.'

'What's that got to do with you?'

He shrugged. 'He disappeared when I was doing building work next door, two years back.'

'Your questioning shouldn't take long,' she said.

'I don't know how long it'll take.' He shrugged. 'Him taking notes. Could be ages. It's a murder investigation.'

'But they can't suspect you of anything!' She stopped, obviously thinking. 'This hasn't got anything to do with you breaking it off with Anne, has it?' She flapped sawdust out of her hair. 'You were avoiding her this morning.'

'We didn't part on the best of terms.' He put down the drill. 'It's nothing to do with Bessie's dad.'

'If I were a cop, I'd follow up on it. You and Anne were having an affair.'

'Hardly an affair. It barely began.'

'What killed it?'

He wanted to shut her up, but figured Fayyad would take the same route. A rehearsal then.

'She had someone else,' he said.

'I see.' She peered at him through narrow lids. 'You know Anne was jailed for murder?'

'Proved innocent in the end.'

'But a second murder,' she mused. 'That looks bad. They'll home in on that.'

True, he knew.

'Getting jailed for one murder was bad luck,' went on Lynn. 'But two? She'll be in for serial questioning.' She turned to Jack. 'And you had a brief fling with her, interrupted by another lover.' She whistled. 'This hots up. Sex, jealousy, murder. You may well be some time.'

'Can we stop this?' He was feeling utterly battered. How could he handle police questioning, if her mild knocks were getting him down? He turned to her, no more of this. 'Anne and I had a short affair. I found out she had someone else. So we stopped seeing each other. Nothing to do with Bessie's dad. So let's get back to here and now.' He gritted his fists in frustration, 'Our date's off. Because the police want to question me. I am not a suspect. And now let's please drop the topic.'

She looked at him for a few moments, was about to say something but didn't, and returned to her sawing. The buzz of it was almost a threat, as if she were doing it deliberately. He looked at his watch. Nearly lunch time. Might as well go now. Get away from Lynn. To think, he'd been kissing her an hour ago, she was talking of working with him permanently. All before Fayyad turned up and told him Frank had been found.

'I'm off for lunch,' he said.

'Right,' she replied. 'You will be back?'

'I'll be back.' And strode out. Time on his own. No questions other than those he'd ask himself.

He left the house, and was about to head off for his van, when he thought he must talk to Anne. Couldn't be avoided, much as he wished it. He checked Lynn wasn't looking out of her window, and then climbed over the low wall and went up the stairs to Anne's front door. He rang the bell.

Anne replied quickly through the intercom. 'Hello.'

'It's Jack,' he said quietly.

'We need to talk,' she said. 'Stay there. I'll come out.'

He pulled himself into the portico as he waited, in case Lynn glanced out. She was already suspicious of Anne and him. Probably compounded of jealousy, but she was making some astute guesses.

Anne opened the door. 'You're white as a sheet,' she said. 'You know?'

'If you mean, do I know about Frank,' he said, 'then yes. The cops have found his body in the forest.'

'They've confirmed it was Frank?'

'My mate's a copper, he was coming here to question Bessie,' he said. 'Didn't he tell you?'

'They were here,' she said. 'But I put them off, said she couldn't be spared.' She sighed. 'They'll be back later. No doubt about that.' She looked about her as if the police might be coming back immediately. 'We have to talk, Jack. Not now though. We're making the children's lunch, I've got to be there.'

'Come over this evening,' he said. 'Early.'

'Right. I'll be at your place at seven.' She pecked him on the cheek. 'Must get back. See you tonight.'

She shut the door.

He stood for a few moments, easing his breathing. So talk to Anne, before Fayyad. Compare notes. Their stories had to fit. He must be prepared. Anne had been through this before.

As he came down the steps, he glanced to Lynn's house. She was looking out of her front window. Their eyes caught. What on earth was he going to say to her?

He gave her a wave. Best not to look as if he was hiding something.

Chapter 26

Nick dawdled along Water Lane picking his spots, too nervous to be aware, or to stop himself as everybody said he should. Unaware of traffic, other people, only where he was going and what might happen there. He'd felt such a bigshot when they'd given him the weed. It was his way in, he'd be the centre. The world would come to him.

They had. He'd been the king for a week. Stoned and selling. There was no tomorrow. The chosen one, homing in the big music deal, instead of the insect his father stepped on.

What did he have of any value? His laptop, his guitar, his sound system, but in a panic sale – what could you get for anything? His dad would never notice the stuff going, running all the time, when he wasn't yelling at aunty Lynn. Tim had told him not to get involved, but he'd pooh-poohed him. He'd wanted to be someone. Lift his life out of the morass.

A weed fantasy.

He'd stayed in bed all morning, but had no weed to inure him. Not a shaving. It couldn't be avoided. Nick just hoped they'd listen, give him time.

He got to the squat as Benji was coming out the front door. The West Indian smiled at him, a gold-toothed beam. He smelt of resin and sweat.

'Got the money, kid?'

'That's what I've come about...' he began.

Benji's smile became a grimace as he grabbed Nick by the throat and dragged him into the house. He slammed the door and thrust Nick against it.

'Where's the money, punk?'

'It got stolen.'

Benji went for him. His hands were protecting his head, but they hardly held back Benji who pulled them away like wrapping paper. And slapped him round the face. A wham that banged his head into the door. First one side of the head, then the other, repeatedly smacking him with his wide hand. Nick collapsed into the door squealing. Benji jerked him to his feet by his nose.

'How much money did you have?'

'Eight hundred and thirty two pounds...' He could barely see Benji, eyes full of tears, cheeks singing in pain. Benji twisted his nose.

'You know what ankling is, boy?'

'No.'

Benji let go of him and took a step back. Nick held his hands up in surrender, in protection, in helplessness. Just let him out of here.

'It's when we shoot a crossbow bolt through the ankle. Here.' Benji indicated exactly where, smiling but there was no shared warmth in the grin. 'You'll walk with a permanent limp for the rest of your life.'

'I got things I can sell,' exclaimed Nick, his hands shaking to emphasise his earnestness. 'I'll get you the money. My guitar, my laptop, my sound system... I'll get you the money. I promise you.'

Benji punched him in the guts. A wham of a haymaker. Nick doubled up, a bundle of pain, barely able to breathe.

Benji grabbed him by the hair and lifted his head. 'I want eight hundred and thirty two quid from you,' he spat. 'Tomorrow. Noon. Or I'll be round with the crossbow. Get me, you lump of pigshit?'

'Yeh,' he managed to gasp. 'I get you.'

Benji pulled open the front door and threw him out on to the path.

'Get the cash. Or you know what.'

The door slammed. Nick slouched up the short path to the pavement, and sank to the ground, head in his knees. He groaned, clutching his stomach, his cheeks, his nose. There was no part of his body without hurt. He was tears and blood. Thought banished, the vacuum taken up by fear.

It was ten minutes before Nick could rise and stagger home.

Chapter 27

Jack returned from lunch with few decisions made. So much was out of his hands. When they questioned him, he'd tell as much of the truth as possible. Round and round, he'd gone on that. But when would the truth edge into a lie? He must stay sober, that was so important. Stress drove him to drink. Not this time. It would get him banged up.

The trouble was all the others. He could claim he was a builder on the job, that's all. But what would they say? And once the first lie was noted, would they all pile in, accusing each other? He had to hope the cops believed none of them were involved. And went their way, crime unsolved.

Lynn was in the sitting room on the sofa, waiting. She rose when he entered.

She said, 'Here's the ground rules. I don't know what you're up to. You are hiding things. But I don't think you're a murderer.'

'There's a show of confidence.'

'I won't ask you why you went to see Anne. Then you won't have to lie to me. We'll get on with the job. Talk about soundproof boards. Nothing personal.'

'Nothing personal,' he assented. 'That's fine.'

'I'll be a Latvian builder,' she said. 'I speak minimal English, just enough to do the work.'

With half a smile, he said, 'You'll have learnt how to swear by now.'

'I might need to.'

They set to work beginning with pieces of resilient channel. They were the crosspieces, metalwork full of holes, screwed to the uprights. Jack explained, keeping to the brief of the non-personal, that the soundproof boards would lay on them to cut direct transmission of sound through the wall. Having said this twice today, he was feeling like an expert. The more you said it, the more you believed it.

Once the resilient channel was in place, they brought in the first of the soundproof boards. Then the second, for there was to be a double layer. Beginning in what would be the new room, they hammered in the two boards through holes in the resilient channel into the uprights, one board squarely over the other.

They discussed as co-workers, the efficacy of soundproofing boards, why two layers on each side, and about the rock wool that would go between the boards filling in the space. About the sounds in a house that needed to be deadened; voices at different levels, music, TV. Hardly aware that they were slipping into the personal, the supposedly forbidden. Either could have stopped, neither did. Music and TV got him talking about Mia, about Alison, his ex, which reminded him.

'You didn't see my phone anywhere?'

'No,' she said, 'I had a look at lunchtime.'

He wondered if she might have thrown it in the bin, having seen him leaving Anne's. Or was that being unfair? When it came to it, he didn't know her. She had her secrets as much as he had.

He said, 'Alison usually phones me about now. Either to complain about what I've given Mia to eat, her un-ironed school shirt, or that she wants me to look after her tonight.' He grinned wryly. 'Maybe we'll hear it ring somewhere.'

Lynn took her phone out. 'What's your number?'

He gave it to her. She tapped it in and rang it. They listened, there was no ring. After half a minute, she shook her head, turning off her phone.

'It's taken me to voicemail,' she said. 'Yours must be out of battery or turned off.'

Or hit by a hammer and in the bin. What a nuisance. Anyone could be phoning him. They probably weren't, but might be. If it was Alison then good riddance. But work calls, responses to his leaflets, he had to give a prompt reply or lose the work. He might have to buy a new phone. More money. Could he get the same number? He had it on the leaflets, on his website, on his van. He might have asked Lynn whether he could, but wasn't convinced she'd be helpful. Best ask no favours.

Not in the van, not here. He couldn't have left it at home, surely? Just about possible. Nothing he could do now. Annoying.

The work, though, went well. They put on as many whole boards as they could on one side, then began sawing boards to size for the spaces at the sides, by the room walls. By mid afternoon, they'd completed one side of the uprights. He and Lynn brought up the bales of rock wool from the cellar.

'This should be the right thickness to fit between the walls,' he said. 'It's flexible and presses in.' He stopped, having had a thought. 'We'll need to buy a lock for the door of the new room. I suppose I could get it in the morning...'

'I could get it now,' she volunteered, surprising him in her eagerness, but then it was to be her room. 'There's a locksmith on Upton Lane. What do we want?'

'A standard Yale,' he said. 'It's only an internal door. Unless you want to replace the door and get a stronger one.'

'Keep the door as it is,' she said. 'No one's going to break in.'

'Go buy the lock then,' he said. 'Get a receipt.'

She saluted. 'Yes, boss. Shouldn't be long.'

And she left him.

He was glad she'd lightened up. It made working together easier. He was the restrained one. She was a good worker though. Picked up things quickly. The marking up, she'd got first time and the sawing.

All the boards on one side had been done. The job was going to be quicker than estimated, as he hadn't calculated on having a mate. He ripped the plastic off one of the bales of rock wool. The stuff was fibrous, dusty. He had a couple of masks in his toolbox, took one out and put it on, then leather gloves. This stuff got everywhere. Heaven knows the long term effects if you were breathing it in unmasked. A powdered mineral, never any good for the lungs.

The slabs of rock wool went in easily, held in by the uprights. The stuff was easy to cut with a knife. Its purpose was to give a middle soundproofing layer, between the soundproof boards that made up both outsides of the wall. He had much of the rock wool in place when Paul arrived, wearing his standard grey work suit, briefcase in hand.

'Moving on, moving on,' he said, rubbing his chin. 'I see you're masked up. Health and Safety and all that.'

Jack pulled down the mask to speak.

'Rock wool,' he said. 'A good sound barrier. Cuts like butter in summer. Dead easy to use. Filthy fibre, but it's springy and fits snug. You mustn't leave gaps for sound to get through.'

'How long you likely to be, Jack?'

Jack thought for a few moments. 'Should finish tomorrow,' he said, 'except for the decorating. Wallpaper would be best, to match the room.'

'I think we've some rolls left over in the cellar,' said Paul. 'Where's Lynn?'

'She's off buying a lock.'

He laughed. 'To keep me out. Oh that woman! You have to laugh.'

'Tomorrow evening, you'll have separate sitting rooms,' said Jack.

'But the kitchen! The kitchen,' exclaimed Paul. 'We need two of those. If I'm in it, she won't come in. If she's got it, I leave it to her. Except when I'm in a rush, and just have to

149

brave her presence.' He shook his head. 'We shouldn't have to live like this.'

Jack said nothing, knowing advice wouldn't be welcomed.

'Maybe she's right,' went on Paul, 'we should sell the place. And I'll buy whatever I can with my share. But I so like it here. It's a great house. And being close to the park... So convenient for a run, just slip into gear and I'm out there. Two, three times a day. See what an obsessive I am.' He gave a short laugh. 'I hate the thought of house hunting, making offers and all that palaver. Buyers trampling all over this place, criticising the wallpaper and cupboards, and ending up where for heaven's sake? I hate the very thought of it.' He shook his head. 'Almost as much as I hate my sister. Do you find that juvenile, Jack?'

'You've got a history,' he said. 'You wind each other up.'

'We don't know how not to.' He held up his hands for a halt. 'Enough on that topic. It must bore you stupid. And I need to do another run before it gets dark. My therapy.' He gave a short laugh, 'It makes me too tired to drink. I'm serious. You should try it.'

'I get enough exercise on the job. So long as the work keep coming in.' And then was reminded. 'You haven't seen a phone around? Have you?'

'Lost it, around here?'

'I was sure I brought it this morning. I need to have it with me, so I can take any work calls. It's second nature...' He looked about him. 'Yes. I remember now. I put it on the table. In the other room.' The boards were now cutting it off, the one room in the process of becoming two. 'Yes. It's come to me. I thought, best not leave it in my pocket with all the sawing and hammering. So I put it on the table.'

'That thieving bastard!' exclaimed Paul. He'd gone white. 'I'm not having this. Not in my house.'

And he was out of the room, into the hallway, and taking the stairs two at a time. At the top, Paul strode along, anger driven, and stopped outside the box room. A cable crossed the hallway, coming out of Nick's room into the box room. There, Tim was on his mattress, sitting upright, a keyboard on his knee, the monitor screen under his chair filled with script, and the tower alongside.

'I got it working, Mr Atwood,' he said eagerly, on seeing Paul at his door. 'I hope you don't mind.'

'Out, you thief!' Paul pointed along the hallway. 'Against my better judgement, I let you stay. I want you out. Right now. Pack your stuff.'

'You said I could stay another night, Mr Atwood.' He'd put down the keyboard and had risen to his knees.

'I've changed my minds. The builder's phone has gone. You are number one, two and three on the list of suspects. So out!'

'I didn't take his phone.' Tim had got to his feet, looking around as if seeking a way out of the confined space. 'I didn't take it. Honest.'

'I'm not expecting you to admit it. Out. Pack your stuff. Get moving. Unless you want me to help.'

'I didn't take his phone. I don't know anything about it.'

'Don't argue. I don't want a thief in my house. Get out. Or I shall call the police.'

Tim began scrabbling his papers together. Paul was at the door of the box room watching him. Then got down and unplugged the extension.

'This is so damned dangerous,' he exclaimed looking at the cable. 'Could burn the house down. That's a cupboard. Never a bedroom. Get your stuff packed. I'm not having a thief in my house.'

Tim was throwing his papers and books into carrier bags. He had no clothes apart from those he was wearing.

'I'm not a thief, Mr Atwood.' But continued packing, as if knowing nothing he could say would work. 'On my mother's life, I swear it.'

'Promise the moon, it won't do you any good. I want you out. We'll all be safer. Out!'

Lynn had come up the stairs, still wearing her outdoor coat.

'What's going on here?'

Paul turned to her, pointing out Tim, 'This thieving magpie took Jack's phone.'

'I didn't,' mumbled Tim.

He had come out into the hallway, stooped, with three carrier bags.

'Stay there, Tim,' said Lynn coming protectively between him and Paul. 'He says he didn't take it.'

'He would, wouldn't he.'

'Don't you need proof before you go around accusing people of stealing?' she retorted.

'Everything stayed put before he came into the house,' exclaimed Paul. 'That's all the proof I need.'

'Shoot first. Investigate later. Great justice,' she declared. 'Perhaps a little examination might help. Though I doubt it will satisfy my flat-earth brother.' She turned to Tim. 'Sorry, love, but we'll have to satisfy the chief of police.'

She took the carrier bags from Tim, and took out the papers and books, leaving them on the carpet as she went from bag to bag.

'No phone in that one.' She gave the bag to Tim who put the items back in. 'Nor this one. Must be in this one, mustn't it, dear brother.' She emptied the papers on to the carpet. 'Not there either. Well, well. I wonder where he could have hidden it. Must be in his pockets.' She turned to Tim. 'And now the LAPD pat down. Sorry, Tim. Raise your arms.'

Tim put his arms up. Lynn started from the top, patting his chest, jacket and trouser pockets.

'Ah, what's this?' She took a phone out of his pocket.

'Mine,' said Tim. 'Let me show you.' He hurriedly took it from her. And with a few clicks, revealed his texts, some to Nick, his employer, and to a few unknowns.

'That's yours,' she agreed. 'Want to look, Paul?' She held the phone out to him.

'No.'

She gave the phone back to Tim, and turned fiercely on her brother. 'You can't go around calling anyone you like a thief!'

'So tell me who took it?'

'Not Tim.' She came up close and shook a fist. 'Why have you got it in for him? He's been kicked from pillar to post all his life.' She took a step away, standing between Paul and Tim. 'It's all to take it out on me. Isn't it? Admit it.'

'I don't want a thief in the house.'

'You have no proof. It's simply me you have it in for. Leave the kid alone.'

'I want him out, Lynn. I want him out now. You pushed me into letting him stay. Well, that's at an end. I have rights in this house too. You can't bring in any waif and stray and expect me to accept it.'

The front door slammed. Lynn went to look who was there. And saw Nick clambering up the stairs, like a four legged thing, groaning. He looked up at her mid scramble, he had a black eye and a bleeding nose.

'I'm going to be ankled,' he cried.

Chapter 28

What on earth was going on up there? First Paul had rushed upstairs as if to rescue a child from a fire. And seconds after, he was yelling at someone to go, calling them a thief. The replies were muted, so Jack was unsure who it might be. Probably not one of his own kids, though you never know. So was it Tim? Had he taken his phone? He recalled him earlier, looking at the half built wall. The phone might've been on the table then, Tim could easily have snaffled it. But then everyone had been in the sitting room one time or other.

Then Lynn had come back. She'd dropped into Jack for a second, gave him the lock, and rushed upstairs. And then the two were going hammer and tongs. Much of the row was lost, but Jack caught the gist. Paul was certain someone was a thief, she was just as certain he wasn't.

And then another entrant, as the front door slammed. He had no idea who and didn't think it right to look. He was the builder, let them rant and rave all they want. So long as he got paid. Rowing was in the air of the house, a gas seeping out of the walls that got everyone shrieking.

No wonder they were all screwed up. Paul and Lynn only have to be in the same room - and boom! The two kids were pretty scatty too. Though he could talk when it came to rows. He and Alison had fought to the last man standing. His mum and dad had fought. Amazing they'd stayed together as long as they did. As a kid he'd leave the house to get away from the dust up, go outside to play with friends, if there were any around, if not wander about, and hope his parents had stopped by the time he returned. Mostly they had, anger replaced by silence.

There were families who got on. Were they lying, because that's what was expected of them? Joyous families dancing round the Christmas tree. The happy housewife contented at home, happy father in his job, bringing home the bacon. Kids doing fine at school, no bullying, not too fat, not too thin, but thoroughly normal, smiling and laughing as if they were in a TV ad.

It wasn't a normal condition, happiness, he'd long decided. You get spates of it. If you're happy all the time then you're an idiot. The normal human lot is dissatisfaction. On occasion, you'll rise above it. On more occasions, fall below.

That was his considered opinion, half listening to the ruckus above. Thoroughly biased. And he might change his mind tomorrow. If he was happy. Though considering what was happening, not much likelihood.

The shouting had stopped upstairs. He listened. Perhaps they're all dead. But no, they were trooping down the stairs. He looked aside as they came past the door, seeing Lynn, Paul and Nick heading along the hallway. Lynn briefly put her head in.

'Sorry, Jack, can't help now,' she said, rolling her eyes. 'Family crisis.'

'So I could hear,' he said. 'I'm grateful for your help up to now.'

She gave him a brief smile.

'I could almost like you,' she said wryly. And left him.

*

Tim was in Lynn's bedroom. She'd pushed him in, telling him to stay there and she'd be back when they'd sorted out Nick. His friend had certainly taken a pasting, and might be liable for worse. He was an idiot getting in with those dealers. Wanting to play the big man.

155

Tim was seated in a chair where he could see himself in the large, oval mirror, the three carrier bags at his feet. This could all go wrong. He had hoped he'd be able to pacify Paul. Be hardly there, so Paul would get used to him. Help out, be the soul of politeness. But then this phone stuff had blown up. He didn't know anything about a phone. Besides, he wouldn't steal anything here. And then he was unsure, looking around at all the stuff in Lynn's room. She had a lot. There was a laptop, must be worth at least £600, a fancy clock radio, a three levelled shoe rack, a dozen or more pairs of shoes filling it, a full bookshelf, and all sorts of knick knacks on shelves and the windowsill. Her jewellery was carelessly splayed on the dressing table, necklaces and bracelets, earrings. She wouldn't even know if he pocketed a couple of those. And didn't he deserve it? He knew nothing about a phone.

Some other time, it might've been him with the phone, but not when he was trying to get in. That would be stupid. And so obvious. Priorities. Even so... He picked up a pair of earrings and a bracelet. That would do. She'd never notice, and she'd patted him down already. Besides, there was another thief around the house.

He put them back again. She might look, having left him in here on his own. A test maybe. And he needed Lynn. But for her he'd be out on the street. And then where would he go? There was that homeless hostel up Stratford. If he could get in. But you were only allowed three nights and then they'd turf you out on the street. He'd try to hang on here, cosy up to Lynn. Nick didn't look like he could help anyone, least of all himself.

Maybe he could stay in this room. Lynn didn't need all this space. She was having that room built downstairs. How many rooms does a woman need? He was happy with the box room. The trouble was Paul wasn't.

Tonight, Tim was working at the casino. He badly needed the money. But payday wasn't for a week. He must get some clothes. His underwear was awful. He couldn't even wash it as he had nothing else to put on. Maybe Nick would lend him some clobber. Not now though, not in his state.

It struck him, that when he came back tonight, in the early hours, how would he get back in? No key. He'd have to talk to Lynn. Warn her that he'd phone about half two, telling her he was outside. And stay out of Paul's way at all costs. Till the heat was off. Nick had got himself in trouble and even Paul had given up on Tim for the time being.

*

Nick had been incoherent when he'd flopped at the top of the stairs. Lynn gathered someone was threatening him, having damaged him already, and was promising worse. That was the best she could make of it in his anxious rambling. Lynn had quietened him down, telling him not to worry, it would be sorted out. She pushed Tim into her room for the time being. It was forbidden ground for Paul, and she took Nick into the bathroom. Paul followed. And there with a flannel, she washed his face, his neck, his hands and the bits of his body she could get to without embarrassment. His arms and stomach were bruised but no bones appeared to be broken. He'd had a sound beating. And was terrified he'd get more.

Following his wash, his father and aunt led him downstairs to the kitchen. Tea was required as well as an explanation.

Chapter 29

Nick gripped his mug, staring into the liquid as if there were an oracle in its depths. His face was shiny clean, pimples the brightest pink, with sticking plasters on one cheek and across his forehead. He had on a long-sleeved shirt with patches on, that Lynn had got from his room. She sat by him, an arm round his waist, his father across the table, the chief interrogator.

'However did you get into their clutches?' exclaimed Paul.

'They had the stuff to sell,' mumbled Nick.

'But they're villains,' retorted Paul, throwing up his hands. 'This is a matter for the police.'

'No!' screamed Nick. 'Don't call the police. They'll kill me.'

'Not if they're in custody, they won't,' said his father.

'And suppose they're not?' said Lynn.

'If you get the police on them,' said Nick, his nails digging into his cheeks, 'they'll get me, and if they don't get me, their mates will. They'll cut me into little pieces and feed me to the dogs.'

'Now don't exaggerate, son.'

'You don't know them,' yelled Nick.

'So why did you damn well work with them then?' his father yelled back.

Like a small boy, eyes closed, forced to tell the truth, he mumbled, 'I never thought anyone would nick the cash. I was just going to make some dosh, pay them off – and that would be that.'

'There's vile people in the drug business,' exclaimed Paul.

'There speaks someone who knows life on the street,' sniped Lynn.

'I suppose you think it's like a market stall,' said Paul to his sister.

'I don't claim to know more than I do.'

Paul loosened his tie and undid his shirt button. 'You were so out of your depth,' he said. 'Sure, I don't know the drugs game. Why on earth should I? But I know it's full of deadbeats. So what are you doing mixing with scum like that?' He threw up his hands in his exasperation. 'Where were your brains? Utterly doped out, I bet. Maybe it would be a good idea if you did get ankled. That'd teach you. Sure as eggs are eggs, we can't.'

'Don't be ridiculous, Paul,' snapped Lynn.

Nick was weeping, head slumped on his arm on the table.

'So what will he learn if we simply pay off the drug dealers?' said Paul, challenging his sister. 'That anytime he gets in trouble Daddy will sort it out. A great lesson for life.'

'It doesn't help telling him off,' said Lynn. 'They've already beaten him up. What more do you want?'

'This has to hurt,' exclaimed Paul. 'What he's been doing is criminal. My son dealing. If we simply get him off the hook, then what's to stop him going back to it?'

'I won't, I won't,' simpered Nick. 'I promise I won't.'

'Easy to say. You'll say anything so long as we give you the 832 quid.'

'So what are you suggesting?' said Lynn.

'Call the police.'

'No! No!' exclaimed Nick, his head still down on his arm. 'I should never have told you.'

'Well, you have. And I'm not having you dealing drugs. This is a matter for the police,' said Paul thrashing the air with a stern finger. 'Then the criminals will get picked up.'

'And your son, too?' queried Lynn.

'So be it,' said Paul. 'It's not our job to get him off punishment.'

'And if he gets ankled?'

'That's all hot air,' he pooh-poohed. 'It'll never come to that.'

Nick was howling, Lynn was rubbing the back of his neck.

'You're such a fool, Paul,' she exclaimed. 'You know nothing about drug dealers. You've said so. You'd let Nick get crippled for life, to prove how right you are!'

'I am not going to pay off drug dealers. That's playing into the hands of criminals. Undermining the rule of law.'

Paul took out his phone and began pressing buttons. Lynn leaned across the table to grab it from him, sending china to the floor. Paul backed away and continued dialling.

'Think, Paul!' she shrieked, coming round the table at him. 'It's your son who'll take the consequences.'

'And about time,' he yelled.

She grabbed his phone hand. Paul pushed her away. She stumbled back, hitting the table, which rocked, spilling mugs and plates. She came back at him, both hands grabbing at the phone. Paul swung an arm, hitting her across the head. Lynn collapsed under the blow.

'Police please,' he said into the phone.

'You unfeeling bastard,' she exclaimed on her knees, nose bleeding. 'I despise you!'

Nick was weeping, head down on the table.

'I want to report drug dealing and assault,' said Paul.

Chapter 30

The row upstairs had simply transferred to the kitchen. Worse if anything. Yelling and banging. And what sounded like breaking china. Jack contemplated going in and finding out if real violence was being committed. Or was it just another shouting match? Paul and Lynn could escalate any little matter into high drama. He knew she could handle herself. So maybe leave it.

He wouldn't be thanked for getting involved in their family affairs.

Work. That's what he was paid for. Though difficult to ignore the racket. He shut the door. Less, but still audible. Carry on. The rock wool was in place. He looked at his watch, should he just get out of here? Tidy up and leave them to it.

He took up the broom and began sweeping sawdust and rock wool pieces. He stopped. Should he just check what was going on? The fact they'd taken Nick in with them, meant it concerned Nick, otherwise the lad would've hotfooted it as soon as they started throwing china. Jack was curious, thinking it could be serious, at the same time wanting to be somewhere else.

But really he should look. Maybe there was more than just crockery breaking. Paul might be murdering her, or she him, for that matter. What a position to be in, this family war, it's not as if he were a cop. He could end up losing the job through interference.

That was a scream. No choice. He put down the broom, went out into the hallway and crept along to the kitchen. Now it had gone quiet. A truce, or someone was dead. He should've brought a hammer. Or a shield.

Jack peered into the kitchen. Paul was strolling, speaking on the phone, something to do with drug dealing, while kicking away pieces of broken china. Nick was whimpering, head cradled on his arms at the table. Lynn was holding on to a side unit, dabbing her nose with a piece of bloody kitchen towel.

Without entering, a hand on the doorpost, he said low, 'Is everything alright, Lynn?'

'Does it look like it?' she said, almost matter of fact, wiping blood off her top lip.

Paul spotted him, but was listening to the phone. He mouthed something that Jack couldn't make out.

'Anything I can do?' he said to Lynn.

'Nothing,' she said. 'Unless you'd like to kill my brother.'

He ignored the suggestion. 'You're OK though?'

'I got my nose in the way of a left hook,' she said with a half smile, dabbing her nose with the tissue. 'But no, Jack, I appreciate you looking in. But you can't help.'

'Just thought I'd best check,' he said awkwardly. 'All the racket. You know. In case someone was being murdered.' He stood, unsure what to say. 'I'll get back to work.'

He left them. No one dead. Just a bloody nose, a crying teenager, talk of drug dealers. Family business, he'd been told. It was like coming in at the end of a play, trying to make sense of the fragments.

Jack returned to sweeping up. The kitchen was quieter, perhaps because they realised he'd heard them. Just as well he'd gone in. He'd needed to know. And they needed to know he was close by.

He was putting away the last of his tools when the police came. Paul opened the front door to them. Two uniformed policeman entered, a man and a woman. Paul led them along the hallway to the kitchen. Jack could hear subdued voices. Civilisation regained. The siblings weren't going to throw china in front of the guardians of the law.

After a few minutes, all three left with the police. Lynn put her head in the room.

'We've got to go to the police station with Nick,' she said. 'No big deal. Let yourself out. And I'll be with you tomorrow morning. Must go.' And she was off.

Jack went to the front window, and watched the family trio accompanying the police to their car. The police took the front seat, the family the rear. There were no handcuffs, but he did wonder what was the crime, who was the criminal. His betting was on Nick, with bigger players elsewhere.

Chapter 31

Tim was sweeping china in the kitchen, when Dawn entered. He'd cleared most of the floor, pushing the fractured pieces into a heap near the bin.

'What's been going on here?' exclaimed Dawn staring at the broken crockery.

'Family row.'

'There's a surprise. Over what?'

'I don't know.' He continued sweeping. He did know, at least some of it, but why should he tell her?

'I bet you do.'

He shrugged.

'You see things,' she said. 'You're always nosing about. Listening in. Looking for what to nick.'

He stopped sweeping, and leaned on the broom, watching her.

'You don't do so bad yourself,' he said.

'Meaning?'

'I know who took the builder's phone.'

Dawn removed her outdoor jacket and put it on the back of a chair. She went to the fridge and took out a bottle of milk and swigged from it. He grimaced; he wouldn't want to drink from that, not with her germs. She took a long draught, daring him to say anything.

She put the bottle on the table, a rim of milk round her mouth.

'So who do you think took his phone?' she said.

'You.'

She didn't reply, and went again to the fridge and took out the cheese dish. With a knife she cut herself a thick slab.

He wouldn't mind some himself but he would not ask Dawn to cut him some, knowing what she'd say.

She put the lump of cheese on a small plate and sat at the table. Tim had cleaned it up, putting the few extant pieces of china into the dishwasher and wiping it down. He watched her carelessly dropping crumbs. A challenge.

'I've got a phone,' she said, as she munched. 'Better than his, I'm sure. Why on earth should I steal his load of old iron?'

Mouth full, she rose and went to a cupboard. She took down a packet of crackers and a jar of pickle. He watched her, curious, as if through glass. She was deliberately not offering him anything.

'You nicked it to get me in trouble,' he said.

She smiled, delicately placing a piece of cheese and lumpy pickle on a cracker.

'Everyone knows you're a thief,' she said.

'Takes one to know one.'

'Any other clichés you have handy?' she said, eating her cracker.

'You took his phone,' he said, 'because you knew I'd get the blame for it. And your dad would kick me out. But as you might notice, I'm still here.'

She blew a raspberry as if to dismiss him. 'Where is everyone?'

Tim knew the builder had left and the family gone with the police, having seen them go from Lynn's window. One of them, he guessed, most likely Paul, had called the cops about Nick's beating up and the dealers' threat. Dumb.

'I don't know where anyone is,' he said.

'You don't know much.'

'I know that you cut yourself,' he said. 'I know not to trust you an inch. And I know you stole the builder's phone.'

'Anything else you know?'

She had decided to be more genteel and poured milk into a glass. Tim was surprised how much she was stacking away, what with the weight of her. She opened a cake tin and cut herself a large chunk of fruit cake. That looked so yummy, all the sultanas and cherries, his stomach wheeled. He should've eaten before clearing up. Mistake. He didn't feel he could take anything with her commanding the kitchen.

'I know you don't like me,' he said.

'Does anyone like you, Tim?'

He wanted to smack her nose with the broom handle, but she was the daughter of the house and he was hanging on by a thread.

'Nick likes me.'

'Nick's stupid.'

He could hardly disagree with that. 'Lynn likes me.'

'Do you give her the soft brown eyes treatment?'

'I don't see anyone liking you,' he said, brushing the china pieces into a pan.

'I have my community,' she said smugly.

'Self harmers,' he said. 'Like you.'

'It's my body, I do what I want with it.'

'Why don't you slice it up quickly, instead of this bit by bit attention seeking?'

'I don't ask you what you do with your body,' she retorted. 'Disgusting things I'm sure. So leave mine out of it.'

He tipped the broken crockery into the bin.

'I don't want anything to do with your body,' he exclaimed. 'What's left of it.'

'Don't put the crockery in the bin like that.' She lifted her eyes in exasperation. 'It'll rip the bag. Wrap it in newspaper.'

He held out the brush and pan. 'Want to do it?'

'I'm happy watching you. But I think I've seen enough.'

She rose, taking a tour of the kitchen opening cupboards and the fridge, picking up bits and pieces: a banana, some biscuits, a yoghurt, more cake, a tomato, some coleslaw. She put the items on a tray with her half empty glass of milk.

'I'll be in my room,' she said with a wry smile, 'keeping my things safe from thieves.'

She marched out of the kitchen, holding the tray in front of her. He waited, listening to her footsteps down the hallway and pattering up the stairs. When he could no longer hear her, he opened the cake tin. There was maybe a third of it remaining. He took the whole of it in both hands, and wolfed it.

Chapter 32

'Please don't be alarmed by this, Bessie,' said Detective Superintendent Nikki Martin. 'It's routine. You've been fingerprinted?'

'When I came in, Miss.'

Nikki didn't correct the 'Miss'. The girl was nervous enough already. Not surprising, being picked up in a police car, being told her father was dead, and with her back story involving abuse. Plenty to terrify her without her necessarily being involved in the killing itself, which couldn't be ruled out. Not at this stage.

Also present were Fayyad and Hayley who had brought her in.

'Your fingerprints will be destroyed as soon as the investigation is over. But we need them for elimination purposes.' Then she added with a brief smile, 'No mucky ink like we used to have. All electronic these days. Quicker, cleaner.'

The door opened and a tray of tea in paper cups with a plate of biscuits was brought in by a WPC.

'Thank you,' said Nikki.

The woman police constable placed the tray on the table and left them. The room was small and bare, one of a series of interview rooms along the corridor. There was a frosted window, through which could just be heard the traffic from the Romford Road.

Fayyad passed round the teas, to Bessie first of all, then to his colleagues. All the time, Nikki's eyes were on Bessie, who was like a trapped animal, panicking in the small space, frantic to escape. They could have interviewed her at home, but the nearest relative is often a vital witness. And sometimes by taking them out of the security of home, the impact of an interview room brought out revelations you might not get otherwise.

'Turn on the video, please,' said Nikki.

Fayyad flipped the switch. Then gave date and time and full names of those present.

'I hope you don't mind us recording this interview, Bessie,' said Nikki.

'No, Miss.'

'It's for your own protection,' she said, 'as well as giving us an accurate record.' She took a sip of tea. 'This is a terrible shock to you, I'm sure.'

'Yes, it is,' said Bessie, barely audibly. She was clutching her cup with both hands as if she'd just been rescued from the ocean.

'How did you get on with your father?'

Suddenly her hands were shaking uncontrollably, spilling hot tea. As Bessie squealed from the burn, Hayley rose, taking the cup out of her hand. She wiped Bessie's hand with a tissue.

'There, there, dear,' soothed Hayley. 'Keep the tissue. Is that better?'

'Yes, thank you,' said Bessie, her eyes filled with tears.

'Leave your tea a while, Bessie,' said Nikki. 'Let it cool down. Or perhaps you'd like a drink of water?'

'Tea is fine, Miss.'

'Are you OK to carry on with the interview?'

'I think so, Miss.'

'Now don't worry, Bessie.' Nikki gave what she hoped was a comforting smile. 'You're not under any suspicion.' Never quite true, Nikki knew, everyone was a suspect at this point. But it's what you said. 'This interview is for information purposes only. But of course, you were one of the last people to have seen your father alive, sharing the flat with him...' She paused an instant before adding, 'I hear he wasn't the best of fathers.'

'He was wicked, Miss.'

'I know this is difficult for you, Bessie, but I do have to ask a little more on that. Could you tell us what you mean by wicked?'

'He used to hit me, miss. All the time.' She was trembling, rubbing her face, refusing to look at Nikki.

'Just hit you?'

Oh that was a clumsy question, thought Nikki, as Bessie broke down. Her face collapsed, she was crying uncontrollably, her hands in her hair tugging and pulling, her body shaking. Hayley went round to comfort her, massaging her shoulders.

'There, there, dear,' murmured Hayley. 'I'm sorry we're bringing all this back. But none of it is your fault. We know your father was a monster.'

Nikki tapped Hayley on the arm and indicated outside.

'We won't be a moment, Fayyad,' said Nikki rising.

Fayyad turned off the video. 'Interview temporarily halted for compassionate reasons,' he said.

Bessie's face was cupped in her hands as Hayley left with her superior. She closed the door.

'This isn't going to work,' said Nikki quietly, aware the corridor was a public space.

'No, ma'am. It's awoken more than she can cope with. Her dad was a beast.'

'I'm sure you're right. But beast or not, we have to find his murderer. You were a family liaison officer for a while, weren't you?'

'For two years, ma'am.'

'Then you can be FLO for this team, Hayley. I want you to take Bessie home. Stay with her for a few hours. Calm her down. And then if you think it'll work, take a statement with Fayyad tomorrow.'

'Yes, ma'am.'

'Win her confidence. Keep her in the picture, within reason, but at the same time be the ears and eyes of the team. Do you understand me, Hayley?'

'Yes ma'am. I am FLO for Operation High Beech.'

'You are. I have a high regard for you, Hayley. Listen, watch, question, but don't push more than she will allow. She will be an impossible witness in court if we can't get her to be more accepting.'

'Accepting of what, ma'am? I am sure her story is awful. A total slave to her father's desires.'

'It's a dirty world we've chosen to work in, Hayley. Do your best.' She put a hand on her shoulder. 'I have a feeling Bessie might be the key in this investigation. Befriend her, help her in any way you think is desirable, but don't forget you are first and foremost a detective.'

Chapter 33

When Jack arrived home, he had a shower immediately. A good wash down, to get the sawdust out of his hair, the grit from under his fingernails, and bathe the disquiet in his head. His body glowed, but not his head. Lynn was talking to him, no bad thing, she'd worked out that he and Anne were involved in something. And so what? The cops were the problem. Her view of him, which was highest on his agenda two hours ago, mattered hardly at all. She could hate him, spurn him, but he'd entered a new universe. A body had been found, one he'd been involved in burying. When the cops had rung the bell when he was working, his immediate thought was that they'd come for him. And it was with much relief to see Lynn, Paul and Nick leave with them.

Fayyad tonight. What to admit. The thought exhausted him. There was one of him. But the police had teams working day and night. Out to get him. To splay him and cut his heart out.

He laughed as he soaped. He was way over the top. There were others in this. There were other crimes to keep the police busy. But so what? There was only one that mattered. He could have no lasting perspective. It was nothing, it was everything. It was all things between.

Work should be finished tomorrow and he could be off. That's if he could fob the decorating on to Lynn. He needed to get away from that road. Frank had been found, Frank had been identified. The cops were asking questions.

He needed another job. Without work, he would obsess even more than he was already obsessing.

Where was his phone?

172

If it were only him, he'd be less concerned. Not true. He'd fill up even if it were him alone. But objectively it was worse when in other rooms Bessie, Anne, Maggie and David were fretting about their questioning. Wondering what each would be saying. The answers wouldn't quite overlap. That could be put down to memory or lying. How long could it go on for? Until they got someone or ran out of money. How long? He'd only found out a couple of hours ago. Would he get used to it or would the strain stay at this level?

Anne was coming at seven. She knew about police interviews, she could prime him. Tell him how to deal with the stress of not knowing. Help him see through his own obsession.

He'd lost his phone. His line for work. Paul had accused that youngster of taking it. What was his name? The mixed race lad. Tim. Whether he had or not, Jack was without it. He had to have a phone. Might still turn up. Concentrate on the phone. See only the phone. Hypnotise himself so he could forget anything else. A phone. He needed a phone more than life. Best assume the worst and get another. Could he get the same number on a new phone? Didn't you have to contact your phone company, and all that palaver – or end up with someone else's bill?

Mia knew more than he did. She and her mates spent half their lives on the phone. Phone the expert. He dialled on his landline.

'Hello, Dad. What's up with your phone? Me and Mum tried to phone you.'

'About anything important?'

'Just can I stop over tomorrow night? She's got a date.'

'Same guy?'

'Same. Could be serious. But you never know. So can I come?'

173

'Yep,' he said warily. There was such a lot happening; he might need to be free. Tomorrow night though was too far away to think about. 'I've lost my phone,' he added.

'Definitely lost it?'

'Pretty sure.'

'Then you have to report it. Straight away to your phone company. Or you could get hammered by someone making long calls to South Africa at peak time.'

'I'll do that. And I need a new one. Badly.' More than life, he thought. 'I might be losing work. Can I get the same phone number? It's painted on my van, on my leaflets...'

'Contact the phone company. They'll probably ask you some stupid questions about your favourite film and your mother's maiden name, but they should be able to give you the same number. Might take a couple of weeks.'

'A couple of weeks! You're joking. I could be losing no end of work...' He was impressed with his level of worry. Good, good. This was the way to go. Change focus.

'You might be able to get them to forward calls to your landline. At least then you could call back after work.'

'Better make a list of this.' He grabbed a pen and an old envelope, and began scribbling.

'Pity I'm not there. And get a cheap phone. The other one might yet turn up. And you don't need to send emails.'

'I want a phone-phone. Just texts and phone calls. I don't want to take photos...' He reflected, might be useful on occasions. Of cops, of people watching him.

'And don't let them push you into an upgrade. They always try. So smooth with it.' She attempted an imitation of a salesperson, 'Do you want an upgrade, sir? For just a few extra pounds a month, you'll get a billion free calls and free texts to the moon and stars...' She dropped the imitation. 'Just say no, and keep saying no.'

'I don't want an upgrade.' He wanted to be free of hassle. His head cool. 'I don't want an upgrade.'

'Tell 'em. Do you want to speak to Mum?'

'No. I need to eat. But I'd better phone my phone company first. Then food.'

'See you tomorrow then. Remember no upgrade.'

'No upgrade. Got it.'

She rang off. He'd been writing down on the envelope what she'd told him: phone lost, same number, no upgrade. What else did she say? Oh yes. Could he get his calls transferred to his landline. Better get started. Keep moving or he'd give up. The phone was all that mattered.

He was making calls for the next forty minutes. No, he didn't want an upgrade, just a new sim with the same number. Each time they passed him on: upgrade, sir? Eventually they conceded he didn't want one, at least he hoped they had. And the new sim would come in a week or so. How long was 'or so' he'd asked a foreign sounding man. Another week or so, he'd been told. Which comes to three weeks, Jack had said, which mystified the man. A joke, Jack had to tell him, though feeling it was all far from funny. But it kept him occupied. Talking to people, having the same meaningless conversations. Were they as meaningless for them?

He had a cheese sandwich, the old standby for a quick bite when he couldn't summon the energy to cook, and a cup of tea. He'd have something more substantial later.

Maybe.

He'd barely finished when the doorbell rang. He went down to the front door. There was Anne in a warm, blue jacket, scarf and red woolly hat, looking serious, over serious. At least, she was worried too.

'Come in,' he said.

'No,' she said. 'I'm not coming in. We have to talk. We might get up to other things inside.'

He conceded they might. Easier than talking.

'Let's go for a walk,' she said. 'Grab your coat.'

Chapter 34

It was a whim that had Lynn following Anne. She'd left the police station, they'd had to walk back, and she'd been arguing non-stop with Paul all the way. All of which was upsetting Nick, as if he could be more upset. But at least the police said they weren't going to charge him. They didn't have any evidence, they said: no money, no dope. 'One dope,' Paul couldn't help adding. No one laughed. The police said they'd raid the squat. With luck, they wouldn't need Nick to give evidence, which should've pleased Nick but he was convinced they'd know he tipped off the law and he'd be ankled anyway. The police said it wouldn't happen, Paul agreed. Lynn didn't.

Once back at the house, Nick flew up to his room to get away from adults. Lynn would have liked to comfort him but felt he needed to be alone a while. Paul began a harangue, she threw up her hands in exhaustion, and left the house. Peace. It was heaven to be alone. She crossed the road to the park, just as it was closing. Pity, trees and sky always calmed her. She continued up the road, following the park railings, until she was beyond the park boundary and at Stratford.

She tried going into St John's church but it was locked, not that she wanted to pray but to get away from the bustle of the rush hour. Her shaking of the door brought a woman out, who told Lynn to come back for regular worship. Lynn said she might, knowing she wouldn't, and crossed the road to the library. She sat there for an indeterminate time with a book in her lap, unaware of even the title. And then a decision was made. She could not let Paul rule the roost. And set off home in the twilight.

Lynn was almost back, when she saw Anne leaving her house. Lynn was about to call out, but instead decided to follow her.

She knew something was up. From her murky conversation with Jack, it was obvious Anne and Jack were involved in something devious. Lynn had seen the police earlier waiting outside Anne's house. And then to top it, when she, Paul and Nick arrived at the police station, there was Bessie with the cops she'd seen previously. She'd asked Bessie if she was alright. And Bessie'd told her they'd found her dad in Epping Forest, confirming what Jack had said. Bessie might've said more, but a policewoman had ushered her away.

All this police activity. The way Jack had changed. She had seen him coming out of Anne's. He had admitted something was up, concerning whatever had happened two years ago when Jack was working at the house. She knew Jack was pushing her away and feared he'd be going to Anne. Mutual aid was drawing them together. They'd be sleeping together. It was all over for her. Desperation is a powerful aphrodisiac.

Lynn put her hood up to be less recognisable, and followed about fifty yards behind her friend, head bowed, crossing to the other side of the road. Up Margery Park Road. Who was Margery? See-saw Margery Daw. Probably no relation. Silly thoughts.

Anne didn't look back but walked swiftly, muffled in a jacket, scarf and woolly hat. She crossed the Romford Road, not waiting for the traffic lights, but skipped through the rush hour traffic, and headed up Norwich Road. By which time, Lynn was pretty sure where she was going.

She was right. Anne went to a house on Earlham Grove. Lynn couldn't see who answered the door, as she drew back behind a parked car, but a minute or two later, out came Jack. And the two of them walked down the street. They weren't holding hands. So this wasn't a lovers' tryst. Anne and Jack had some talking to do before they made love.

They didn't trust themselves to talk in the house. Lynn wondered if she herself was still in with a chance. A joint problem could bring a couple closer, but could as easily blow them apart. If every meeting reminded them of what you wanted to forget. Then watch this space.

Her jealousy hardly assuaged, she followed down the tree-lined road. The couple were deep in conversation. At one point, she dared get ahead of them on the other side of the road, striding quite quickly to the end of the street, where she tried analysing body language. Lots of talk, arm movement, mostly Anne. Her friend had the habit of taking over a conversation, giving advice often unasked for. Lynn was in no mood to flatter.

No touching though. Which didn't mean they might not end up in bed, once the words dried up. Though they might want to get away from each other. Run a mile from the intractable problem. Whatever it was. She was consumed by curiosity. All those cops. A body in Epping Forest somehow involving the two of them. She hardly knew Jack, so what he was like deep down she had yet to ascertain, if she ever would, but Anne she knew had a shady past. She'd been falsely accused of murdering her husband, did two years in jail, having to survive among tough, screwed up women, before the mistake was righted. What had that bruising done to her? She certainly hated cops and would spit at lawyers.

The couple came out on to Woodgrange Road, Lynn was behind them again, keeping back as they passed the Co-op supermarket and on towards Forest Gate station where a train from the City had just come in, with commuters flooding out of the entrance. Eighteen months ago, she'd have been one of them. No, it would have been later than this, maybe two or three hours later, later still when she had to get the magazine out ready for the morning. City workers were easy to spot amongst the travellers, the uniform, one of the few things she didn't regret losing. Lynn had four dress suits, she should dump them all, give them to a charity shop. She was never going to wear them again.

A wave of depression struck her. Her illness, allergy, her God knows what, had thrown her on the scrap heap. Rendered her useless in the eyes of the working world. Made her a nobody, going nowhere. Earlier today, she'd thought, I could be a builder. Admittedly, a thought intermingled with sexual attraction. To hell with Jack. But really, working today, she'd seen there wasn't much Jack was doing she couldn't do with a bit of training. OK, she'd have to learn about materials, use of tools, but there were courses. DIYers sawed, drilled and planed every Sunday. She'd picked it up quickly. A lot of it was confidence, not believing you couldn't do it.

She let Jack and Anne go. What was the point of following them further? They were heading down towards Wanstead Flats. A big, wide space to walk and talk in. She had seen as much as she needed to see. And was hungry. Ever since lunch, she'd been rushing about. Then she was working with Jack, off to get the lock, and returning to her brother ejecting Tim. Mini row, you might call that one, compared to the one that followed when Nick turned up black and blue. No time for food what with breaking china, bleeding nose and down en famille to the cop shop.

She was alone, she would always be alone. Hadn't she always been? Her brief marriage, if anything, illustrated it, in her illusion that she wasn't alone then. She'd best get used to it. Stop trying to grab a man, any man. She might live another fifty years. Then live her own life. On her own, not rowing with her brother and following her best friend.

That was why she wanted to help Tim. Needed to. There was someone, only just out of childhood, alone too. Those sad eyes. Thrown out by his parents, going from foster home to foster home, kicked out of a squat even. And then by her brother, who had the sympathy of a louse. Except she wouldn't let him. The kid needed love, protection. The elemental stuff. If she couldn't give that, then why bother?

She went into the Forest Café, more settled once she'd given up following the pair. She ordered a fry up, nothing healthy. A builder's dinner: chips and burgers, beans and eggs with a big mug of tea. She would be her own person. Whatever that meant, she would be it.

Lynn had finished eating and was drinking her second cup, when she saw Jack and Anne returning. She had a table by the window, so had a good view. If they hadn't been in animated conversation, they might have seen her. And so what if they had? She was simply eating out. No sin. She could've waved at them.

She paid up, and went in pursuit. By the time she was out of the shop, they were no longer in sight. They must have turned up Earlham Grove. Did she really want to know whether they were going to end up in bed? But she was moving and following, turning on to Earlham Grove herself; there they were, ahead. Now they were holding hands. It simply needed a door to shut and all would be confirmed. A night together.

Presumably they'd reached agreement, and now would pursue it physically. Sealed and delivered. What a walk can lead to. A breeze had come in from the east, shifting the purple clouds, sprinkling leaves on to the pavement, like orphans starving in the street. No alms, no salvation will be given. No one gives a damn about leaves.

No stars were visible, the street and house lights burnt them out on the clearest night, Jack had said.

To hell with him. He wasn't worth it. Anne could have him.

The street was a grove, once a posh part of town. Less so now. Many of the houses were turned into flats for rent, though some were owner occupied, a mixed street where most of the dwellers didn't know their neighbours. The good and bad of the city. Where you could be left alone. Where you could die of loneliness.

She wouldn't, she insisted. She would remake her life.

The couple ahead had stopped. Oh, what was going on? They were being approached by a man. Lynn was on the far side of the road and walked on past them, taking a quick glance as she passed. It was that cop, the Asian one, he seemed to be everywhere.

She went on for maybe fifty yards and then ducked behind a car. Looking back, she smiled. Who'd have guessed it? Jack was going in to his house with the cop. While Anne was going off. Lynn was sure that had never been their plan.

PART THREE:
PRIME SUSPECT

Chapter 35

'Jack!'

He turned as he was walking up the path to his front door, holding Anne's hand. He dropped her hand instantly. And they separated, as he watched Fayyad coming towards them. Jack grimaced and looked at his watch. Eight forty-five. He'd hoped Fayyad wouldn't be here when he got back. Yes, he'd made the appointment, but one he'd decided not to keep.

'I'm sorry, Fayyad. I forgot completely you were coming.'

The policeman was at his side.

'Eight o'clock we'd arranged, Jack. I tried phoning you...'

'My phone's been stolen. Sorry,' he said, with a weak smile, trying to excuse himself. 'We were out on the Flats, walking, talking, went for a coffee. I lost track of time. Busy day, it just slipped my mind. You know how it is. So sorry. Have you met Anne?'

'Yes, we have met. Small world.'

'It is,' said Anne. 'I'd best be off. Thanks for the chat, Jack.'

Jack wanted her to stay but there was no way out of the interview with Fayyad. He could hardly invite her up with him present. In fact, it was stupid of them walking down the road hand in hand. Back to the real world. Fayyad must be dealt with.

'Good to have seen you,' he said to Anne.

'See you in a while,' she said with a wave as if they were just acquaintances who'd happened to meet on the street.

He watched her go with disappointment. And turned to his visitor.

'You'd best come in,' said Jack, trying to appear agreeable. There was no other way. Fayyad was here, he couldn't tell him to go. He'd agreed the meeting. And sooner or later, it had to begin. So begin it now. He'd had a good chat with Anne. Cleared his head. They'd wandered on to the Flats, had a coffee on the way back, and talked of just such occasions. How to deal with the cops. As much truth as possible. They'd said as much as could be said. Anne was going to stay the night, she hadn't actually said so, but the pressure of her hand told him it was her decision. And now, all change. No wonder no one liked the law.

'The least I can do is offer you a coffee,' he added with a forced smile. 'It was just meeting Anne, you know how it is.'

'I faintly recall how sex trumps everything,' grinned Fayyad, 'even interviews with the police.' He punched Jack lightly on the shoulder. 'In my single days.'

Oh dear, thought Jack. He and Anne should have parted on Woodgrange, not come up to the house. Now Fayyad knew they were in a relationship of sorts.

Bad start.

Fayyad followed Jack into the house. He carried an attaché case. In his suit and short coat, he looked more like a banker than a detective. Be wary, thought Jack. He's a cop first and foremost. Friendship was way down the list. As they mounted the stairs, Jack was considering what to say. So far, the police had nothing on him. He'd simply been around when Frank disappeared. A builder doing a job. And had met Anne. Well, so what? They were friends, a bit closer than friends. Such things happened.

Once inside, Jack said, 'Let's go in the kitchen. I'll make us a coffee.'

He led his friend into the kitchen. At least he'd washed the dishes before going out for the walk with Anne, thinking she'd be coming up, as she so nearly had. Away with regrets, deal with the cop at the table. Fayyad had sat down, taking out his notebook, snapping into professional mode.

'Let's get a move on,' he said. 'I've a home life too.'

Jack considered that he'd apologised enough and said nothing.

'We need to get the dates straight, Jack. Let's be clear when you were working at Ham Park Road. From when to when.'

'I'll get my laptop. My work calendar is in there.'

He left the kitchen thinking what Anne and he had been discussing. As much truth as possible. Lie only when you have to. Omit. You can always claim you'd forgotten after two years. In the sitting room, he picked up his laptop from the table, and went back to the kitchen. He switched the machine on, and as it warmed up put on the kettle and got the coffee things together.

'OK,' he began, as he put the mugs on the worktop. 'Two years ago, let me get my head together. I was employed to knock down the garden wall,' he mused, safe ground, his work at the house. 'It was leaning, a dangerous structure. I had to knock it down, put the debris in a skip and get it taken away. Then replace it with a wooden fence.'

'I've seen it,' said Fayyad. 'It's a nice job. How long did it take you?'

Jack sat down, opposite Fayyad at the table, and began getting into his files on the laptop. 'I think it was a week. This'll tell me.' He didn't say four days of actual work. One day he'd had to take off. After the burial in the forest, they hadn't got back to the house till six in the morning, and then he'd helped Anne get rid of blood-stained furniture. And was too washed out to work that day. A sickie, you might say.

'Here we are,' he said, turning the screen so Fayyad could see. 'My work diary two years ago. October. There.' Pleased to be able to speak the truth, more or less. 'I was at the house from Monday 19 October to Friday 23 October. A week's work.' He was confident Fayyad wouldn't know he'd done the job in four days. Even a builder couldn't be sure. Taking a wall down can have all sorts of unforeseen problems. He was prepared to exaggerate them if needs be.

'I'll need a copy of that page,' said Fayyad.

'Fine. I'll just turn the printer on.'

'I'll finish making the coffee,' said Fayyad.

Jack went out to the sitting room, and turned on the printer, it was set up for wireless printing. Work was safe ground. Nothing on his computer to incriminate him, if they should ever take it away. He and Anne hadn't emailed. Face to face, the odd phone call.

Back in the kitchen, Fayyad had milked and poured out two mugs of instant coffee. Jack sat down, taking a sip of coffee.

'Hot and wet,' he said, putting it down. And with a few taps of the keys, he sent the page to print.

'I'll need to take your fingerprints, Jack,' said Fayyad. 'I've a portable electronic gizmo. So no hassle.' He took a small machine and attachments from his attaché case. He plugged it in at an electric socket. 'Doesn't hurt,' he said with a laugh. 'I'm not a dentist out to fool you. So no sweetie.'

'No nasty ink I see,' said Jack, looking at the machine which was like a fat phone.

'Long gone,' said Fayyad with a wave of the hand. 'All digital these days. Let's have your hands one at a time. Spread your fingers, palms up. That's the way.' He slowly brushed the reader over Jack's finger tips. 'Other hand.'

'What's this in aid of?' said Jack.

'Elimination purposes. You've nothing to worry about. A fingerprint has been found. A single one. Everyone was amazed. Two years and still there. But it was protected in a fold of the plastic. On a builder's bag one of the bodies was in.' Fayyad laughed. 'Could be your bag, Jack.'

Jack attempted a smile. 'Or a thousand other builders.'

'We've been told to take the prints of everyone we question. Now the machine has to check with the database. Takes a few minutes. Don't worry, these prints get deleted when the investigation is over.'

When the hell will that be, thought Jack. It had barely begun. Everyone in Anne's house at the time had to be questioned, there could be stories in the papers, TV coverage. And that fingerprint. Could be his. Could be Anne's. Could be David's. They were the only ones who'd had contact with the bag that night. Though, he reflected, it could be none of theirs, perhaps someone at the wholesalers where he'd bought the bag. Or even at the manufacturers.

He should've worn gloves, should've wiped down the bag before dropping it in the hole. Should never have got into this mess in the first place.

'Any more questions?' he said, disguising his wandering thoughts as he drank the coffee.

'Just a few more, Jack. I don't want to stay much longer. Nothing personal but I need to get home. My dinner will be burnt to a frazzle. And we've a case meeting in the morning.'

'Sorry about being out.'

'Forget it.' He waved away the apology; it was history. 'Now where was I?' He consulted his notebook and nodded, more to himself than Jack, then continued. 'You told me earlier you'd met Frank Brand.'

'Nasty bit of work. Yes, I saw him once. He was in the garden, putting out meatballs with tacks in on the lawn. He stopped soon as I came into the yard, I pretended not to see what he was doing. We had a bit of a chat. I told him I'd sent off his daughter, Bessie, to do an errand for me. I got the feeling he didn't like that. Her doing errands. She was his skivvy. Can't remember what else we said. Then he went in the house. And I had a good look at those meatballs. Each one had a half inch tack inside.'

'What for?'

'The old lady. What was her name?' He flicked fingers. 'Nancy. She had this cat. Can't remember its name. Me and names, two years ago though. Frank was out to get the cat. A real psychopath. I picked up all the meatballs I saw, but must have missed a few, as later on one got stuck in the cat's throat. Tickles – that was its name. I got it out.'

'And you never saw Frank again?'

'Just met him that one time.' Alive was the omission, but that was for Fayyad to find out.

'Can you remember what day it was?'

Jack scratched his head. 'Now you've got me. The Monday or the Tuesday, most likely the Tuesday.' He took a sip of coffee. 'You know he was abusing Bessie?'

'So we've noted. We interviewed her earlier. Well, hardly an interview, as she got into such a state when we brought up the relationship between her and her father. It was too painful for her to handle. She became hysterical. We sent her home with a family liaison officer.'

'Poor girl.'

'Did you ever meet Bert Long?'

'Another nasty bit of work,' said Jack. 'He came to the house looking for Frank, Bessie told me. And then moved himself in, taking over from Frank. Rape, physical abuse. What a scumbag! Do you really need to investigate who killed them? Shouldn't society be grateful they're dead?'

'That's mob rule, Jack. You can't have people being judge and jury.'

'Even when you know they're wicked?'

'Why have a police force? This isn't the Wild West,' he said. 'Though sometimes I wonder. But no, I agree they were rats, but the law has to take its course. You were telling me about Bert.'

'I met him only the once. Bessie told me what he was doing to her. I knew he was in Anne's place, so I went in to have it out with him...'

'What happened?'

'We had a shouting match. I told him to leave Bessie alone or else.'

'Or else what?'

'I'd knock him into next week. And that was the last I saw of him. It was towards the end of the week.' He waved a hand in recall. 'I remember now. I'd arranged to go to Brighton for the weekend with my ex, Alison, and Mia, my daughter. Alison was going to move down there for her work. She's a teacher, a head now. Mia wasn't too happy about moving, so we were going to see the town as a family. A weekend at the seaside. I didn't want to leave Bessie in the house alone for the weekend, not with Bert prowling around. So we took her with. Stayed in a bed and breakfast.'

He was content telling this stuff, when he was out of town in Brighton, away from the scene. And all true.

'We came back late Sunday,' he continued, 'dropped Bessie off, no sign of Bert. Maggie told me he hadn't been there all weekend. And, although I'd finished the work, I checked in with Maggie and David during the week. Bert was out of the picture.'

'He's one of the bodies in the forest, Jack.'

'Which accounts for his absence.' He shrugged. 'Can't say I miss him.'

'He's got a family, friends, enemies, I dare say a lot of those. We'll be exploring every avenue.' He shut his notebook. 'That'll do for now, Jack. You'll have to give a proper statement at the station. Sorry about the bureaucracy, but it all helps us to get a picture of who was about at the time. The last people to see Frank and Bert. You never know what's important at the beginning of an investigation.'

191

'Pity they couldn't have just rotted in the forest.'

That had been the intention. Let the worms and bugs do their work. Stupid, not removing that plastic bag before burying Frank. He didn't need to be buried in it. But the corpse was such a mess, leaking blood and body fluids. Even so, it wouldn't have taken so long to drag the bag off him. Burn it. Wash off the stink, throw away any stained clothing. It had occurred to him at the time: get rid of the bag, the body will rot quicker. But it'd been late, he was tired, neither Maggie nor David, who were with him, suggested doing anything. So it was left.

And was coming back as Exhibit No 1.

'Oh, what's this?' Fayyad was looking at the fingerprint machine screen. He turned to Jack. 'We've got a match.' He screwed his eyes in puzzlement. 'There's something odd here.'

'What's up?'

Fayyad showed Jack the screen, showing two prints side by side. 'The print on the bag. It's yours.'

Chapter 36

Paul knocked on the bedroom door. There was no answer. He hadn't expected one, so took a deep breath, knowing this was likely to be thankless, but he had to try. He glanced at his watch, just past 10 pm, not so late. He quietly opened the door. The room was in darkness, he turned on the light. Nick was lying face down on the bed, head cradled on one arm.

'Are you awake?' he said.

'Go away,' murmured his son, without changing position.

Paul came close to the bed.

'There was no other way, Nick,' he said. 'You must see that.'

'Leave me alone.'

'The police said they'll raid the house,' went on Paul. 'They'll pick them all up, and won't say who tipped them off. They'll hold them in custody...'

'You know nothing, dad!' yelled Nick. 'You're a half-baked accountant. Way out of your depth. And I'm going to get ankled!'

Paul dropped on to the single bed. He put his hand on his son's back. Nick shrugged it off. Paul was soaked in guilt; his son was right. He knew little about the drug scene, hoped there'd be no repercussions. The police said it would probably be alright. Probably. A worrying uncertainty. He knew it was Lynn, in the kitchen, telling him not to phone, that had pushed him. She was against it, he must be for it. So juvenile. It had been his childhood excuse: *she made me do it, Mum!* But it was true. How could he agree with her, especially when she was haranguing him.

'We can't let those dealers get away with it,' said Paul, trying to comfort his son as well as defend himself to himself. 'They deal in poison. They threaten, they kill I dare say. And if everyone just pays them off, then on and on it goes. Victim after victim.'

'I'm going to get ankled!' Nick screamed into the pillow. 'Don't you understand?'

'Not if they are picked up, you won't.'

'They've got mates. That's how they operate. No one crosses them.'

'It'll be alright,' said Paul feebly. 'You just see. They'll be picked up, jailed for years...'

'And I'll be crippled!'

'It's just the way you're thinking now...' said his father.

Nick turned over and sat up.

'That's all so much crap,' he spat. 'You don't know what you're talking about. And too damned tight to pay them off. That's always the way with you. You'll pay anything for Dawn's therapy. I need something once in a while – and you dump me in it.'

'You dumped yourself in it, Nick.'

'Eight hundred measly quid could have got me out of it,' said his son bitterly. 'And does my dad pay up?' He shook his hands fiercely. 'Course not. He's a bloody accountant. It's not a cost benefit to pay up. So let's chance it. It's only an ankle.' He coiled up into a ball, arms gripping his head. 'Go away. You're useless. When I need you, you're never there. Get out of my life!'

'It'll be alright, Nick, I assure you. That police inspector, he said...'

Nick threw a pillow at him, and screeched. 'Leave me alone. You've done too much damage already. Piss off!'

Paul retreated. He'd lost. The lad wouldn't be comforted. Fear had taken control. Whatever he said was thrown back at him.

'Would you like a coffee?' he said meekly at the door.

'Get out of my life! I don't want anything from you. Ever again. Turn off the light. Go!'

Paul turned off the light, and left his son's room. In the hallway, he leaned against the wall breathing heavily as if he'd just come in from a run. That was awful. He was public enemy number one. Nick saw it as betrayal. Was it too late to pay off the dealers? Even now. Of course it was. He'd have to ask Nick for their address. That would be admitting he was wrong. Maybe he was, maybe he wasn't. Besides which, Nick wouldn't tell him. It was all set for a police raid in the morning. He couldn't stop that. It was out of his control. Once he'd called the cops, there could be no paying off. The police had taken over. There was nothing he could do.

It was Lynn's fault. She'd goaded him. She knew what she was doing. Always the way with her. Such a cunning cow. Force him into a corner, so he'd have no choice but do the opposite to what she wanted. He couldn't allow her to control him like this. Play him like an automaton. Now he had Nick hating him. She must be stopped. He couldn't spend his whole life reacting to her.

He must deal with her, once and for all. But first Nick. He had a duty as a father, especially if he'd made a wrong decision. But who could say it was wrong? If they'd paid off the dealers, they could well be back for more. Go for the whole family even.

Maybe someone else could do better. He took a few steps along the hallway and knocked on the door.

'Who is it?' called Dawn.

'It's me. Can I come in and talk to you?'

'If you must,' she said wearily.

He opened the door. She was laid out on her bed with her laptop. Any other time, he might have told her to sit at her desk. That's why he'd bought her a desk in the first place. Only children worked on their beds.

Instead, he said, 'Nick won't talk to me.'

'I heard him yelling at you,' she said without looking at him, her hands busy on the keyboard.

'I wondered if you could help.'

She looked at him, screwing up her eyes. 'In what way?'

'Talk to Nick.'

'He never listens to me.' She shrugged, 'Along with everyone else round here.'

'You're his age,' he said. 'You could try. Assure him what I did was for his own good.'

'He thinks he'll get ankled,' she said.

'What do you think?'

She shrugged. 'I really have no idea. By all accounts, they are nasty people, so wouldn't think twice about it.'

'But they won't know he called the cops.'

'He didn't,' she said.

He backtracked, holding up a hand in admission. 'OK. I called them. I am a parent. I had to. It's what any responsible parent would do.'

She blew a raspberry. 'Responsible parent? Since when?'

'I do my best,' he sighed. 'I feed you, I clothe you, I pay for your electronic gadgets...'

'And you run round the park whenever there's a problem.'

'I pay for your therapy.'

She clenched her fists and shook them at him. 'Have you never thought why I need therapy?'

'Many times,' he said. 'I'm not a fool. I know your mother and me breaking up was bad for the pair of you. I know my drinking made things worse. I was a pain, a fool. A neglectful parent. I am sorry. What else do you want me to say? At least I'm not in Australia like your mother.'

'I can't help you with Nick,' she said and returned to her keyboard, responding to something on the screen. 'He won't listen to me. Thinks I'm an idiot. I think he's an idiot. And we're both right. Don't you agree?'

He wanted to tell her to stop emailing or whatever she was doing, but knew that was counterproductive. But he didn't know what was productive. Neither for Nick nor her. They were supposedly grown up. He wished they were off his hands, but knew he'd be stuck with them forever.

He said, 'How did I lose you both?'

'Don't bother yourself,' she said. 'It's a phase. Life. Soon be over.'

He wanted to slap her for her facetiousness, the way she kept on with her keyboard while he was trying to have a serious conversation. He closed his eyes, overwhelmed by hopelessness. Nobody took any notice. Everyone pushed him away. Even so, he could but try. He was here. Love was his weakest suit. Offer at least.

'Are you alright?' he said. 'I haven't got just a son. A daughter too. Are you OK?'

'Fine.' She tapped on.

'No more of the cutting?'

'All under control.'

'Then I'll leave you to your business. I'm sure it's more important than I am.'

She looked at him quizzically.

'He doesn't listen to me, Dad. I'd talk to him if he would. But it would be a complete waste of time.' She considered then said, 'You could ask Lynn.'

He stiffened. 'I could. I might.' Knowing he wouldn't. 'I'm glad we've had a chat.'

And he retreated from her room, closing the door, but she'd already shut him out as she clicked and tapped into a world that was far more important.

In the hallway, Paul considered. He'd tried. There was nothing he could do. Let it not be said he hadn't tried. It would be alright, he was sure. Time had to pass. The police raid and so forth. In the meantime, he could clear out the box room. The boy had gone somewhere, Lynn was out. He would empty the room and lock it.

Chapter 37

'So what did Bessie tell them?' asked David.

He was in the armchair, in his shirt sleeves, tie off, collar button open. Relaxed mode. Maggie was straddling one of the chairs at the table, showered, face clear of make up. Anne, their focus, had the sofa to herself.

'Not much,' said Anne. 'She came back with a cop who stayed with her a couple of hours. I couldn't get to her. That's the way they play it.' She looked at her notebook. 'Police constable Hayley Amis. Clever little madam, comes over as so supportive, but she's a cop, she'll wheedle her way into Bessie's confidence and worm the whole tale out of her, you bet your life.'

'But what has Bessie said so far?' insisted David.

'I popped in just before I came up here, the cop had gone, thank goodness. Bessie said she hadn't told them anything; it was only a short interview. She'd started crying and they let her go.' Anne waved her hands in frustration. 'But believe me, they know she's the weakest link. They'll use every trick in the book to get her to talk.'

'She doesn't know the whole tale,' said Maggie. 'Nothing about Bert.'

'Too much about Frank though,' said Anne. 'She saw the body...'

'Didn't we all,' said David. 'All clustered in your nursery planning what to do with it.'

'What japes!' exclaimed Maggie in mock humour. 'It was as if we were all stoned. A group of hippies playing bongos. A body to be disposed of. Screw the pigs. Why not help our downstairs neighbour...'

'Very kind of you,' said Anne disparagingly.

'All great fun,' went on Maggie, 'until my husband lost his keys in the forest, with a very telling Nigerian flag on the fob.'

'You left your phone, dearest.'

'I wouldn't have left the damned thing if we hadn't had to go back for your keys...'

'Stop quarrelling, the pair of you,' said Anne.

'And you with that bloodstained dress!' exclaimed Maggie turning on her. 'Fancy putting it in a skip where Bert could find it. Why didn't you burn it?'

'Why didn't you leave your phone at home?'

'Stop it, you're doing my head in!' exclaimed David.

The two women glowered at him, but said nothing, brooding on the mistakes that necessitated them killing Bert. He'd found the bloody dress, thought it was Maggie's, followed the couple when they went back to the forest looking for the keys, chanced on the keys himself. And stole the phone from Maggie's parked car.

'I think we are fairly tidy on Bert,' said Anne. 'Only the three of us know about his killing.' She stopped for an instant, reflecting. 'What did you do with the knife, David?'

'It's in the Thames. Along with the keyfob.'

'Was that wise?' said Anne raising her eyebrows. 'The two of them.'

'Not in the same place,' he said with an exasperated breath. 'And why should a key fob be associated with a knife anyway? I had to lose the fob. I didn't want to see it every day and be reminded of my folly.'

'Your murder, darling. Beware euphemisms.'

'I'm not alone in my euphemisms, sweetheart.'

They were quiet again. Anne hoped Maggie and David would stay together, because if they ever split then what secrets might be revealed to future lovers? Some of the most lovey-dovey pairings split ten years down the road. David and Maggie had a child they loved, but this situation was a dreadful strain on any relationship. And she was no marriage counsellor. She could only hope the two of them stayed together until the cops departed.

'It's Bessie I'm worried about,' she said. 'I've seen Jack. He'll be alright. He's working next door.'

'Are you sleeping with him?' said Maggie. 'That's usually the way you function.'

Anne gave a thin lipped grin. 'Jack won't be a problem.'

'So you are sleeping with him.'

'That's neither here nor there.'

David laughed. 'It's not the best way to handle complications.'

'Why not?' she snapped.

'If the relationship turns sour...' he began.

'And if you two split up?' Anne interrupted.

'Let's not deal in ifs and ands,' said Maggie raising her palms to pacify. 'We have an immediate problem.'

'We most certainly do,' admitted Anne. 'We'll all be questioned. The way to handle it is to tell the truth as much as possible.' She turned to David. 'You should admit to hitting Frank at the leaseholders' meeting. Frank probably told others in that dreadful organisation he belonged to. He hated the two of you as a mixed race couple...' She halted this train of thought. 'You two will be fine.' She hoped. 'It's Bessie I'm worried about. That cop she's got hanging about with her... She might tell her anything when she's in a state.'

'What can we do about it?' said Maggie with a shrug.

Anne didn't speak for a second or two, biting her lower lip. She looked from one to the other, saying, 'We must think the unthinkable.'

'Oh God, here we go again!' exclaimed David, throwing up his hands.

'What's the unthinkable?' demanded Maggie.

Anne peered at her through half closed lids. 'You know as well as I do.'

Chapter 38

Jack couldn't sleep. His fingerprint was on the bag Frank was buried in. Great. He most certainly would get the third degree tomorrow. No pleasant chat and coffee with Fayyad, but down to the station and in the interview room, tape recorder on to catch him out. One slip and they'd be in there like a hawk after a hare.

After a couple of hours of tossing and turning, he thought of phoning Anne. And then rejected it. She'd said it all on their walk. What could she add? The same words in a different order. There'd be the solace of love making, followed by the frustration of talking all night. And really, he couldn't take that. Going over and over what to say when.

Ultimately you're on your own. That's what he'd learnt when he split from Alison. That's what he'd learnt in his drinking days. No one could save him but himself. Anne would get sick of him, he'd get sick of her if all they had was this one topic of conversation. Pity he couldn't pick up with Lynn, but not now. There was too much he couldn't say.

He got up, dressed and had a brief wash in cold water. It was 2.54 am. No glimmer of daylight. But he was better standing up, less self pity, more able to deal with the world. The flat was too confining, sleep was out. He decided to go for a drive. The tank was near full, after Lynn's payment.

Taking his jacket off the hook, he left the flat. It was blowy in the street, no stars in the ruffled blanket of purple cloud. The road was devoid of traffic, and when he drew up to the high street, little there either. He turned north, heading towards Wanstead Flats. Forest Gate station was closed, the shops shuttered, a drunken man staggered on the pavement. That was an option, lose himself in booze. Drop out of existence for X hours.

The cops would still question him. Hold him in a cell until he sobered up, watch him vomiting every ten minutes. He couldn't evade them. He looked at the time. Just before three, he could still go to Anne's. What would she make of the fingerprint? She'd tell him what to say. She was good at that. But what would she really think? Idiot builder.

He was driving across the Flats, the vista clear over the grasslands on both sides. It was only last night he'd been out here with Mia. Not the best night for stargazing but tonight was worse. Pity, it always calmed him looking at the stars, picking out the constellations on a clear night, with or without a telescope. Getting light years away from his own little mess.

Lights were flashing in his mirror. Someone behind. He guessed who it might be. They drew closer, and yes, it was a police car. Jack pulled up by the side of the road. This should be OK. He was sober, no body hidden in the back.

He let down his window and waited for the cop to come. Surely they wouldn't be sending out someone to arrest him so late at night? Fayyad had told him to go into work, and they'd come for him after he'd talked to his boss.

A young policeman in uniform appeared at his window. Behind him, he could see a policewoman.

'Driving late, sir.'

'Couldn't sleep,' said Jack. 'So just driving around.'

'Would you get out for a moment, sir?'

Jack did so, closing the door lightly behind him.

'Have you been drinking?'

'Stone cold sober,' he said.

'I don't smell any,' said the cop.

'I'm off the stuff,' said Jack. 'I need my van. I'm a builder. If I lose my licence that's my work down the chute.'

'Same here,' said the cop with a laugh. 'Can I have a look in the van?'

'You can,' said Jack, going to the back. 'You looking for anything in particular, like timber or a box of tools?'

'There's been a robbery on the high street, sir,' said the policeman. 'And we'd like to rule you out.'

Jack opened up the rear doors. The two police officers looked in. Jack stepped away, stretched and took a deep breath of cold night air. Oh he was tired. It was going to be a tough day tomorrow. Work, cops. The work he'd get by on, but the cops – they'd be testing. Sleep would be an asset.

'You can close up, sir. Might I see your licence? Always as well to go by the book.'

Jack fished it out. He did think the man was being exceptionally thorough. But maybe it was good practice. A dummy run, with nothing to hide.

The policeman looked at Jack and then at the photo.

'Make a good mug shot,' said Jack.

The cop laughed. 'You should see mine. Thank you for your co-operation. You can be on your way.'

Jack thanked him. Never annoy a cop. A good tip for the future. And got back in his van. He wondered where to go. What about that all night café at Whipps Cross? Get some breakfast in, a mug of tea. Then see if he could sleep for an hour or two.

He set off. Turning off at Bush Road for the Green Man roundabout. When he got to the all night café, he found it shut. Most definitely not all night, or not tonight anyway. Was it ever? He felt sure it was. Maybe it wasn't. And set off home.

Back at the house, he saw a note on the mat. It was from Anne saying: *I called round. I could do with some comfort. Sorry you weren't in. Anne*

He thought of going over there. And rejected it. At this hour? He'd have some breakfast. 3.45 am. And try again for sleep.

Chapter 39

The police came early in three vans. The strategy was to catch them unawares and to have few onlookers. Though it wasn't early for the residents and hangers-on, as they slept by day. The sun was close to rising, the invaders saw light through the shutters of the squat and heard heavy metal thumping which would have kept any neighbours awake, if there'd been any in the corrugated iron clad houses abutting. The whole stretch was intended for demolition.

A third of the police went round the back, while the rest were at the front. At the signal there was a hammering on the door and a chorus of 'Armed police!' Followed seconds later by the thudding of the short battering ram, which crashed repeatedly into the door until it splintered open.

The police rushed in yelling. They were in uniform, men and women, all armed. They went from room to room pulling people out. A couple making love were allowed only to put on the rudiments of clothing before being pushed out, handcuffed and thrown in the prison van. A group smoking weed made no attempt to hide what they had. The atmosphere was smoky and obvious. Scattered about were the apparatus and materials for a panoply of illegal substances: pins, penknives, pipes, papers, bottles and syringes.

A couple of men attempted to get out the back way, but were caught and handcuffed by officers who had come over the fence. Nine in all were pulled in and taken away before the search of the building began.

A young man watched the ruction, hiding behind a car on the street. He had a rucksack and carried a guitar case, a hood concealing his face. When the first of those arrested were pushed into the street, protesting in their handcuffs, he ducked lower, but stayed, watching until the last occupant was removed.

Chapter 40

Jack arrived at the house just past eight thirty. His start time was eight but this morning around 6 am he'd fallen asleep and not set the alarm. He'd woken at eight and rose in a rush. Two hours' sleep was better than he'd expected, so maybe he'd get by today.

Lynn was waiting when he arrived.

'Sorry,' he said. 'Overslept.'

'You must have a clear conscience,' she said.

If only, he thought, but said, 'Let's get the last panels up. Then there's just the lock to put in. And all done bar the decorating.'

'I'd like to have a bolt on the inside too,' she said.

He raised his eyebrows. 'You going to be watching porn?'

She laughed. 'I want to keep the house out. Claim my space. Make it clear who it belongs to.'

He didn't respond, regarding her attitude as ultra territorial, but then she was the customer.

'We'll need to buy a bolt then,' he said.

'There's one in the cellar,' she said. 'I'll bring it up.'

While she was downstairs, Jack sorted out his tools. Where was his drill? The tools that he'd been working with yesterday, he'd left tidily in a corner, thinking they'd be safe here. Idiot, he thought, considering what had happened to his phone. He searched both sides of the partly constructed wall, went out to his van to check whether it was there. It shouldn't have been, and it wasn't. But he did have another drill which he brought in.

When he got back, she was there with a large door bolt.

'That's fine,' he said. 'Seen my drill?'

'What's that?' she said, indicating the one he was holding.

'My second best. The other one's a Bosch. Cost me. And I definitely left it here with the other tools.' He put down the drill he'd brought. 'My phone, a drill... You've got a thief in this house.'

'I don't know who,' she said, though perhaps she did. 'I'll pay for it.'

He didn't argue. Someone had to.

'I shall have to lock everything away,' he said.

'Sorry, Jack.'

He shrugged. She'd said she'd pay, though she might be surprised at the cost of a Bosch. It had cost him over one hundred quid.

'Let's get moving,' he said, not knowing how long he had before the cops came to take him in for questioning. Or worse. Keep working until it happened. Maybe they'd forget. As likely as winning the Jackpot, without having bought a ticket.

They'd nailed all the whole boards on before stopping for a break. All the inside had been covered with boards on the previous day, leaving the outside they'd just completed. The middle was filled with rock wool. All that remained was cutting part boards to fill the gaps and so complete the partition wall.

She said, 'Would you like to make a coffee and toast, Jack? Sorry, tea. I need to go up and talk to Nick. He was in a bad way yesterday.'

'I noticed there was a situation,' he said carefully.

'And a half,' she said.

'I'd better stay here and guard my tools.'

She was about to say something and thought better of it. A phone and drill had gone; he had every right to guard his gear. And, if she was paying for his losses, she shouldn't stop him.

'Won't be long,' she said.

She headed upstairs. Some soothing to do. And some waking up. Tim had come in late last night after his stint at the casino. And had slept on the floor of her room. Her brother had put a padlock on the box room, as if he owned it. Every time she came up to the upstairs hallway the lock infuriated her. Her brother had taken possession of the cupboard. Though now he was out for a run, so she could tell Tim he could get breakfast without danger. But first, some more immediate business.

She knocked on the door.

'Who is it?' called Dawn.

Lynn entered. Dawn was laid out on the bed, doing something on her laptop. Lynn didn't believe it was college work. Tim was the only one in the house who seemed to be doing any.

'Give me the drill,' she said, holding out her hand.

Dawn sat up abruptly. 'What drill?'

'The one you stole from the builder. Give me it.'

'I don't know what you're talking about.'

'You took his phone. And now you've taken his drill. Why?'

'Why does everyone accuse me? There are four others living in this house...'

Lynn had gone to the mattress and was heaving it up.

'Hey stop it! How dare you! You can't search my room. You're tipping up my laptop. Who do you think you are!'

Lynn pulled out a drill, hidden mid bed.

'This yours?' she said holding it up like a trophy, cord dangling.

Dawn burst into tears, hands over her face. Lynn had known it had to be here when two items had gone. The phone could have been Jack's carelessness, but she'd seen the drill last night, left there with his other tools. Tim wouldn't be daft enough, still trying to keep a foothold here, Nick had other concerns, leaving Dawn. Lynn should have

209

thought that straight away. It was her pattern. And now the tears. But only for being caught.

'What did you do with his phone?' asked Lynn.

'It's in the river,' mewled Dawn.

Lynn was at a loss what to do. It was impossible to be in a temper with the bedraggled girl on the bed.

'You don't need a phone, you don't need a drill... Why do you do these things?'

'I can't help myself.'

Lynn thought, what am I to say to Jack. And had a disturbing thought. What might she find in this room if she did a real search? It was unlikely Jack was the first victim. Though no one else in the house had complained of things missing. That left college, shoplifting, friends – did Dawn have any friends left?

Lynn said, 'I've got the drill now, I'll tell Jack that someone borrowed it. You haven't killed anyone. So let's get things in proportion. I'll pay for his phone. Now you dry your eyes.'

'Thank you, Aunty Lynn.' She was sniffing, dabbing her eyes with a tissue.

'I'm going to make coffee and toast,' said Lynn. 'I'll make some for you. You stay here, I'll bring it up.'

Lynn left her. One scene dealt with, but only temporarily. What would the girl do next? How do you get her out of the pattern? Lynn was halfway down the stairs when she remembered she hadn't gone in to see Nick. And was about to go back up, when she saw Jack at the front door with an Asian man and a woman she recognised from yesterday.

'I've got to go to the police station, Lynn,' he said. 'I don't know how long I'll be.'

Chapter 41

Paul was running at a good pace, pleased with himself. He was so much fitter with two to three runs a day. At first, he'd been so stiff, but gradually his body had got used to it. Yesterday had been a three day, today was two stints. And he was so strong. There were five months until the London Marathon; he'd be in top form. He enjoyed passing other joggers in the park. He'd speed up to show how much faster he was, and take them. Only when well ahead would he ease down.

Today was a steady run, five miles. He'd like to do more resistance work, strengthen the legs. Up the sand dunes at Camber Sands or the North Downs. But he couldn't leave Nick in his state. He must go and see him when he got back. The boy should've calmed down after yesterday's hysterics. The police had phoned Paul just before he left on the run. They'd told him the house had been raided and everyone taken into custody. So, Paul reasoned, his son was safe, a total alarmist. You mustn't give in to these people.

It was a relief to be right. He daren't think of the contrary. He had stuck to his guns, disregarding his son's tantrum. Stood up for law and order. What would Lynn say now? Some sharp remark, no doubt. The day she ever admitted she was wrong would be a national holiday.

A good day for running, the wind had dropped. It was cool, but that was fine as it counteracted the heat he built up. Some runners took bottles of water with them. He never bothered for less than a ten, otherwise you were swigging all the time, instead of concentrating on your pace.

Four laps of the park. He'd worked that out as 5 miles. An easy distance after yesterday's workout. He'd weighed himself this morning. 65 kilos. He'd like to lose another couple of kilos. He'd seen an article in Running magazine, extra weight slowed you up. Only to be expected. You had to carry it round. Lose the fat, and gain minutes in a marathon.

He needed another pair of trainers. Later today, he'd get a couple of pairs, and be ahead. This pair was losing its tread. And you have to bear in mind the jarring as the soles get thinner. Though it was better running in the park, more than half of it was on grass which was easier on the feet and calves. Hard pavement, week in week out, could be a killer. He was so lucky to live close to West Ham Park. Just out the house, across the road, through the gates and he was away. It was why he could never concede the house to Lynn. Let her do her worst, he would stay.

He had to go into work in the afternoon. Another of those assessments. What are your goals for this year, Paul? Two years, three? He couldn't tell them his London Marathon goals, the only ones that mattered to him: three hours 10, three hours dead, two hours 50. But clients, that's what the firm wanted. How many new clients do you expect to bring in, Paul? So make up a figure for them. Everyone else did. Of course, they'd catch up with you in a couple of years when you'd fail to reach the target, but he'd hoped to have moved on by then. Somewhere more local. Easier to fit in with training.

Paul had come into the ornamental garden. There were flower beds here and shrubberies, a rose garden with a pergola, an iris garden. He enjoyed the seasonal changes as he ran through the days; how summer eased into autumn. The rhododendrons coming out in a blaze in late spring, fading so quickly, the sun getting higher in the sky with the passing months, to peak on midsummer's day in June. But now autumn, the sun in the same place in the daily arc, just lower to suit the time of year. That was a discovery. A secret almost. And of course it was why a sundial worked. They should get one for the back garden.

He was on the back shrubbery at the bottom of the ornamental garden. Outside the shrubs, almost hidden, though audible, was the main road, beyond the railings. Here, he was on tarmac, and would be till he left the ornamental garden through the avenue of tall trees. This was a favourite section, quiet, little visited. Green peace. As was the park itself. His place, a refuge.

Paul passed the rhododendron bed with the bridge over a gully. In the gully was the winter garden, half blanketed in leaves with a few aching white flowers. He glanced at his watch. Good going, and he wasn't aware of pushing it.

Out of nowhere, Paul was knocked off his feet. A man had simply crashed into him from the shrubbery. Paul staggered, struggling to keep his feet. And then fell in a heap a few yards along.

'What the hell are you up to?' he yelled at the man.

And then held up his hands in fear. The man's face was hidden in a brown balaclava with holes only for mouth and eyes. In his hands was a crossbow, a bolt in place. He came in close, standing over Paul.

'Don't move!' he shrieked, 'Or I'll nail you through the skull.'

'I've no money,' whimpered Paul. 'Nothing with me.'

The man held the crossbow a foot from Paul's face.

'Lay on your back,' he ordered. 'Now!'

Paul did so, stretching out full as if waiting to be crucified, trembling with fear. Why him? Why here? Someone come, please. He could not see the man, but the sky and the high branches of overhanging trees, a magpie flying past. What could he do? What could he offer?

'Please, mister, I've money at home...' he pleaded.

There was a thud. Simultaneously, Paul screamed.

Chapter 42

Fayyad identified who was present for the recording. There was himself, Hayley, his boss Detective Superintendent Nikki Martin and Jack Bell. Jack was alone on one side of the table, his inquisitors the other, Nikki in the centre with an open folder full of papers and photos in front of her. There was no other furniture apart from the table and chairs; the walls were bare.

The questioning began. At first, covering the ground Jack had been through with Fayyad last night but in more detail. When he was working at the house, doing what, his interaction with those in the house. And coming on to Frank, of course, and Jack's one encounter with him. That was gone through several times; how Jack had come in with a wheelbarrow through the garden gate and seen Frank scattering meatballs with tacks in. Jack hadn't confronted him as he hadn't known what he was doing or who he was. Only later realising he was out to kill a cat.

A little more of this, and then Nikki, who was doing most of the questioning, put the big one. It had to come, Jack knew this. The rest was just build up.

'Your fingerprint has been found on the sack Frank Brand was buried in, Jack. Can you account for that?'

Jack had had all night to think of an answer. It was fortunate that Fayyad had come over last night, otherwise the question would've come out of the blue. And that would have really got him rocking on his feet. Prepare, Anne had said. Imagine it's an interview for a job, try to think of an answer to every question they might ask. On their walk, she'd quizzed him, playing the hard cop. But she hadn't known of the fingerprint.

He said, 'I use large builder's bags all the time. I keep a few in my van. Someone could easily have stolen it from the van. When I'm working, I often leave the back open as I'm going to and fro. Anyone could have taken it. I'd never have noticed. They're cheap enough. Or perhaps,' he added, 'I might have touched it at the wholesaler's. I use Jewson's in Stratford a lot.'

'Just coincidence it should be yours then,' said Nikki.

'I'm a builder,' he said. 'I was working at the house. My van was there every day.' He opened his hands dismissively. 'Anyone could've taken it.' He thought for a second, then said, 'It would get the heat off themselves and implicate me. Lead you up the garden path.'

Nikki grinned slightly. 'We're not so easily led, Jack.' She looked down at her notes, and said, as if interested in his hobbies, 'Do you ever go to Epping Forest?'

'From time to time,' he said. 'Me and my daughter, we have a favourite place, Barn Hill. We go up there sometimes on clear nights with my telescope. I'm into astronomy. I was there last week in fact.'

'Is Barn Hill anywhere near High Beech?'

'Not far,' said Jack. 'A mile or so away. There's that tea stall at High Beech. We'd sometimes grab a hot drink there before going up the hill.'

'Ever buried a body nearby?'

'Never.' That was his first lie.

'If you had,' went on Nikki, 'that would be a very good reason for a fingerprint of yours to be on the bag Frank Brand was buried in. Don't you agree?'

'It would be a reason,' he said grudgingly, 'but I think the bag was stolen out of my van while I was working at the house.' And then added, almost cheekily, 'That would be the best reason for a fingerprint of mine on the bag.'

Nikki gave him a thin smile.

'Do you have a spade?' she asked. 'One suitable for digging.'

'I don't,' he said. 'I have a couple of shovels, for moving cement and sand. But they are useless for digging.'

'I expect you could get one easily enough,' she said.

'Anyone could,' he retorted. 'From any garden centre.'

He hoped there was not to be much more. The room was hot, stuffy too, with the four of them and no window open. Maybe that was standard practice. Keep you uncomfortable. If so, they'd succeeded. He was worried they might keep him in. Anne had said they could hold you for up to 48 hours before having to charge you. Though there had been no mention of that when they picked him up. Probably it depended on his answers.

'Might I ask a question or two, ma'am?' said Fayyad.

'Go ahead.'

'I saw you with Anne Tucker last night, Jack. Are you having a relationship with her?'

Jack reflected on this. A tricky area. Fayyad had seen them holding hands last night, so no point being in denial, but how much to say?

'We have begun one,' he said carefully. 'I knew her from two years back when I was working in her house. And now that I'm working next door, well, I bumped into her. A couple of days ago. And things developed.' He stopped, reflecting. 'Might be a fling. Might not be. Who can say?'

'Where had you been last night when I saw you?' asked Fayyad.

'We went for a walk,' said Jack. 'Over Wanstead Flats. I was going to show her the stars. You get a good view to the horizon. Only it was cloudy, so hardly any stars for us to see.'

'You say you are close at present,' said Fayyad. 'What about two years ago, when you were working at the house? Did anything happen between you?'

'We had a brief relationship,' he said.

'Why brief?'

Jack shrugged. He had talked this through with Anne. It was bound to be asked. What to say, what not to.

'She was having a relationship with someone else.'

'Who was that?'

'I've forgotten his name,' said Jack. He hadn't but Anne had said it was a useful ruse to blame memory, two years having passed after all, then it could be used whenever needed. 'A tall skinny bloke. A butcher I think.'

'This man?' Nikki slipped a photo across the table.

Jack picked it up and looked at it.

'Yes,' he said, 'that was him.' He passed the photo back. 'He turned up looking for Frank. And when Frank didn't show up, he moved himself into Bessie's place. A nasty bit of work.'

'Bert Long,' said Nikki. 'He was your competition with Anne?'

'Bert. Yeh, that was the name. I left her to him,' said Jack. He waved a brusque hand as if to erase Bert. 'I knew he was messing around with Bessie. And that turned me off Anne.'

'So why did you pick up with her recently?' asked Nikki.

Jack shrugged. 'Time passes. She told me he was a charmer but she was beginning to realise what he was like beneath the charm, when he disappeared. So two years on, I meet her again. She's free, I'm free. Why not?'

'Not because of any joint involvement in murder?'

'Most definitely not,' said Jack. 'You can't leap from a single fingerprint to that.'

That fingerprint, along with his involvement with Anne, were sticking points, he knew. His interviewers knew their importance and took their time moving on, but eventually they got on to Bessie, and he was able, more or less, to stick to the truth. The questioning went on for a further half hour. Jack had the feeling it was fizzling out. He certainly hoped so, tiredness was catching up with him in the heat of the room. A second's loss of sharpness and they'd be on him.

And then abruptly, Nikki said, 'Thank you, Jack. I think we'll terminate this interview. But I'm sure we'll need to talk to you again.'

'Can I go then?' he said, hoping he hadn't got it wrong, and had heard what he thought he had.

'You can go,' she said, 'You're not planning to go on holiday?'

'Most certainly not.'

'Good,' she said with a thin smile. 'You must realise you are a suspect, Jack. You were there at the time, you know the forest, we have a fingerprint of yours on the bag that contained Frank's body, and you know both Bessie and Anne... In fact, you were in a relationship with Anne two years ago and are having one now. We will most certainly need to talk to you again. Please don't leave town. Or we'll have to pull you in.' She looked down at her notes and thought for a second, before adding, 'I'd like you to check in at Forest Gate police station every day, Jack. Just a signature, so we know you're around.' She gave him a broad smile. 'I'm sure that will hardly inconvenience you.'

Chapter 43

The children in the nursery were exasperating, probably no worse than usual but Anne had slept badly. She hadn't just the police to worry about but the wishy washiness of Maggie and David. They would worry and bicker till the cows came home, helping no one. Their precious baby, Lenny, the light of their lives, was having a tantrum while she walked up and down with him over her shoulder.

There was Jack, of course. She could probably trust him. He was smart, not likely to give anything away, but you couldn't be sure. Was he simply too honest? At least, he didn't know anything about Bert's death. That was between herself, Maggie and David. Their shared skulduggery. Stupid Bert, too clever for his own good. He had the key fob and Maggie's phone. He'd planned to leave them at Frank's burial site and call the cops anonymously to implicate the mixed race couple.

Two years ago. Anne shuddered at her recall. She'd had to sleep with him to gain his confidence, go along with his racism. Be his girl. Had no choice when he'd shown her the bloody dress, thinking it was Maggie's, not realising it was Anne's. The one she'd worn when she'd smashed Frank on the head when he tried to rape her in her flat. Luckily or unluckily, Jack had arrived for dinner to find her covered in blood with a body on the sofa.

Too obliging Jack.

The whole house had awoken. Everyone keen to help. Frank carted off to be buried in the forest while she and Bessie cleaned the flat. What a team!

Until Bert showed up two days later.

She thought of her last moments with him. Walking through the forest to the site, where Maggie and David were in hiding, Bert thinking he was oh so clever with his woman by his side. He'd dump the evidence, call the cops, and leave them to arrest the mongrel couple. They'd kissed at the site. All arranged. The signal for David to stab him in the back.

All went to plan.

Smart as far as it went. But burying Bert in the same grave as Frank wasn't smart. They had a whole forest for choice. But who wants to stick around with a body? Especially when they were at Frank's grave, easy digging, so freshly dug.

Last night in the early hours, sleeping, she'd had the image of Bert's face, the cry of betrayal as the knife went in. In reality an incoherent cry, in her half dream, it had become, 'Bitch!' And his taloned hands had gone for her neck. She'd awoken with a shriek, sweating and fearful.

As she walked with Lenny over her shoulder, she was watching Bessie. There, with the children, in her element, in the nursery. She loved talking baby language, reading picture books, probably making up for what was missing in her own childhood. Bessie was a big worry. A fragile young woman, but worse than that, she was both innocent and knew too much. Nothing about Bert's death fortunately, that was strictly between herself, Maggie and David. But Bessie certainly knew what had happened to her father. She'd seen the body when Jack and herself were dragging him out of her flat in that plastic bag. And she was there in the nursery when the house had the powwow about what to do with the corpse. Off went gallant Jack, Maggie and David with the spades, while she and Bessie mopped up blood.

The cops had Bessie in their sights. They'd kindly given her a police constable minder. To comfort her, but more importantly to listen, to encourage loose talk, which would come given time and circumstance. They knew it.

Anne was determined she would not go back to jail. Once in, how do you know you'll ever get out again? She recalled her hopelessness once the door banged shut, found guilty of murdering her husband. Controlled and commanded, surrounded by other hopeless women. A life without purpose. It was almost two years before the real murderer was discovered. An awful time, everything she'd said had been twisted at the trial. And then the jail. Everyone's innocent here, one of the screws had said. That shroud of desperation, days on days of petty, bleak conversations. Shut in, ordered about by hard women with keys.

Anything but go there again.

Bessie was having a tea party with four of the children, almost a child herself, passing round a teapot of cold water, filling the tiny cups, the children getting splashed, giggling. It would be a pity to lose her. She was good with the children, she lived in the house, always willing to do extra hours. Anne never had trouble with her. Not about childminding, that is.

But the pigs were snuffling, their snouts into everything. Removing Bessie would not be easy. It had to have the appearance of an accident. Falling over a cliff or down the stairs, something like that. The fuzz could believe what they liked. It was proof that mattered. The rest was hot air.

Lenny had stopped bawling but she knew from experience that she couldn't put him down just yet, although he was quite a weight. The cops could come in an instant, another interview with Bessie. And that policewoman guardian, due back later, so understanding, leading her on.

Impossible to talk to Bessie now; seven infants were too demanding. You began a conversation and one of them was pulling at you, demanding a drink, or the toilet or another story. All the time, every instant of the day, you had to keep them occupied, encourage them, say nice things about their scribblings. How long could she keep up childminding? Though what else could she do? The money wasn't bad, and she'd been in prison. The fact that she'd been found not guilty after two years, didn't wash with employers. Why take a risk with an inexperienced worker?

And now all this. The cops back. Her turn soon enough. They'd be sure to drag up her prison days, what had happened to her husband.

Today was a drag. She must get some sleep tonight, if not then go to the quack for some pills. She couldn't function like this. If it was just herself, she could tough it out, but it was the others she had to rely on to keep their mouths shut.

There was a sudden racket amongst Bessie's group. Two boys were hitting each other and yelling. She put Lenny in the playpen. He started bawling. Well, he'd have to bawl, she could only manage one fight at a time.

Chapter 44

Fayyad offered Jack a lift back from the police station as he was going up to Stratford. Jack hesitated, unsure whether to accept as he'd had more than enough of cops. But Fayyad gave a tap on the nose, and Jack realised Fayyad might have something useful to say.

When they were in the car and on their way, Fayyad said, 'She wanted to hold you, Jack.'

'What, on a single fingerprint?'

'People have been convicted for less,' said Fayyad. 'The boss thought to hold you for 48 hours, and see what we could get out of you.'

'I've told you everything,' he said.

'I said you couldn't have done it. It wasn't in your nature.' He turned down Upton Lane, following behind a 325 bus. 'I hope I was right.'

'You were right,' said Jack. 'Thanks, mate. I'd hate two days in the nick.'

'The food's not too good,' said Fayyad with a grin. 'I thought she was being hasty. Not that I said that to her. I said what a good chap you were. I said it wouldn't look good at a press conference, especially if we had to release you.'

'That's all I need, the papers banging on the door,' retorted Jack.

'They can be a pain,' said Fayyad. 'Turn over your life just to fill a quiet day. And then we'd get in trouble for stirring it up. Anyway, the boss took it on board.'

'Thanks for sparing me that.' He was sweating, genuinely thankful but at the same time eager to get away from his friend. Whatever else he was, Fayyad was a cop.

'It wasn't simply the fingerprint, important though it was,' said Fayyad, 'but your involvement with Anne Tucker. You know she was up for murder?'

'Found not guilty after two years,' said Jack.

'There's some who wonder about that,' said Fayyad, as they passed the Spotted Dog, still boarded up after ten years and falling to pieces. Henry the VIII's hunting lodge. It had been a thriving pub in his drinking days. And now looking the way he felt.

'Anne was innocent,' said Jack. 'The culprit confessed.'

'There's people who'll confess to anything,' said Fayyad turning on to Ham Park Road.

'You've got cynical in your old age.'

'It's the people I mix with, Jack. I don't believe anyone about anything.'

'Me included?'

Fayyad shrugged. 'You're hanging on by a hair, mate. If anything else turns up, you heard the boss, she'll pick you up. And won't listen to anything I've got to say.'

The car pulled up on the side of the road by the park railings.

Jack said, 'Thanks for the lift, Fayyad. And for the word. I appreciate it. But I swear, I'm clean.'

What else could he say? Almost clean, half clean. They shook hands and Jack got out of the car. He took a deep breath, free at last. He waited for Fayyad to leave and then crossed the road to the house. Suddenly aware that he was hungry. Nerves had held back the pangs while in the police station. But he'd left Lynn's just before their tea break in the morning, and it was now well into the afternoon.

He rang the bell. Lynn answered.

'How did it go?' she said as he came in.

'I'm still a free man,' he said. 'Only just.' He attempted to laugh that off. 'Information only. I was working next door when Bessie's dad disappeared. I'm not in the running.'

She eyed him quizzically. 'I would have thought everyone is at this point. Besides, I know you and Anne have some secrets.'

Oh not that again, he thought.

'We all have secrets,' he said. 'Let's do some work.'

'Have you had any lunch?'

'That's why they let me out,' he said with a laugh. 'Kept me any longer, then they'd have to feed me.'

'I'll make you a quick bite,' she said.

They went into the kitchen. She began getting food from the fridge.

'Nick's gone,' she said.

Jack could barely think who he was, so preoccupied with his own circumstances. Then remembering, the youngster yesterday that the row had been about. The one Lynn and Paul went to the cop shop with. He'd got it. Paul's son.

'Gone where?' he said.

She shrugged. 'Don't know. I went up to his room to offer him some comfort after yesterday and found a note. He wrote that he couldn't stand it here, didn't want to get ankled, and he's going away for a while.'

'Ankled?'

'A drug dealer threatened to shoot him through the ankle if he didn't pay what he owed.' She gave a wry smile. 'Charming people he got in with. Totally out of his depth. Poor kid.' She shook her head wistfully. 'I hope he can manage wherever he's going. I've put a couple of hundred into his bank account.' She placed cheese and salad on the table followed by plates. 'You're not the only one to be visiting the police station. It's all the rage round here. Me, Paul and Nick yesterday. I saw Bessie there, all about her father. Talk about ring a ring of roses. You know Bessie. And where does Anne come into it?'

He held up his hands to fend her off. 'Please, I've had one inquisition today. And that was way too much. Can we just eat and talk about the weather?'

She put out bread and margarine. 'I've eaten,' she said. 'You fill up. I'll make us tea.'

'Make it coffee,' said Jack. 'I need to keep awake.'

She didn't ask why. And they talked about the work. Jack was blinking rapidly, almost nodding off as he ate. He drank two cups of black coffee and washed himself in the downstairs toilet, splashing copious cold water on his face, rubbing his eyelids.

They went back to work. He was surprised to see Lynn had already cut out a couple of make-up pieces of board.

'Pretty good,' he said when he put them in place. 'You're getting the hang of this.'

'I thought I'd have a go myself,' she said. 'I saw how you did it yesterday. And I figured if I made a botch of it, we had enough spare for you to do it.'

He thought for a moment, then said, 'Why don't you carry on. Nail those bits of board on, then cut out the rest of the make-up pieces. And I can get on with putting the lock in.'

'You're letting the apprentice free on her own?' she said beaming, plainly happy with his encouragement.

'That's the way it's done,' he said. 'You've picked it up quickly. So go ahead.'

His boost was genuinely meant, but had the added advantage that they'd work separately, too far apart to chatter. Better for the work, better for his head. He took the tools he needed into the hallway as her phone rang. Jack was curious who it was. Could be anyone. Nick maybe. Or someone he didn't know.

He couldn't hear, he was out in the hallway and she'd gone to the far end of the room. He caught the odd word, but not enough to make any sense of it. He was getting as nosy as a cop. Work, the only therapy. He marked up where to put the lock. Satisfied, he drilled a hole for the barrel, and had just completed it, when he saw her standing by him.

'Paul's in hospital,' she said. 'Newham General.'

'What's happened to him?'

'I'm a bit confused,' she said. 'I didn't speak to him but to a nurse. Seems he was out running in the park and someone shot him through the ankle with a crossbow bolt.'

Jack gasped. 'That must be painful.'

'I reckon it was meant for Nick,' she said. 'Don't you?'

'Seems a mighty coincidence otherwise,' he said. 'Poor guy. Are you going to visit him?'

She gave a short laugh. 'Of course not. I might go to his funeral. But unfortunately, it's not life threatening.'

'I'll go,' he said. 'And give him your love.'

'He'll know you're lying.'

Lynn returned to her work.

Chapter 45

The dividing wall was finished, the lock was in on the door of the room that they now called the new room. A bolt was in place at the top of the door, on the inside. Filler had been squirted into cracks. Jack and Lynn went out into the hallway and through the door into the new room.

Lynn turned about, enchanted, like a child taken into a newly decorated bedroom. Jack was gratified at her pleasure. The new wall was a divider. But did it keep out sound? He didn't remind her.

'The dining table will have to go,' she said. The wings had been folded down. 'Could go in the hallway. Be a sort of shelf to put hats and gloves on. These chairs, I don't need more than a couple here. The other two can go somewhere or other. I've got an admiral's chair in my bedroom. I'll bring that down. I could do with a small table to work on.' She went to the French windows. 'I love this light. That's Clapton Football Club beyond the back fence. We hear the matches on Saturday, always feel I should go one day. Would you like to come?'

'Maybe.'

'Not while you're with Anne. I understand.' She said this with a light laugh and continued planning her room. 'It's all right without an overhead light. The two side lights will be enough. And I've got a standard lamp I could bring down. Some shelving there, I think.' She turned to Jack. 'I'd like to put that up myself, if you don't mind.'

'I charge commission for my apprentices,' he said.

'I haven't signed the papers,' she said flippantly. Her eyes lit up as she had a sudden thought. 'Let's try it out for sound. You go out and put his TV on.'

Jack left her. Well, she had to get to it sooner or later. This would be the test. Did the wall work as more than a separator? With double layers of soundproof boards both sides and rock wool in the middle; was it enough? Lynn was elated now. Would she be in a minute?

Silence was golden.

He went in the old room. Lynn had done a good job putting in the make up pieces in the wall this side. She'd cut them neatly, and nailed them in place. Not that it was difficult work. A matter of marking up, not being afraid of tools and materials. Just the decorating tomorrow.

Jack turned on the TV. A cooking show was on. Plenty of chat and shouting. He turned up the volume. And up more. He waited for her response.

He called, 'Can you hear anything, Lynn?'

And when she didn't reply, he turned off the TV and went back to the new room.

'Why didn't you turn it on?' she said. 'I've been waiting.'

'I did,' he said, breaking into the widest grin. 'I had it on full volume.'

'Liar!'

'I swear to you, I had it on full volume.'

'Not possible. I couldn't hear a thing. Stay here.' She went out, closing the door on him.

He knew what she was going to do. Turn it on herself and come back. Fine. Let her prove it. He waited, looking about the space in the meantime. It was a pleasant room, and of course in summer she could have the French windows open, spread out on to the terrace. But would it really make much difference to her and Paul's life?

She came back in. As the door opened, he could just hear the TV. Gone when she closed it.

'It works, Jack!' she exclaimed with a leap. 'We did it.'

She threw her arms round him and kissed him on the mouth. Jack was caught unawares, hesitated for a second and then grasped her back, their bodies pressed together, lips sucking and melding. They sank to the carpet, she pulling out his shirt, his hand massaging the round of her belly.

'One moment,' she murmured, a finger on his lips.

She rose and went to the door. And slipped the top bolt across.

Chapter 46

She was sawing through one of the large eyehooks with a hacksaw while Tim watched nervously. Lynn was manic, she had her new room, her brother was in hospital. The house was hers. Claim it!

The eyehook fell in half, the closed lock dangled uselessly. She opened the box room door. There was just a few files inside, along with two cardboard boxes. Why on earth did Paul need all this space? To spite her, of course.

'Dump it all in his room,' she said.

'Are you sure?'

'He's in hospital,' she said, a hand on Tim's shoulder. 'Been ankled. Could easily be there a week or more. When he gets back he'll be in plaster. I don't think you'll have to worry about my brother.'

They carried the files and boxes into Paul's bedroom. The room smelt of sweat and unwashed sheets. Scattered around were underwear, socks, and running shorts. The double bed was unmade, the desk a pile of papers, almost covering a laptop.

'I don't know how he works here,' she said. 'Does he never open a window? He throws things everywhere. Like a kid.'

She wrinkled her nose in distaste at the odour, jealous though of his en suite bathroom. Why did he have it and not her? He didn't have the chore of waiting for Dawn and Nick to finish. He could ignore their mess.

Forget him. Enjoy his time in hospital! She was ebullient, her brother out of her life for however long. She had a new room. It was quiet, his TV dumb. She hadn't planned the escapade with Jack. It had happened. She'd been overjoyed at her new space and ecstatically threw her arms round him.

And he had welcomed them. What would Anne make of that? she thought smugly.

Her friend, was she a friend? had a hold on him, but Lynn was sure she could get him away. Go on his next job with him. Work for nothing for a while, for the training. Learn to be a builder. And maybe sex thrown in. Her teacher had been pleased with her work. So she'd given him an apple.

'Let's get your mattress in,' she said to Tim.

'Are you sure, Lynn?'

Any other time she might have told him off, but she was too over the moon. And wanted to share her mood. Tim's insecurity was understandable, considering how Paul had railed at him. He'd been hiding from him ever since. Going to the kitchen only when he was out, looking warily out of her bedroom when he had to go to the toilet.

'Treat it like a holiday,' she said. 'And when Paul comes back, he'll be hobbling. He won't be in much of a state to throw anyone out. In the meantime, reclaim the space, honey.'

They laid out the mattress in the box room, along with the duvet and pillow. Then the computer and monitor from the attic. She helped him make the bed with clean sheets and pillowcase. Tim brought his few things from her room and laid them out.

She looked at the space. It was hardly a room, and when you thought, Nick's was vacant, though he could be back any day, so it wouldn't do to put Tim in there.

As if he read her thoughts, Tim said, 'I got a text from Nick. He says thanks for the money.'

'Do you know where he is?'

'No. He says he stayed in a hotel last night.'

'He'll have to get a job wherever he is,' she said. 'I don't mind subsidising him for a week or two, but after that he'll have to look after himself. Or come home.' She reflected a second. 'It might do him good being away. Get him off drugs. No one to bankroll him.' She considered for a second. 'As long as he doesn't start stealing, or become a rent boy. I do hope he can stand on his own feet. Let's say it's a test.'

'He's scared,' said Tim.

'Did you tell him they'd ankled his dad?'

'I didn't think that would help.'

She nodded, not knowing what to make of it herself. Could Nick ride it, or would he come running back? Tim was staring at her, waiting for her to decide what to do. She was held by his eyes; she could look at them all day, the deep brown. And such beautiful lashes. Any girl would be jealous. Best not tell him, she thought, young men not finding that a compliment.

'Come and see my new room,' she said. 'Oh wait a minute. Let's not waste a journey. We'll take some things down with us.'

They went into her bedroom, tidier now with Tim's mattress gone, though she hadn't minded him sleeping on the floor. She felt about him almost like a favourite pet dog. One that she wanted to stroke and cuddle, though she couldn't do too much of that. Or he'd get the wrong idea.

'I'll take the admiral's chair. You carry the standard lamp.'

Chapter 47

When Jack arrived home, delayed by impromptu sex, Mia was already there. She was doing her homework, which he was quite grateful for as it gave him time to reflect. He automatically said a few of the usual things parents said when kids come home from school, how was your day and such like. He didn't react to her abrupt answers but took them gratefully. He didn't want to talk either. And had a shower. As he washed, he thought of what had happened that day. The work had gone well. Lynn was a good worker, she'd picked things up so quickly. The sex had been an utter surprise. Out of her joy at the room, his praise of her, genuine enough. As for himself, he'd simply let it happen. Twenty minutes' forgetfulness. No police, no body in the forest, swept away on a crest of emotion. Quite where it left him, he was unsure. Washed up on a bank, but where?

There wasn't much left to do at Lynn's. A little tidying up, the decorating which she could do herself, but she hadn't volunteered to do it, wanting him back for another day he surmised. As a teacher, as a lover perhaps.

Was this smart? He and Anne had just got talking. Needed each other. Had he jeopardised this? Would Lynn tell her? Then what might Anne do? But then Anne needed him too. Him and her against a couple. He was a suspect, Fayyad had said they were going to hold him but for his intervention. Thank God he'd survived that round of questioning. They'd be back. He needed Anne. He didn't need Lynn, at least not to keep him out of jail.

He dried himself and dressed. He'd told Lynn that he'd go to the hospital, not that she cared whether he went or not. He would, but first needed to go through his emails and answer any that might mean work. For half an hour he busied himself on work related communications. There was a phone message on his landline that could mean a job. He phoned but there was no one there, so he left a message. That was the pain of having lost his phone; he couldn't answer at once, that meant chasing them, often fruitlessly as they'd gone elsewhere. His phone company had promised a phone with the old number but it could take ten days. Ten days! Nothing he could do, but swear and wait.

Chores done, he said to Mia, 'How much more work have you got?'

'I must do this science,' she said without looking up from her laptop. 'I'm late with it already.'

'Can you work in a hospital?'

She turned to him, puzzled. 'Why?'

'Someone I know had a crossbow bolt shot into his ankle.'

'Really?'

'Really. Let's go. We'll find you somewhere quiet to work, while I visit him. Then we'll get a pizza.'

Chapter 48

Paul was in the orthopaedic building at the far end of Newham General. Jack left Mia in a lounge area. There were a few patients there, a couple in wheelchairs and another two on crutches. A TV was on but no one was watching. Mia wanted to turn it off but it didn't seem possible without a remote, as it was high up on a shelf.

'Won't be too long,' he said, and went to search for Paul.

He asked at a nurses' station. When he told the woman he was looking for the man who'd had a crossbow bolt through his ankle, she immediately knew who Jack referred to. And gave him directions.

Paul had his own room. Jack wondered how this was decided. Who went on to a ward, who got a room. Maybe it was simply the luck of what was available. He found Paul in bed, sitting up, pillows behind him, morose.

'What a hell of a day!' he greeted Jack.

Jack had picked up some grapes at the hospital shop. 'Where shall I leave these?'

'Take 'em home. Buggered if I want them.'

Jack took a seat by the bed.

'I gather you're not happy,' he said.

'Would you be?' retorted Paul. 'Some bastard comes out of the bushes, floors me, and shoots a bolt through my ankle. The cops wanted to know whether he was black or white. In a balaclava, I told them. They said what colour were his hands.' He threw up his arms in exasperation. 'I wasn't looking at his hands, Jack.'

'Why did he pick on you?'

'Karma,' he spat. 'The cops reckon he was after my son, saw me leave the house. I don't know. Mistaken identity.' He blew out his cheeks. 'Maybe he just had a spare bolt.'

'I'm very sorry,' said Jack. 'It's an awful thing to happen.'

'Awful? Horrendous!' Paul lifted the duvet off the injured leg, showing the ankle, most of the foot, and half the calf, covered in plaster. 'I've got to have an operation in a week. They'll put in a pin or six. The doctor says I'll be walking with a limp for the rest of my life. I'm a cripple.' He clapped his hands to his head. 'I'll be hobbling on a stick. Can you imagine?'

Jack didn't know what to say that wouldn't be rejected.

'I'm so sorry,' he said. 'It's an awful thing to happen.' Aware that he was repeating himself, but he had no advice. Maybe he shouldn't have come. He was worse than useless.

'It means I can't run anymore. Finished. This is not just an injury, it's done for me. The end of my running days. I am so sick and miserable. You can't imagine how I'm feeling.' Paul closed his eyes, a tear seeped through the lids. 'I was so fit. I was going to get close to three hours for the London Marathon, I know it. I was the fastest of the Wanstead Flats Trotters. And now? Kaput. Busted. What the hell am I going to do?'

Jack was at no less of a loss, but managed, 'There are other things in life than running.'

'Not for me, Jack.' He was sniffing, dabbing his eyes. 'Excuse me blubbing, but how can anyone understand?' He bit his lip. 'Maybe you can. One ex-boozer to another.' He stared at Jack as if daring him not to. 'Running got me off alcohol. Running kept me off alcohol. The routine, the goals. It's my religion. I don't give a monkey's toss about my job, if the truth be told.' He flapped a dismissive hand. 'I'm a wage slave. If they fired me tomorrow, no one would notice. The agency would send in another clone.' He shook a fist. 'The only time I'm alive is when I'm running. Then I have hope, I have goals.' He stopped, burnt out. 'I shall be walking with a limp. With a stick, like a crabby pensioner off to the chemist to collect his medicine. Look at me, Jack. I sound like one already.'

'It's too soon,' said Jack. 'You need to find something else to do. Like painting or gardening.'

'I could join a flaming choir, couldn't I? Do flower arranging at the church. Join a book group. Collect fountain pens...' He shook his head. 'My sister will love this. She'll be leaping with joy. Paul has got his comeuppance.' He stopped, a thought. 'You know what? She'll take over the house. Get that mixed race kid in. And God knows who else she'll have in.' He swung out of bed with his good leg. 'I am damned if I'll let her.' He turned to Jack. 'Will you give me a lift home?'

'You can't leave,' exclaimed Jack.

'I poxing well can. I'm not letting her have the house.'

'You need to be in bed, Paul. You need to recover.'

'I can recover at home. My leg's in plaster, so what else can they do for me? Will you give me a lift, Jack? Or shall I call a taxi?'

Jack could see Paul was going to leave with or without him. He could walk away and let him do it himself. He watched Paul trying to get dressed. It was painful but the man was determined; he was going to go home, one way or another.

He helped Paul to dress, giving up trying to persuade him to stay. Jack disliked hospitals himself, though he was sure this was too early for Paul to go. But it was obvious he wasn't in the mood to listen, sense or not. Paul had decided.

Once dressed, Paul pointed out the wheelchair near the door. Jack brought it over and Paul hobbled in.

'Wheel me out,' said Paul. 'Give me the crutches. I'll need them at home.'

Jack put the crutches on Paul's lap and wheeled him past the nurses' station. The woman on duty protested. Paul told her this wasn't a prison and he was leaving. She continued protesting. He told her he was a free born Englishman and she couldn't hold him. She told him he was a fool. He said he had every right to be a fool. And he was leaving. The nurse gave up, and gave him a form to sign saying the hospital wasn't responsible. Paul signed it.

On the way down the corridor, Jack picked up Mia. And wheeled Paul on to the car park. At the van, Jack helped Paul into the front seat. Jack had been about to wheel the chair back, but Paul insisted they keep it.

'Get me out of here!' Paul ordered. 'They won't chase us in a police car.'

Jack drove off. It was the least of his crimes.

Mia, in the middle, said, 'Should you really be leaving hospital?'

'Yes,' Paul snapped.

Mia said nothing more all the way to Paul's house. There, Jack wheeled him to the steps. Paul gave him the keys. Jack opened the front door. Then he helped Paul up the steps, then went back for the wheelchair. Mia followed holding the crutches.

Jack wheeled him along the hallway to the front room. Paul said he wanted to go in there. Jack wheeled him in. Mia came in with the crutches. Jack stripped off the decorating sheets and put them into a corner.

'God! Look at that bloody wall she's had built. This room feels like a dungeon. Half a room. Why ever did I agree? Do I need a drink!' He turned to Jack, and pleaded. 'You wouldn't like to get me a bottle of whisky.'

'You're asking the wrong person.'

'I just want to get blotto. Absolutely out of my skull. I've had enough of this damned world. It's a shit hole. No one'll miss me. No one cares. Look at this leg. I'm going to be limping for the rest of my days. Do me a favour and push me over a cliff. Save me the hassle of living.'

From the kitchen, Jack brought in some bread and cheese, some fruit, a jug of water and a glass. He washed the grapes he'd brought from the hospital. Paul was driving him crackers. He wished he'd never gone to visit him. The man was misery on wheels.

As soon as they decently could, Jack and Mia left.

Chapter 49

Detective Constable Hayley Amis and Bessie were in Bessie's flat. Hayley had just made a cup of tea which they were drinking at the kitchen table. She'd brought some chocolate digestive biscuits which she put out on a plate for them to munch. She noted that she was eating more than Bessie. Maybe she'd let her choose the biscuits next time. Hayley was in navy blue trousers and a light blue denim shirt. Her outdoor, half length black coat was on the back of the chair.

They'd been talking about Bessie's day at the nursery. Hayley was keen to get off the subject as her boss had no interest in the topic. Nor had Hayley, but she wanted Bessie to talk. Chatter away about anything. But she'd been ordered to get a move on. Or as DCI Nikki Martin put it pithily: 'You're not a paid companion.' Which got a laugh at this morning's High Beech meeting.

'I have to win her confidence, ma'am,' she said in her own defence. But was aware she was a cost, and she had to bring results. The public rebuke had stung and dominated her thoughts. Maybe a matter she and Bessie had talked about yesterday should be taken more seriously. She should be less dismissive of her silliness. There might be something in it. Or maybe she should request to be taken off this posting, and do something useful.

Hayley said, 'You know you told me you did black magic when your father died.'

'It was the magic that killed him,' said Bessie.

That's what Bessie had said yesterday, and Hayley had brushed it aside. Today, she'd follow it.

'Did you cast a spell?' she said.

'Me and Nancy did. She was the old lady that died. I really liked her.' Bessie stopped and stared at Hayley. 'It's not a crime to cast a spell, is it?'

'No, it's not.'

'Even if it kills someone?'

'Do you really think your spell killed your father?'

'Yes.' Bessie was scratching the wooden surface of the table with a fingernail. 'Lots of people don't believe in black magic but it shouldn't be underestimated.'

This was more or less where they'd got to last time. Bessie had killed her father with black magic. How could she tell that to her boss unless there was substance to it? Passing on such a fanciful notion would make her look stupid. Of course, Bessie wanted her persecutor dead. And might use any superstitious nonsense on the planet to that end. But the fact that it had worked this time was coincidence. Or so she'd thought yesterday. Maybe yes, maybe no. Most likely no, but there could be some truth hidden in the mumbo jumbo. As it was, everyone wondered what she was doing, nursemaiding Bessie. She needed to do more than buy biscuits.

'Your spell must have had words,' said Hayley.

'Yes, it did.'

'Can you tell me the words?'

Bessie shook her head vehemently. 'No. You must never tell the words to anyone. Or you'll be cursed.'

'Someone must've have told you them though.'

'A witch. She can tell. She has the powers, she has the permission. I don't have it. I can only be given it temporarily in the spell she grants me.'

'I see,' said Hayley, though she didn't; it was all gibberish to her. This was what had stopped her last time. So pursue it; see if there's more than wishful thinking to it. 'You surely had to do something too, Bessie. Like dance or throw things into a cauldron. Things like that.'

'I had to gather things,' said Bessie. 'I can't tell you what. I'm not being difficult but it's a condition. And put them in a box. And leave the box under my father's bed for a whole night.'

'Why was that?'

'So he would infuse the vapours.'

'I see,' though she didn't. 'What are the vapours?'

Bessie looked at her as if she were a fool. 'The magic of course. The potency of the curse. The vapours soak into the soul of the victim.'

She'd taken on the language, thought Hayley. It's like a religion.

'And was that the end of it?' she asked. 'Once the soul was soaked in the vapours. Had you anything else to do?'

'We had to bury the box and contents in the garden under the moon.'

'And you did?'

'We did. Me and Nancy. She used to live on the floor under mine. Died last year. But I don't think it was anything to do with the black magic. She was old.'

'How do you know the black magic worked?'

Bessie rolled her eyes. 'It killed Dad, didn't it?'

'How do you know it did?'

'I saw him dead. With my own eyes.' She tapped her eyebrow. 'And although Anne said she did it, she didn't. And although Jack said that I didn't, I did. I made the spell, I did the ritual with Nancy. They had no choice. They had to go along with the magic. They were its unwitting ministers. '

Hayley wondered at the lingo, probably straight off a website in mystical cyberspace.

'You say Anne and Jack had no choice?'

'None at all. They might think they did, but they were the playthings of the spirits. Made to do what they did.'

'Did they bury him?'

'The spirits made them.'

'Made them what?'

'Bury him.'

Hayley was getting frustrated. She had two names, but anything else Bessie had said was nothing that the girl couldn't have learnt from the story in the papers. It would sound potty under cross examination. Boxes buried under the moon, incantations. Defence counsel would ask whether a black cat and broomsticks were involved.

'So Anne was made to kill him,' Hayley reiterated, hoping she would get something extra. Real confirmation of involvement. 'And Jack was made to help her.'

'It's not their fault,' said Bessie. 'You must understand that. It's all mine. I did the spell. You see, he tried to rape her. He had to. The spell was in him. She hit him on the head with a vase. She had to. Jack came, and had to help her. They weren't in control. It was the working of the magic.'

'I understand,' said Hayley. 'It was the magic that killed him. They were merely instruments. They were used by the forces of black magic.'

'Have you done black magic?' said Bessie, looking at her family liaison officer in wonderment.

'I haven't, Bessie. I think it's too strong. There would have to be some real wickedness for me to try it.'

'My father was wicked,' said Bessie. 'He had to be stopped. I'm sorry I used Anne and Jack, but I had to stop him. You do understand, don't you, Hayley?'

'Of course, I do. Your father tried to rape Anne and she hit him on the head with a vase. She didn't have any choice in the matter. And then Jack came and he didn't have any choice. And he took the body to Epping Forest.'

'Not by himself.'

'With Anne?'

'No, Anne stayed here with me. Maggie and David, they were taken over by the spell too. The whole house was infused. And they went with Jack. People don't understand how powerful black magic is. You mustn't meddle with it lightly.'

'I see that,' said Hayley. She had been recording the conversation, though whether anyone would make head or tail of it was another matter. But she felt she had something substantial. 'Shall I make us some scrambled eggs?' she said brightly.

Chapter 50

Anne had waited two days for them to come. They'd taken in Bessie for questioning and she now had that cop coming to see her all the time. Jack had had the third degree. All day Anne had meant to talk to him, see if they'd got anything out of him, but it was such a tiring day, Jack had lost his phone and she'd have to leave the nursery to see him, and what with one thing and another, she hadn't got round to speaking to him before they'd come for her.

All she could do was look after herself. Hope Jack, and especially Bessie, had kept their wits about them.

They were in a bare interview room, containing a table and chairs, and a video camera, just below ceiling level and focused on her. The window was frosted glass, letting in a ghostly light from an outside world that was rumoured to exist. That Asian cop again, the one who'd been around the house on and off, and his boss. It was too reminiscent of the time she'd been pulled in for the murder of her husband. Six years ago. A lifetime. Yesterday. A room just like this one. Oh that vicious cop! He still gave her nightmares.

The questioning began with routine stuff, DS Nikki Martin doing most of it. Who Anne was, what she did. How long she'd lived in the house. Then it came.

'You were arrested six years ago for murdering your husband,' said Nikki.

'An incompetent investigation,' exclaimed Anne. 'They were determined to get me, no matter what.'

'You did two years for it.'

'As if I could forget,' said Anne with mock nonchalance. 'I might still be there, protesting my innocence to the screws and all those crazy banged up women. If someone hadn't talked.'

'Lucky.'

'Two years inside, lucky? I don't know what your life is like, but that doesn't count as luck in my book.'

'Some say you were lucky,' pressed Nikki. 'To get out at all. Some say you did it and got off on the appeal. Guilty as sin. Lucky.'

'You lot never admit you're wrong, do you?'

'We don't like it when murderers get off.'

'I am not a murderer. I didn't get off. If you want to know why I hate cops, it's for this very reason. It was a botched investigation. Once you had me in the frame, you were determined I would get done. And now, I'm out, found innocent on appeal, six years later you're still trying to stick it on me.' She stopped, breathing deeply, fingers rapping on the table. 'If I'd have known this was going to be a retrial, I'd have brought a lawyer. I will not answer any questions about my conviction. I was found innocent on appeal. End of. What else do you want to ask me?'

She had silenced them. It was her intention. Whatever it was, this was not going to be a run through of Malcolm's murder. She still had some rights. Do they never let go?

'How long did you know Frank Brand?'

She gave a grim smile. The cow had got the message.

'About eighteen months,' she said. 'Eighteen months too long. He was a complete bastard. He made a slave of his daughter. A beast. I suspected incest at the time...'

'Why didn't you tell anyone?'

'What!' exclaimed Anne. 'And get involved with you lot. Even now you won't let me forget.'

DS Martin stared at her, Anne stared back. She would not be pushed around, or goaded either. They'd deliberately made her angry, so something might slip out. Sneaky. She half admired the technique.

'What do you know about Frank's disappearance?'

Anne shrugged. 'Nothing. One day he was there, then he wasn't. I wondered of course, we all did. His daughter worked for me, so of course we talked about it. But what had actually happened to him, I hadn't the slightest idea.'

The door opened and Hayley entered. DS Martin turned in irritation at the interruption. Hayley crossed to her chief and whispered something in her ear. The two went outside, leaving Fayyad as Anne's minder.

'Don't stitch me up,' she said.

'That's not our intention,' said Fayyad. 'We want the truth.'

'Whose?' She smiled wryly. 'Yours or mine?'

'There's only one truth,' he said. 'And we'll find it.'

'Well, stitch up someone else this time.'

The two women returned. Hayley took her boss's place, Nikki sat to the left of her, Fayyad on the right stayed put. Anne assumed the younger woman was going to have a go at her. Catch her off guard with some revelation. But she'd be a match for them.

'For the record,' said Hayley to camera, 'I am Detective Constable Hayley Amis. Just arrived in the interview room.' She turned to Anne. 'I think you know me, Anne.'

'You've been chaperoning Bessie, the last couple of days.'

'I have. It's a difficult time for her. Finding her father's body and the awful memories it brings back. I am her family liaison officer.'

And chief snitch, thought Anne.

'Did Frank attempt to rape you?' said Hayley.

That caught her unawares. Tread carefully. She must've got it from Bessie.

'No,' she said. 'Wherever did you get that from?'

'And did you then hit him on the head with a vase?'

'Me?' She acted bewildered. 'Are you accusing me of killing Frank?'

'I am,' said Hayley. 'He was attempting to rape you, so you grabbed the nearest thing handy and smashed him on the head with it.'

'Fiction. Total fiction.' She swished her hands to dismiss the assertion.

'Did you then call in Jack Bell to help you get rid of the body?'

Anne caught her breath. It had to be Bessie. She'd been talking to her minder. Stay focused. It was just Bessie's word, and Anne knew she could be very muddled.

'All nonsense. Are you trying to fit me up again?'

'You had an affair with Jack Bell at the time?'

'The briefest imaginable. Hardly more than a one night stand.'

'Perhaps because of your killing of Frank Brand, he wanted to get away from you. Don't you agree?'

'What am I to say to this story she's making up?' she exclaimed, looking to Fayyad and Nikki as if they would confirm how hopeless were Hayley's charges.

'Jack and your upstairs neighbours, Maggie and David,' went on Hayley, 'ferried the body to Epping Forest and buried it there. Do you agree?'

It had to be Bessie. The woman had been with her so much of her free time and had wormed the essence out of her. She must keep her nerve. Bessie was only one person. There were four of them to deny it.

'You're talking rubbish,' she said disparagingly. 'You've been listening to Bessie. She makes things up, you know. Did she tell you about the black magic? Can't tell fact from fiction half the time. I'd be wary of hanging around her too much.'

'Thank you for the advice,' said Hayley. She returned to her theme. 'There would be a lot of blood, when you smash someone on the head with a vase. And broken glass too. Don't you think?'

'If you say so.'

'So, while Jack, Maggie and David went to the forest, you and Bessie cleared away the evidence.'

'I have never heard so much codswallop.' She appealed to Nikki. 'Are you going to simply let her go on with this travesty? Without a shred of evidence. Please control your junior.'

'I have a nose for these things,' said Nikki, peering at Anne through narrowed lids. 'Been in this game long enough. Too long some might say. And I'm bothered by the fact that a woman, implicated in a murder six years ago, is involved in two murders that happened two years ago. Of course, lightning can strike twice in the same place. Unlikely, but one mustn't rule it out.'

'I think you've already made up your mind,' said Anne bitterly. 'I know how you lot work.'

'You're not under arrest, Anne. Yet. Though far from cleared,' said Nikki. 'We need further evidence as yet. But let me try this on you. We found a chip of blue glass embedded in Frank's skull. What do you think that might be?'

'You tell me.'

'We think it's from a vase that someone hit him with. You perhaps?'

'No.'

'We think it might well be. But we'll keep an open mind, Anne, while we do our searches and conduct our interviews.' She turned to her colleagues. 'I think we'll leave questions on Frank Brand for the time being. And move on to the other corpse in the forest. Bert Long.'

PART FOUR:
BEHIND THE WALL

Chapter 51

Jack had a better night of sleep. It had helped that it had been a busy evening. And Mia was there. All that business with Paul had given them plenty to discuss. Mia had said he was more miserable than Eeyore. The simile had escaped him and she had to remind him who Eeyore was.

'The donkey in Winnie the Pooh,' she'd said. 'He never expects any presents or anyone to help him anytime ever. Everything is awful for Eeyore, and he knows it won't get any better. In fact, it will get a lot worse.'

Yes, that was Paul alright, depression on legs, or rather on crutches. Discussing someone else's bad fortune had kept his mind off his own. Given them a topic to thrash about. She'd been fascinated about Paul's running.

'He was never going to win the London Marathon,' she'd said. 'Come about 500th if he was lucky.'

'That's pretty good,' he'd said.

'What, to come 500th? How is that good?'

'It's better than coming 35 thousandth,' he'd said, but wasn't sure what he was defending. 'Do you only enter if you're going to win?'

'I can see entering, running all that way and collecting for charity,' she'd said. 'But it's the making something big of it, like he was crossing Africa on foot. The London Marathon has been done millions of times. Alright, run it if you have to. But don't make it your life.'

'He's too competitive,' he'd said. And realised he had a handle on Paul. All his life was a competition. The London Marathon, the battle with his sister, work most likely. He wanted to be a winner, and only a winner. But he wasn't. There weren't many ways to deal with that. The bottle?

Hardly, that was simply a refusal to acknowledge you weren't a winner.

Or hand back your number. And stop competing.

But Paul hadn't handed it back. His number had been snatched from him and torn up. He'd had a dream, count it as silly, meaningless in the scheme of things. What isn't, when you look up at the stars? Just time on a watch. Smashed by a crossbow bolt.

Don't judge, said Alcohol Halt. Mia was a fierce judge. The preserve of youth. But Jack could judge too easily himself. He had no right to. Running was Paul's way out of alcoholism. Desperate, you might say, stupid. But you need purpose in life. Jack had found it in work, in astronomy, in his relationship with Mia, but knew too his fragility. Too aware of how it could be lost, now the bodies had surfaced.

Jack and Mia left the house together. She to go to school, him to work. He offered her a lift but she said it was only a ten minute walk, and he'd get stuck in traffic. So they parted.

Jack drove to Lynn's, arriving almost dead on 8 am. He hoped Paul would be feeling better after a night's reflection. At home again, getting beyond 'Why me?' Or would he still be Eeyore?

Lynn opened up for him. She gave him a welcoming smile and a kiss on the cheek. She still had yesterday's bounce, that had led to their lovemaking. Today was tomorrow. A job to finish off and who knows what to follow.

She was wearing tight jeans and a check shirt, hair light and curly, as if coming out of a cowboy musical. Quite unsuitable clothing. What she'd been wearing yesterday was fine, old clothing. Maybe she didn't intend doing much today. Not that there was much to do.

They went into the sitting room, well, Paul's half of the sitting room. Jack expected to see him there in the wheelchair. But he wasn't, nor the wheelchair. There were his things on the sofa, a half eaten sandwich, an apple core. An ominous smell of whisky.

'Where's Paul?' he said.

She shrugged. 'I don't know. He was in a foul mood last night. I came in here once. I asked him how he was – and he blasted me with both barrels. As if I'd shot the bolt through his ankle. He went through his life story, accusing me of ruining everything, his marriage, his relationship with his children and being responsible for him being crippled.'

'A lot to lay on you,' said Jack looking over the detritus of the room, wondering who was going to clear it up. It was Paul's room now.

'I threw some back,' she admitted. 'Shouldn't have done, but he does wind me up. I'd almost got to the point of feeling sorry for him, but managed to hold back.'

Jack had seen her in action; he knew she'd be poor comfort to Paul. So he'd hit the bottle. Little comfort there either.

'How did he get the booze?' said Jack. 'He asked me to get him some and I refused.'

'Don't know,' said Lynn. 'Probably phoned for it. You can get anything delivered these days.'

'Where is he?'

'I haven't the slightest idea.'

'He was in a wheelchair,' exclaimed Jack. 'Could just about hobble on crutches. He can't have gone out, surely?' He stopped, reflected. 'Might they have picked him up drunk? Could he be back in hospital?'

'The front door was open this morning,' she said reflectively.

'He could've wheeled himself to the front door,' surmised Jack. 'To pick up the booze. Stayed there to drink it. Got absolutely out of his skull. Collapsed. A passer-by saw him, called an ambulance.'

'Sounds possible.'

'He was in a state when I left him,' said Jack, looking over his tools. They were tidier than he left them, probably courtesy of Lynn. 'What's this?' He picked up a sink plunger. 'How did this get here?'

'It's from the kitchen,' said Lynn puzzled. 'We use it to unblock the sink.'

'Why should it be here?'

She clicked her fingers. 'I know. Let me have it.' He handed it to her. 'Watch, and learn. *Blue Peter.*' She went to the bookshelf and took out a book. She placed the book flat on the floor. 'Suppose I was in a wheelchair and dropped a book. How might I pick it up?'

'With a plunger! Brilliant, professor.'

She put her fingers into a half full glass of water, and wetted the bottom of the plunger.

'It has to be wet,' she said. 'Or it won't work.' She depressed the plunger on to the book, forcing the air out. And then lifted the plunger with book attached high in the air. 'It's ze little grey cells, monsieur,' she said in a cod French accent. Detaching the book, she said to the plunger, 'Back to ze kitchen avec vous.' She dropped the French accent. 'And us too. I've made a coffee, a quick one before we get started.'

They went to the kitchen. Lynn put the plunger back in the cupboard under the sink. And then poured them both a coffee from the cafetière.

'I hope Paul's alright,' he said as he sipped coffee. 'He was in the blackest mood last night. Like Eeyore.'

She laughed at his reference. 'With his tiddly bit of balloon that Piglet gave him!' She took down the biscuit tin. 'Except Paul isn't so philosophical. Eeyore has learnt to live in a disappointing world. Expecting the worst. Paul keeps thinking he'll get the prizes and is knocked flat when he gets nothing.'

Paul would never get compassion from his sister. How the two of them tormented each other. He wouldn't try to be peacemaker. A thankless, useless task. He helped himself to a couple of bourbon creams, having only had toast for breakfast, thinking it likely he could fill up here.

She said, 'I'd like to decorate the whole of the new room. Not just the new wall. So, we'll need to move furniture. Buy paint.'

'Fine,' he said only half listening. 'Do you think we should phone the hospital?'

'They'll ring us,' she said slightly irritated.

He knew better than to challenge her. Lynn didn't want to be brought back to Paul. Her thoughts were on her new room. Though Jack felt guilty about bringing Paul back last night. He should've left him in hospital. But Paul did say he'd get a taxi if Jack wouldn't give him a lift.

He shouldn't be so obliging. That's what got him in trouble with Anne. She was due to be questioned. Had to be her turn. Maybe now even. There was nothing he could do about that. Or about Paul.

'Let's do some work,' he said. 'I want to have a look at the new room. See what condition the walls are in.'

They took their coffees and went into the hall. Jack went to open the room door.

'It's locked,' he said. 'Have you got the key?'

'Somewhere.'

She was about to go and find it, obviously not in her tight jeans which couldn't hold a ticket, when he stopped her. 'The door's not locked at the lock. I don't get it.' He pulled at the door and shook it. 'It's the inside bolt at the top. See.'

'That's not possible,' she said perplexed. 'How can it be bolted?'

'Unless someone's in there.' He called, 'Paul? Are you in there? Paul!'

'He's probably drunk,' she said.

He sniffed. 'Yes. There's a smell of booze. He's in there all right.'

'Passed out in my room... What right has he?'

'Drunks don't care,' said Jack. 'We could try the French windows.'

She headed off, he followed, through the kitchen and out the back door, and on to the patio. He'd not been out here before. It was like a stage set, awaiting actors, with an ironwork table and four chairs, pots with bedraggled plants. They crossed to the French windows of the sitting room.

The door was locked, the curtains almost completely drawn shut. They could see a key in the inside keyhole of the French windows. Jack turned the handle to check. Locked. A light was on in the room.

'He's there,' exclaimed Jack, angling his head back and forth in the thin crack between the curtains, to see as much as possible.

She put her head close to his and peered in. 'Yes, there he is. King of the castle,' she exclaimed, 'in the wheelchair. In my room. Oh my God, Jack. Look!'

He tried to see where she was pointing. She backed away to give him space, and he peered in, shielding his eyes with his hands to see more clearly. Jack squinted. Paul was in his wheelchair, head thrown back. There was a deep, bloody gash in his neck.

He turned to her. 'I think he's dead.'

'Why pick my room?' she exclaimed, looking out across the tired garden. 'He knew it would hurt. The bastard.'

'We'd better call the cops.'

Chapter 52

They sat in the kitchen, having phoned the police. Lynn made more coffee and offered toast. He took up her offer in spite of what he'd just seen. His stomach didn't care.

'Of all the places,' she said.

She was obsessed with where the deed was done. Not that it was done, he thought.

'Paul was so depressed last night,' he said. 'I should never have brought him home.'

She sat down at the table, buttering the toast. 'How would you cut your own throat?' she mused. 'Like this?' She demonstrated with a mock swipe of the butter knife. 'I suppose so. If the blade is sharp enough, you slice through the windpipe before you choke.'

Jack shivered, imagining Paul severing the windpipe and arteries. Would you be conscious to see the spurt of blood or too involved in choking, like a hanging man?

'Chickens run around with their throats cut,' she said as she handed him two slices of toast on a plate. And then added wryly, 'But then Paul couldn't run.'

'Please, Lynn.' He waved her away. 'I know your relationship was bad. But he's cut his throat. Lay off. The police will get the wrong idea.'

'They won't,' she said crunching toast. 'He locked himself in. Deliberately. Chose my space to do it in.'

The bell rang.

'The law,' she said. And went off to answer the door.

He took a bite of toast and washed it back with coffee. In the midst of life there is death. Poor Paul. Had he ever been happy? When he was running maybe. That's why the ankling hit him so hard.

Jack wondered if he should have stayed with him last night. Might he have been able to talk him out of it? Though he was in the blackest of moods. But then Jack had Mia, so couldn't stay. All Paul had was his sister.

Lynn led Fayyad and Hayley into the kitchen.

'Jack! Wherever I go, you're there!' exclaimed Fayyad.

Jack put down the slice of toast. 'I'm working here, remember?' he said. 'I went to go in the new room to get it ready for decorating. And found it locked from the inside. So we went outside and looked though the French windows... And saw Paul with his throat cut.'

'Paul's my brother,' offered Lynn.

'Let's check this out,' said Fayyad to Hayley. He turned back to Lynn. 'Where's the door to the room?'

Lynn led the detectives back into the hallway. Jack stayed, they didn't need him. He could hear them talking, the door rattling as they shook it. He shouldn't be eating toast and drinking coffee. Though what should he do? His mind was blank on the matter. Work was out, and he couldn't leave as presumably the cops would want to talk to him. Go where, anyway? He pushed the toast away.

The three came back. And Lynn led them through the kitchen and out to the patio. Redoing the route he and Lynn had covered twenty minutes earlier. Jack stayed put, knowing what they'd do. The same as he and Lynn; peer through the crack in the curtains at the man in the wheelchair, almost in a spotlight, noting the gash in the neck. Cops would be much more matter of fact. A man was dead, a man you had no relationship with. Another body. How many had Fayyad seen? He was such a nice chap; Jack could never have imagined his school friend in such a macabre role. But then who knows what a school kid might become? A billionaire, a builder, a detective, a corpse in a wheelchair.

Jack snapped his fingers. He had a role in this. He rose and went out into the hall, and into the TV room. There, he picked up a pair of leather gloves, a hammer and screwdriver. They would need to get in the room.

He went out to the patio. The threesome were about to come back in.

Jack said, indicating the tools, 'If I smash a small pane, you can get in.'

Fayyad held a hand up. 'Not quite yet, Jack. We need to fetch our crime scene gear from the car. Then you can get us in.'

Chapter 53

Jack and Lynn were in the kitchen, having been banned from the TV room as well as the new room. They were crime scenes. Hayley and Fayyad had returned togged up in paper outer garments, from head to foot, and latex gloves. Jack had broken a small pane in the French windows for them, so they could reach the key in the inside keyhole, and so get into the room. Jack watched as the police went in, not allowed in himself, but could see little of what they were doing as they didn't draw back the curtains.

Though he could imagine what they were seeing. The slashed throat, the blood. And recalled Frank, two years earlier, when he'd come into Anne's sitting room. Head smashed in, blood everywhere, the dribbling mouth. The variety of ways of dying. A vase to the head. A knife to the throat.

A doctor had arrived and a few other cops. Chatter, photographs. It might have been a social gathering, with the greetings and banter. Lynn had tried closing the kitchen door on them, but they insisted on coming through to the patio this way, even with the new room door now open and the back door too.

'I wonder how long they'll be,' she said.

He thought, ask Anne. She's the expert on cops and crime scenes. But didn't say so.

'We won't get any work done for a while,' he said. 'Maybe not today at all.'

'They have claimed the territory,' she said. 'But we could go out and buy paint.'

'If they'll let us.'

Fayyad came in, dressed in white paper coveralls, including overshoes. He pulled his hood down. He was holding a small plastic bag.

'Is this yours, Jack?'

Jack took the bag. In it was a carpet knife, blood on the short blade.

'Probably,' he said. 'I had one in the toolbox in the TV room. I haven't checked whether it's gone. Is it the weapon?'

'Yes,' said Fayyad, 'dropped on the floor along with an empty whisky bottle.'

'Never occurred to me he might use something from my toolbox,' said Jack. 'I wasn't thinking. The mood he was in, I should have taken my tools away.'

'He could've used a kitchen knife,' said Lynn.

'I suppose so.'

'No one will blame you, Jack,' said Fayyad.

'Thanks.' Though he didn't feel much comforted.

'Do you want a coffee?' said Lynn to Fayyad, holding up the half-full cafetiere.

'That would be most welcome,' he said, sitting down opposite Jack. 'At least, a simple case this time round.'

'Is it easy to cut your own throat?' asked Lynn.

'The doctor thinks so. Sharp knife.' He held up the bag with the evidence. 'And this is sharp enough. A determined swipe across the windpipe. And you're through, windpipe and gullet. And no return.' She handed him a coffee. 'Thank you, Lynn. There'll be an inquest. You'll both be needed as witnesses. But it's obvious to anyone what happened.'

'He was so depressed last night,' said Jack. 'I've never seen someone in such a bleak mood.'

'You brought him home from hospital, I hear.'

'Wish I hadn't.' He blew out his cheeks in regret. 'But he'd said he'd get a taxi if I wouldn't give him a lift.'

'You weren't to know, Jack,' said Fayyad.

'He was so down. The hospital doctor informed him he'd be walking with a limp for the rest of his life...' Jack sighed. 'He was training for the London Marathon. Every day going out running, two or three times. And then he gets ankled. And his world collapses.'

'I'm so sorry,' said Fayyad to Lynn. 'This must be very distressing for you.'

'We didn't get on,' said Lynn. 'Though I'd rather it hadn't happened.' She took a sip of coffee. 'I know you've a job to do, sergeant. And I don't want to rush you, but how long are you likely to be?'

Fayyad shrugged. 'Another couple of hours I expect. This is straightforward. Your brother shut himself in the room and cut his throat. Full stop. No one else involved. We'll take photos of the scene. The body will go off to the mortuary in an hour or so. You never know what's needed, so we have to overdo it. But it's an obvious suicide. No one else had access. We had to break in ourselves. Say two to three hours.'

'I wondered whether we could leave you to it,' she said. 'Go and buy some paint.'

'Don't see why not. We'll need to take statements but there's no rush. No point sitting around watching us. You go out, and we'll get on with our business.'

Chapter 54

They went in Jack's van to Jewson's, the builders' merchant, in Stratford. They parked up and went in. Jack felt estranged; the man he'd brought home from hospital had killed himself. Did it show? Everything was normal, the traffic, the pedestrians. What's another death? It means little when a hearse goes by. You might take your hat off, might wonder for a few seconds about all the people dressed in black in the following cars. Are they really mourning him, or glad he's gone?

They were in the paint aisles with a trolley. She was busy looking at the cans, he hardly aware of them.

'Will you go to his funeral?' he said.

She thought for a little while, gazing at a can of *Azured Sea*. 'I don't know,' she said. She put the can back on the shelf. 'I suppose I have to. It would look odd if I didn't. Though everyone knows our relationship. I suppose I should see him off. We have to phone relatives. What a chore! Tonight's work. I think Tim's in contact with Nick. Will you come, Jack?'

'Yes. I'll come. I knew him from Alcohol Halt. Both hapless divorcees trying to keep off booze. The co-ordinator played one of those games when you pair up with someone. I had Paul as my partner. We each had two minutes to tell the other about ourselves. As honestly as possible.'

'Did he mention me?'

'I don't recall. It was a couple of years back. He talked about his ex wife, the difficulties he was having with his kids, how his business had gone bust and he was having no luck job hunting.'

'Two minutes wasn't long enough to talk about me,' she said. 'What equipment do we need?'

'I've got brushes and rollers, plenty of sandpaper and Polyfilla,' he said. 'We'll need white spirit. Undercoat for the walls. Emulsion for that. And oil based undercoat for the woodwork. Then whatever colours you want for topcoats.' He picked up a couple of paint charts and handed them to her. 'You have a look through these and make your choices, while I calculate quantities.'

He'd noticed she was getting attention from other builders, her tight jeans. This wasn't a usual female habitat. Why ever had she put them on? Useless to work in, he really could have done without the distraction. Though she was plainly in her element, looking through colours and paint cans.

She should be in black, he thought, not going through the rainbow palette. Rationally, Paul was dead, beyond caring. But the world expected some grief. Lynn would do as little as she could get away with. Would she invite the mourners back to the house, give them tea and sandwiches, or not bother? She had Dawn and Nick to think about. Funeral directors. She'd go for cremation, he was sure. No gravestone to inscribe, or visit.

She was bobbing up and down, along the aisles of paint cans. As if he and she inhabited different universes. He hardly knew Paul, a little acquaintance from Alcohol Halt, but not that much really. Its mantra was 'support each other' which was why he'd gone to the hospital last night. The thought of him being there on his own, injured, without support. But then Jack had abandoned him, once he'd got him home.

But Paul had asked him to take him home. He said he'd have got a taxi if Jack hadn't been there. Jack should've removed his tools. He could've put them in the cellar. But as Fayyad had said, or was it Lynn? he would've used a kitchen knife. Something sharp. There is always something.

Where did he get the whisky from?

Lynn was approaching him with pots of paint dangling from each arm. He hadn't done any calculations. Had a notebook out, a pen. And a blank page to be filled.

'What do you think of lilac for the walls?' she said holding up a can, 'and this canary yellow for the woodwork?'

Chapter 55

Back at the house, the police had gone. They carted the paint into the hallway, stacking it against the wall, out of the way.

'I must get out of these jeans,' declared Lynn, 'if I'm to do any work. Get yourself a coffee.'

'I'll get hyper if I drink any more,' said Jack, but she was already charging up the stairs.

Jack headed for the kitchen. Maybe he needed to be hyper. One way to survive in a universe where you encounter friends with their throats cut. He still had that out of the world feeling, looking from a distance at human oddity. But caffeine might keep him up all night, if dread from what was going on in Anne's house didn't. Though since the glimpse of Paul in the wheelchair, Jack had hardly thought about Frank, Anne and Bessie. One death at a time was all he could handle.

He put a kettle on as Dawn entered.

'Hello,' he said.

'Hello,' she said, with a slight smile, quickly withdrawn. 'I want to apologise for taking your phone.'

'I wondered who had,' he said.

'I did, and I'm sorry.'

'Do I get it back?'

She shook her head. 'No. It's in the river.'

He stared at her, eyes screwed. She was a skinny thing. What was she up to? Daring him in some way? He couldn't be bothered with this. Another day, he might have admonished her but she caught him at a time when a lost phone didn't amount to much. Especially as she'd lost her father. Not that they balanced out. But how could you yell at someone whose father had cut his own throat the night before? Nothing mattered that much today.

'Why are you telling me?' he said.

She sat down on a chair, biting her thumb. 'Lynn said I should. My therapist said I should.'

'Are you really sorry?'

She looked at him, unblinking. 'Yes, I am. Lynn said you might lose work.'

'Very likely,' he said. 'The phone number's on my leaflets.'

'I could pay you,' she said vaguely.

'Forget it.' How much did she have? What would he ask? Then added, 'And my drill? Did you take that too?'

'You got that back,' she said defensively.

'Why did you take them?' he said. 'You've got a phone. And anyway, you just threw mine in the river.'

'I need to be the centre of attention,' she said.

Jack shook his head. 'I can't believe someone is admitting that.'

'I wanted Tim to get blamed.' She was pulling at her hair.

'So which?' he said.

'So both. I can't be ignored. I get manic.'

'So why take it out on Tim?'

'He was playing heavy metal at two in the morning. In Nick's room. Can you believe that?'

'He's staying here now?' enquired Jack, hardly knowing the situation.

'And taking over my brother's room,' she exclaimed. 'We had a hell of a row. I told him what I thought of him. But Lynn protects him. He's her favourite. He can't do anything wrong in her eyes. He's an orphan. Brought up in care.'

Jack had lost her logic. She'd come to apologise, now she was having a go at Tim.

'He's a thief,' she said.

'Then you should understand each other,' he said.

'That doesn't mean I should like him. But I am stuck with him. With Dad gone, that little prick is well and truly here.'

'I'm sorry about your father.'

'I'm glad someone is.' She sighed, still tugging at her hair. 'Anyway, I wanted to say how sorry I was. And that I won't do it again.'

Standard fare. It's what teacher tells you to say.

'Thank you,' he said. 'And actually, I don't know why I came into the kitchen. I don't want another coffee. I've had enough to keep an army awake. I'll go and do some work.'

'I really won't do it again,' she said, as he left her.

He'd bet she would, but not to him. Anger was welling as he left her. Attention seeking. Even the apology was. Coming into the hall, he was aware of hammering. The door of the new room was ajar. As he came in, he saw Lynn on her knees in a corner. She was banging nails into a bit of soundproofing board, low down in the new wall. Her back was to him, so he was able to watch her. It didn't quite make sense.

'What are you doing?' he said.

She turned to him, her face drawn in annoyance. 'What does it look like?'

'I don't understand,' he said. 'Why are you banging in nails? We did all that yesterday.'

'Missed a bit,' she said.

He took the hammer from her and got down on his knees. They were close, almost touching. He could feel her heat, her annoyance. The wall had been covered both sides with soundproof board, nailed into the wooden uprights. Here, at the end, there were part boards. Yesterday, they'd cut them as large as they could. But here was a small piece, about two feet wide and a foot high off the floor. Lynn had banged in a couple of clout nails, but there were nail holes without nails. Who had taken out the nails? Why?

He rubbed his fingers on the panel. 'I don't understand this. How is it staying in?'

She didn't say anything.

He stared at the rectangle of board. An inkling worming in his head.

'Will you let me finish what I'm doing?' she said sharply, holding her hand out for the hammer he was holding.

Jack put the hammer some distance away, then placed a hand on the side of each of her shoulders, as if measuring the width of her body. With his hands held apart, he placed the width in the rectangle.

'What are you doing, Jack?'

He turned to her. 'There are no nails in it, apart from the one you were putting in,' he said.

'So?'

He pushed her aside and got down to floor level. He looked on the floor and wiped his finger along the edge picking up fibres.

'We cleaned up thoroughly. Why are there bits of rock wool here?'

She shrugged. 'Easy to miss a bit.'

Jack looked at her, she held his look as if daring him. He turned back to the wall and with the claw of the hammer, pulled out the single nail. He put the nail and hammer down.

'That make-up piece has no nails in. So how is it staying in place?'

'I don't know.'

He pushed the piece of board with both hands. 'Absolutely firm,' he said. 'But no nails. Can you think why?'

She had come down to floor height, where he was, close, kissing distance.

'I think you are about to tell me,' she said.

She was staring him out, her face fixed, hard. He stared back at her.

'You killed your brother.'

Chapter 56

'You'd better explain your ridiculous assertion,' she said. 'And I'll put you right.'

He was watching her, still in otherworldly mode. Half caffeine, half reaction to Paul's death. They were topping up the caffeine in the kitchen. He'd more or less worked it out, but was unsure what to do. What do earthlings do with murderers?

He said, 'You were banging nails into a bit of panel that should have already had nails in it. In fact, it had but they'd been removed. There are nail holes. You hoped to have the nails in place before I came back in.' He clicked his fingers at a thought. 'You persuaded Dawn to apologise to me, thinking that would hold me long enough. Only I decided against another coffee, being caffeined out.'

'An apology from Dawn was only right, Jack.'

'I came into the new room and saw you, banging in a nail. And saw nail holes but no nails in that small piece of board. And so I started to work backwards,' he said as if she hadn't spoken. 'I'd been bothered by the bottle of whisky. How Paul got it in the first place. And how he could do anything once he'd drunk it, let alone cut his throat. But then he didn't have to, as you did it. In fact, you bought the whisky. You saw how depressed he was, and knew he'd succumb. All you had to do was buy it and give it to him. Then it was a matter of time.'

She smiled thinly, humouring him.

'Once he was out cold, you wheeled him into the new room. Convenient, the wheelchair. He'd have been an awful weight otherwise. Then using the claw hammer, you took out a make up piece of the soundproof board at the end of the wall. There are slight dents from the hammer head if you look closely where you pulled out the nails. Once the board in the new room was free, you took out that bit of rock wool behind it. And then sawed off a small piece at the bottom of the outer wall, just big enough for you to crawl through into Paul's TV room.'

'That's an awful lot of trouble,' she said.

'It is,' he said, 'but you had all night. I said you were a quick learner.'

'Thank you,' she said.

'You then went back in the new room with my knife, wearing gloves I should think. You cut Paul's throat. Then you were committed. No going back. You put his fingerprints on the knife, and dropped it at his feet. You then slipped the bolt in the room, closing the door from the inside. Now you had to get out.'

'It's a good story you tell,' she said with a wry smile. 'Carry on.'

'It gets better. You crawled through the rectangle you'd cut out, and into the TV room. Now you had a problem. You had to put that rectangle back in the murder room, if I may call it that. And do it from the TV room. You of course couldn't nail it back, as you were in the other room.' Jack sucked his lip. 'I think you used superglue instead of nails. But to do that, you'd have to hold it in place for it to set. How could you do that from the other room?'

'I don't know, Jack. You're the one telling the tale.'

Jack went to the sink, and opened the cupboard below it. He took out the sink plunger. He waved it at her.

'You used this. Compressed it on to the bit of soundproof board, then superglued the board edges. Then held it in place, for say a minute, for the glue to set. So inside wall back. You then put in the rock wool. You'd been a bit careless with that, which is why I found the fibres. But rock wool in place. All that you had to do was hammer back the board on the TV side. All done. Brother safely inside a locked room with his throat cut. You could go to bed.'

They didn't talk for a while. She was playing with crumbs on the table with her forefinger. He was watching, waiting on her, having told her what he'd surmised. It was clear from her reaction that he wasn't far off. She was brooding, sucking her lip. This is what lie detectors pick up, he thought. She knew he knew. Now what?

'Almost right, Jack,' she said at last, looking at him. 'You've got it. More or less. Except there were two of us involved. Me and Tim. He hated my brother too.'

'You could have done it alone,' he said.

'I could have. But I didn't.' She was silent for a few seconds, working out what to say. 'Paul was in a frightful mood last night. Tim and I went in to see how he was. He lashed out at Tim with his crutch. Quite a blow on his wrist. That's what decided us. So unnecessary. Why take his anger out on the poor boy? I sent Tim out to buy the whisky. A big bottle, full strength. Tim took it in to him with a glass. He tried apologising, as if it were a gift, but Paul swung at him with his crutch, missing this time. So we left him with the booze. In an hour, he was unconscious. Most of the rest you've got. Two of us made it easier. Tim held Paul's head back by his hair, so I could make a clean slash of his throat. And then we slipped the bolt, got out through the small panel in the new wall. Then superglue and plunger as you worked out.'

'Though I should think nailing back the bit of board in the TV room would have been noisy,' said Jack contemplating. 'In the early hours. Why didn't Dawn come down?' He slapped his head. 'Of course! She didn't hear, as Tim had put on heavy metal in Nick's room.'

'Did she tell you that?'

'She demanded he turn it down and get out of her brother's room,' said Jack. 'And when he wouldn't, they had a fearful row.'

'While I banged in the nails. And when I'd done, I went upstairs and told Tim to be more considerate.'

'Nice of you.'

'I am her aunt.'

'So it was all done,' he said. 'Paul shut in the room, throat cut. You could go to bed, sleep sound, and wait for me to arrive in the morning.'

'You were perfect,' she said, clapping her hands. 'Did all the right things. Tried the door, locked, so tried the French windows. And saw Paul shut in the room. And then phoned the police like a good, solid citizen. Along they came, out they went, thinking what they were supposed to think.' She held his gaze, with a thin smile. 'Are you about to change their mind?'

'You murdered your brother, Lynn. What other course is there?'

She waved a finger at him, as if to teach him something. 'You have it wrong, Jack. I didn't kill Paul. How can you say that? You of all people.' She poked him in the chest. 'When you did it.'

Jack laughed. The cheek of her. She was beyond words.

'This was a builder's crime,' she said. 'How could I have done it? Don't be so ridiculous. All I did was hold tools for you, fetch and carry, make coffee, while you built the wall. I'm an editor, I can't handle tools.'

'You watched me,' he retorted in exasperation. 'You picked it up quickly. You know how the wall was assembled. You cut some of the boards yourself. Admit it.'

'All lies to protect yourself, Jack. I'm cack-handed. An office person. I wouldn't know which end of a hammer to use.'

He gave up, unable to argue further with her, 'We'll let the police decide.'

She smiled at him. 'Are you sure you want to do that?' She put a hand on his, he withdrew it as if scorched. 'I'm in a tight spot, Jack. I will lie till the seas run dry. This is clearly a builder's crime.' Her eyes widened, 'But aren't you already in trouble? Some dirty work next door, involving Anne and Bessie's father.' She waved a finger at him. 'Mind, Jack. If you cry murder in this house, they might not pull me in. Not when they hear what I have to say.'

'You killed Paul,' he exclaimed, too aware of what she'd been saying. 'Deliberate murder.'

'You did it,' she retorted. 'Let's see who they believe, should you be fool enough to go to the police.' She rose. 'And now, I'd like you to leave, Jack. Thank you for your work. Pack your tools and go. I'll sort out your payment.'

She marched across the kitchen and left him. He stayed put, in spite of what she'd said, finishing his coffee, the last he'd have in this house. He knew too much. She'd lie him into a prison cell if she had to. His legs were hollow as if he'd just climbed a mountain. How little we know of people when we are kissing them. All that had gone on last night after he'd left here. She and Tim killing Paul, locking the room from the inside, and taking out a section of wall to get out. Hours to do it in. To put back the bit of wall, all set for him to walk into in the morning.

What should he do?

Jack threw back the remnant of coffee and left the kitchen. Decisions. He went along the hallway and into the TV room.

There was little packing to do. Most of his tools were in the toolbox, he'd hardly got any out today, the morning interrupted by finding Paul and then the cops all over the place, preventing any work being done. There was his hammer in the murder room, through the wall. The one he and Lynn had built. The one where she'd dismantled a piece and put it back together, barring a few nails.

He went out into the hallway and into the room to get the hammer. He'd put it on a chair. But it wasn't there. This time, he knew, it wasn't Dawn who'd taken it. Her aunt was the culprit, and she wouldn't give it back. As soon as Jack left she'd hammer the remaining nails in the rectangle.

He went to the corner, the exit from the room, the un-nailed piece. Lynn was a good student. Top of the class. He ran his finger round the edge. Paul's throat cut, she and Tim had crawled through just here. She'd fooled the police. He, himself, would have been fooled if he hadn't built the wall.

She mustn't get away with it.

There was a landline phone in the room. He must call the police now. Why hang about? It was cold blooded murder. Jack crossed to the phone and lifted the receiver. Three numbers, that's all he needed to tap. But he reflected, who would they arrest when they arrived? He was in the frame in Anne's house. Only Fayyad had stopped them keeping him in. Should he really draw them into this house too? Where she would claim her complete innocence and throw it on him.

Or should he leave the law comfortable with suicide?

What he ought to do was phone the police, stay in this room, stop her doing any hammering and destroying evidence. There might be blood stained clothing about. Though she'd been pretty thorough. And where was Tim? Maybe he'd already got rid of any clothes they'd been wearing. Perhaps that was why Lynn was wearing tight jeans; the working clothes from yesterday she'd worn for the act, Tim could be dumping them in a bin ten miles away.

There was a case for murder. Examine the small rectangle of soundproof board, he'd tell them. See the dents where nails had been pulled out, see the superglue. Yes, a murder. But who might they hang it on? His fingerprints abounded, as well as hers. As she'd said, it was a builder's crime. She would claim she wasn't capable. Just an editor. All she'd done was make coffee and get tools for Jack.

The builder done it.

How ironic. He wiped his brow. If he evaded next door's crime, he could still be stuck with this one. Or worse. Get done for both.

Lynn came in, holding a white envelope.

'Your payment, Jack. I've added extra for your phone.'

He didn't mention the hammer, just said, 'Thank you,' and took it from her, stuffing it in his pocket.

'I'm sorry it has to end like this,' she said. 'I wanted to work with you. I think we could have made a good team.'

'You're a quick learner,' he said.

'I'd hoped we might have been more to each other. But...' She sighed. 'There we are, reality intervenes. I wish you all the best, Jack.' She held out her hand.

He didn't take it and walked past her.

'Jack!' she called. 'I'm not your enemy.'

He ignored her, going into the TV room to pick up his toolbox. Without looking behind him, he strode out of the house, slamming the front door.

Chapter 57

Jack kept away from Ham Park Road. The pair of houses he'd worked in had brought nothing but ill fortune. He wanted nothing more than to forget they ever existed. Impossible of course. The two corpses disturbed his sleep, Frank slumped on the sofa, head bashed in and Paul, seen through the gloom of the curtains, head back in the wheelchair, throat cut. The hardest time was home alone. In the evenings, he would go for long walks, and drive out to nowhere.

A little work came in. Some of it for just a few hours, re-hanging a sticking door, repairing a window. A leaky roof took him longer than expected as Jack had trouble finding where the water was coming in. He had to pour water over it and follow the leak back, along the rafters to a tile that was shifted by a small fraction.

Several times Anne phoned but he ignored her.

About a week after the events at her house, he saw Lynn on Woodgrange Road, the local high road. She was with Tim, out shopping. Jack crossed to the other side of the road to avoid them. But she had seen him, and gave him a cheery wave. He managed a half hearted wave in return, and she pointed to the Forest Café, miming drinking. Jack shook his head and went down a side street. From his brief glance, Tim seemed happy enough. Safely ensconced in the house. Threat removed by his guardian.

Did she really think they could be friends, lovers even, after what he knew of her? When she was no longer the woman who had charmed him, but the woman who'd cut her brother's throat. And left him, so calculatingly, in a locked room. How could he sleep with her, literally sleep with her? He would be wide awake through the night, hands over his neck.

About a fortnight after Jack had left the Ham Park Road job, Fayyad came over. Jack was watching TV, his attention only half on the hospital drama when Fayyad rang the doorbell. Jack invited him in, wondering on the occasion of this visit, remembering the last, when his fingerprints had been taken and matched with that on the sack.

They sat in the kitchen, drinking tea almost like old pals, except there was a chasm of knowledge between them. Fayyad was, as usual, smartly dressed in a short overcoat over a brown suit. He undid the coat buttons without taking it off, leaving Jack to assume this wouldn't be a long call. And, he hoped, not an official one.

After a few niceties, Fayyad said, 'I'm not here to ask about your health, Jack, pleased as I am that you're OK. But to put you in the picture.' He rubbed the side of his nose with his forefinger, a habit of Fayyad's. 'We're calling off the investigation into Frank Brand and Bert Long's death. The boss has made sounding with the Crown Prosecution Service – and they don't think we have a strong enough case. Our key witness, Bessie Brand, would be torn to shreds in the witness box. What with her black magic rigmarole.'

'It would be an ordeal for her,' said Jack.

'And you could talk your way out of that fingerprint.' Fayyad threw up his hands, 'And what's a single shard of blue glass? Nothing unique. Found in Frank's hair, corroborating Bessie's tale. But so what? It wouldn't jail anyone.' He took a sip of tea, having given his news.

'So it's over then,' said Jack, hoping he had heard correctly.

'Yes, it is. We have all been assigned to other cases, you'll be much relieved to hear, I'm sure.' He leaned forward, eyes screwed tight. 'It doesn't mean we've not a good idea what happened.' Then shrugged and sat back. 'We just can't prove it.'

'I didn't kill anyone,' insisted Jack, holding his friend's look in the hope he'd be believed. 'I did someone a favour. A stupid favour.'

'For a woman,' said Fayyad with a grin. 'Might I guess Anne?'

'You can guess all you like,' he said.

'She's a tough nut,' said Fayyad, as if Jack had agreed with him. 'We held her for two days. After the first session of questioning, she wouldn't say anything without her solicitor. And did she have a good one! A woman from Wanstead, hard boiled, no nonsense. We went round and round the houses and got nothing new. So we brought in her upstairs neighbours David and Maggie Ayodele. Do you know them?'

'I've met them,' said Jack carefully. 'Nice couple.'

'We interviewed them separately, of course. They'd done their homework on solicitors too. Neither would say a word without them present. Their stories were so perfect, you wouldn't believe two years had passed.'

'Both graduates,' said Jack helpfully. 'Good memories.'

'And lots of practice.' He pushed his empty cup away. 'I thought I'd best pop round and tell you the team's disbanded. You looked rather worried last time we spoke.'

'I wish I could be completely honest,' said Jack. 'But whatever else you are, you're a cop. Just believe me when I say, I didn't kill anyone. And I didn't assist in any killing. I was a mug who helped someone out.'

'Anne,' said Fayyad, 'we both know it was Anne. She struck Frank over the head with a vase. He may have been attempting rape; he's the sort. But there was no black magic involved. And you, Maggie and David took the body to the forest and buried it.'

'No comment.'

Fayyad showed his empty hands. 'You needn't worry, our evidence is lousy. The key witness too flaky.' He paused for an instant to gather his thoughts. 'In a way, I'm glad. I know you're not a killer. It's not in your nature. You went there, as a builder, to put up a fence. You had no reason to kill Frank.'

'Or Bert.'

'Or Bert,' he accepted. 'Strange though, he should be buried in the same grave.'

'That's what I thought,' said Jack. An uncomfortable grin slipped out. 'I was amazed when I heard it. I didn't know he was dead until you told me. Not that I miss him.'

'It stays on record as an unsolved crime,' said Fayyad. 'It's doubtful anyone will pick it up again.' He rose, doing up his coat buttons. 'I just popped in, Jack. Thought I'd give you the good news. So you can sleep at night.'

'I appreciate it.'

Fayyad adjusted his lapels and collar. 'I went to Paul Atwood's cremation today. At Manor Park cemetery. To pay my respects. I expected to see you there. Wasn't he a friend?'

'I knew him slightly,' said Jack uncomfortably. 'Same alcohol support group. But I wouldn't call him a friend.' He took a swallow of tea to soothe his dry throat, aware his hand was shaking. 'I didn't know it was happening.' Not adding, he wouldn't have gone anyway, not with Lynn there. He put the cup down and pressed his hands on his knees.

'Quite a few there. His daughter was there, not his son, I don't know why. Families. His sister Lynn was very smart in her long black coat and matching fur hat. And a lot of his running mates. They said he was one of their best and improving all the time.'

'It was a sad death.'

'Yes. Depression can be a killer,' said Fayyad. 'Once he knew his running days were over, he didn't want to live. Horrible way to die.'

'Are there any nice ways?'

'I don't see many of those. Though there must be people who die peacefully in their sleep after a short illness. But that's not my game.' Fayyad put out his hand. 'Look after yourself, Jack. Don't do anything stupid.'

They shook hands and Jack saw him to the door.

'Thanks for coming, Fayyad. You always were a mate.'

Fayyad slapped him on the shoulder. 'Count yourself lucky. You're a free man. Make the best of it.'

And headed down the path.

Back in the flat, Jack wondered who he should inform that the heat was off. Not Anne. Anne had got him into the morass in the first place. Besides, she was a friend of Lynn. He could phone Maggie and David. They'd be relieved.

Paul cremated. And Lynn in full possession of the house. He wondered how thorough she'd been since he'd left her. She'd had plenty of time to remove that small piece of board with the superglue on the back, throw it away, and replace it with a pristine piece. All clean and tidy, with her brother gone up in smoke.

Leaving nothing that Jack could've told Fayyad, if he'd been minded. But having got out of one mess, he wasn't about to shuffle into another. The cops would have to solve this one. Or not. He hoped he didn't bump into Lynn for some time. Or Anne either, for that matter.

His phone rang. Alison. A woman less troublesome these days. Though he could guess what she wanted. It was mostly the same.

'Hello,' he said.

'Can you have Mia tomorrow?'

Thank you!

I am grateful to every reader who finishes one of my novels. I have taken you on a journey which I hope you have enjoyed. There are plenty of things you could have been doing, other than reading this book. So, thank you for your time.

If you liked Jack Recalled, here's what you can do next:

I'd appreciate a review on Amazon. In that way, you can help me tell other readers about my books. Without reviews authors get few sales on Amazon. So I'd be grateful for your review to help this series get on the move.

You can get a FREE ebook of Jack of Spades if you sign up for my readers' list. You may give it to a friend if you wish. Every month a lucky reader from the list will be sent a free, signed paperback of their choice from the series. Sign up using this link:

http://eepurl.com/buAh5H

When you sign up for my readers' list you will receive my regular newsletter. This will give you news about me, what I'm reading, tell you about my future books, PLUS a variety of giveaways.

Books by DH Smith

DH Smith is the name I use for my Jack of All Trades series. The books are all standalone novels and can be read in any order.

Out Now:
- Jack of All Trades
- Jack of Spades
- Jack o'Lantern
- Jack By The Hedge
- Jack In The Box
- Jack On The Tower
- Jack Recalled

Coming Soon:
- Jack at Death's Door
- Jack at the Gate

Books by Derek Smith

All my books, other than the Jack of All Trades series, are written under the name Derek Smith.

Mystery/Crime
Murder at Any Price

Fantasy
Hell's Chimney
The Prince's Shadow
Elektra

Other
Strikers of Hanbury Street (short stories)
Catching Up (poetry)

Young Adult Novels
Hard Cash
Half a Bike
Fast Food
Frances Fairweather Demon Striker!

Children's Novels
The Good Wolf
Feather Brains
Baker's Boy

For Younger Children
The Magical World of Lucy-Anne
Lucy-Anne's Changing Ways
Jack's Bus

About the Author

I live in Forest Gate in the East End of London. In my working life, I have been a plastics chemist, a gardener and a stage manager before becoming a professional writer. I began with plays, working with several theatre companies, and had a few plays on radio and TV, as well as on the stage. In the early 80s I became involved in running a co-operative bookshop and vegetarian café in Stratford, learning to cook, and having my first go at writing a novel. The first was a mess, and, after too many rewrites, binned. The transition from drama to novels took me a couple of years to get to grips with. My first success was a young adult novel, Hard Cash, published by Faber. Buoyed up by this, I stuck with children's work, did school visits, and made a hand to mouth living as a full time author, topped up with some evening class work in creative writing at City University and the Mary Ward Centre in Holborn. A few adult fiction titles appeared from time to time, between the children's list, and I have since been working more in that direction with my Jack of All Trades series.

My full name is Derek Howard Smith. I write as DH Smith for my Jack of All Trades series; all other books appear under Derek Smith. Earlham Books is my own imprint.

www.dereksmithwriter.com

The book you're holding was designed by Lia at Free Your Words...

Contact lia@freeyourwords.com for a quote

www.ingramcontent.com/pod-product-compliance
Lightning Source LLC
Chambersburg PA
CBHW061944170626
46813CB00006B/2526